The Polish Gang

Detroit 1929

Karl J. Niemiec

LapTopPublishing.com
A Paperless Press

P.O. Box 3501 Carmel, Indiana 46082

The Polish Gang

ISBN 978-0-9833663-3-1

Though this story is a complete work of fiction loosely based on my grandfather's family, the naked girl in the back seat of my pop's convertible on the front lawn of Michal's Bar was not.

This is a 'what if' she was promised to someone else —
a love story set in 1929 Detroit.

For Pop, Bronislaus (Benny) Niemiec…thanks for being you.

Michal, Benny, Edward, and Stanley Niemiec

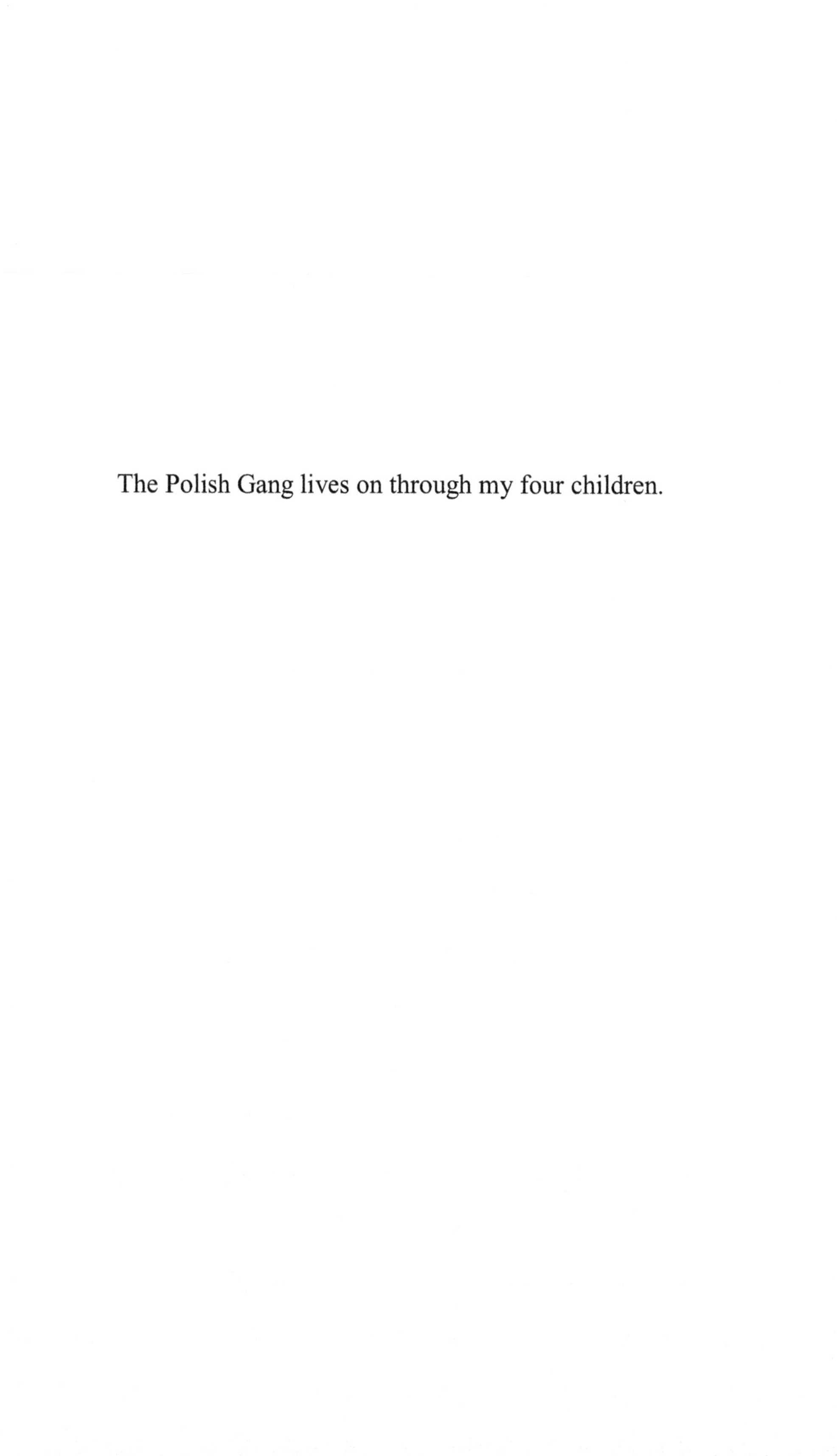

The Polish Gang lives on through my four children.

PROLOGUE - PROLOG

In the grips of the 'Roaring Twenties' Detroit was wide open to bootleggers and murderers. Dollars by the fistful were there for the taking by anyone strong, cunning and murderous enough to chance dying for them. A city in a stupor, gone mad with drink, where blood ran at the drop of rum, Detroit became a civilization taken over by strong-armed gang members.

During this time of social unrest, at the very height of prohibition, there existed — now only in old-timers' porch swing tales that grow mysteriously dim as time slips by — a small band of young men known as The Polish Gang.

Just what happened to The Polish Gang? Where did they go? And why do so few people remember? And why, in a time of such profound documentation and national scrutiny of one city is there but one small newsprint article hinting about this elusive band of young men?

These mysteries and more are revealed in The Polish Gang.

1 - JEDEN

It was less than a dog's tick from eight-thirty in the morning and already the molting sparrows were stilled by a heavy sweat that comes most often when a gutter cleansing summer storm is much overdue. The daunting humidity hung in the streets, filled with industrial perfumes; a breathless mixture of molten steel and in this particular Detroit Westside neighborhood — baked bread. So constant was the scent that only strangers seemed not to have dabbed it behind their ears, or splashed it on their clothing.

It was Wednesday, July third, 1929, the very height of the Roaring Twenties… and Prohibition, also known as The Noble Experiment, a period from 1920 to 1933, during which the sale, manufacture, and transportation of alcohol for consumption were banned nationally as mandated in the Eighteenth Amendment to the United States Constitution.

Only sun-parched Pittsburg Street divided Tasties Bakery from Michal's Bar, and only five rows of white painted garages divided Michal's Bar from the matching bricks of the 6th Precinct and the fire station. Most of the people who patronized Michal Niemiec's establishment either had worked for the newly built bread bakery or the Police and Fire Departments at one time or another — or had friends and relatives who did, or at least had spent a wet-eye or dry-night there.

Through the years, Michal's had become a very important social point in the small Westside, predominately Polish community, and the Niemiec family the center of that collective spectrum. As the bakery, Police and Fire Departments became the most influential employers for this tight knit neighborhood, so did Michal's Bar as a place to meet and rejoice. And Michal was good to the neighborhood. Rumor had it that a smart guy could make extra dough being friends with the likes of Michal and his family. Since The Volstead Act — the popular name for the National Prohibition Act, passed through Congress over President Woodrow Wilson's veto on October 28, 1919 — certain off the ledger things had to be done. After a while, they all became Michal's big extended family. Some people even went as far as to fondly call them 'The Polish Gang'. And up until this fateful morning the family was seldom interfered with by outsiders, because rarely did the family need to reach out beyond its own community for profit. It was the way of these Poles, to be left alone, to live and to enjoy their lives as they saw fit.

Exiting their nearby homes three young Tasties loading dock workers, two hefty Caucasians and one meaty Negro, rambled lazily along Martin Avenue. They side-stepped the excited children who silently fought for a position to bathe in the spray from garden hoses held by their mothers. The mothers washed away the night's gift from nearby Henry Ford River Rough Plant that welcomed them nearly every morning since the world's largest industrial complex started operating along the banks of the Rouge River, near the intersection at Dix, in South Dearborn. Construction had begun during the late 1910s and early 1920s and the massive River Rouge Plant included all the elements needed for automobile production: a steel mill, glass factory, and automobile assembly line. Iron ore and coal were brought in on Great Lakes steamers and by railroad, and were used to produce both iron and steel. Rolling mills, forges, and assembly shops transformed the steel into springs, axles, and car bodies. Foundries converted iron into engine blocks and cylinder heads that were assembled with other components into engines. By September 1927, all steps in the manufacturing process from refining raw materials to final assembly of the automobile took place at the vast River Rouge Plant, characterizing Henry Ford's idea of mass production that began raining its rough granulated coal ash at night across most of the Westside of Detroit, depending on which way the wind blew.

It was still early for the morning shift at Tasties Bakery so the workers, in their crisp white short-sleeved uniforms, made a detour from the squirming children toward the vertical red and white sign reading "Michal's" hanging above a narrow red cloaked window that cut across the front of the two story brown brick building. At both ends of the window a heavy red door hung three steps up into each front corner. The young men headed toward the door two strides off Pittsburg Street leading into the bar and restaurant. The other door led directly upstairs to where Michal Niemiec lived with his wife and four grown children.

Oddly, parked between the two doors, angling across the manicured lawn, was a new cream convertible Buick series 116-25 sport Touring car with its top down. The three young men stopped at the bottom of the steps, studying the unusual parking of the car, considering the care put into keeping the small front yard looking healthy, and decided to do Mr. Niemiec a favor. The tallest of the three got in behind the car's wheel while the other two pushed it towards the street.

Back across the street the mothers' heads played Dominoes as an unfamiliar yet expected sable 1929 Cadillac, an ever-popular and spacious limousine for seven passengers, the Fisher style #163, grudgingly slithered through the murk heading south on Martin Avenue. It hesitated just long enough for its occupants to scrutinize the three bakers as they finished properly parking the convertible.

The three bakers stopped to return steadfast looks before making a move again toward Michal's. One half block up Martin Avenue the Cadillac made a right turn onto McGraw, slid past the fire station and pulled to a stop in front of the 6th Precinct.

The V8 motor, described as the supreme achievement of automotive engineering, heaved a sigh as it ceased and the driver's door sprung open. Walter, a prematurely bald man in a crumpled dark suit, with deep stuffed alligator-eyes, tiptoed his five foot five, well-developed frame, around the car and stood at the passenger's door nearest the curb. He quickly removed his driver's cap to wipe his brow. Cigar smoke struck him in the face as he opened the door and replaced his cap. Out stepped a square-jawed Lorenzo Mangione, looking well-groomed in a custom-tailored, stylish camel colored summer suit. He took in a short breath. "Phew, get a whiff of this neighborhood." He dramatically spat in the direction of the gutter with distaste in case anyone watching was wondering how he felt about having to come all this way to the Westside of working class Detroit. A strand of saliva hung from his thick lower lip. He wiped it away with the back of his stubby, hairy, Italian hand.

Angelo stuck his head out behind Lorenzo. He too was perfectly tailored like his older brother, but in a gray silk striped two-piece suit, though slightly less effective, due to the acute ugliness of his moonscape face and overly waxed back hair. His even blacker eyes darted around taking in the watching neighborhood. "Factory workers," he surmised after testing the hot air for himself.

Caruso, the second oldest of the three young Mangione brothers, emerged but unlike the first two, he had thin black curly hair running wild in the humid air and sported a pinch-back black linen suit. He flicked away his cigarette with the two remaining nicotine stained fingers on an otherwise digit-less left hand. "I'd like to pin an ear back on this clay pigeon," he said as he reached into his coat pocket and lit up again. Walter waited diligently for Bartolommeo Mangione, last and shortest, to grunt his way out of the Cadillac. Finally, with help from his oldest son, Lorenzo, Bartolommeo managed his ill-tempered exit. Walter closed the door, tiptoed back around, slumped behind the driver's seat and pulled a Free Press up to his pummeled nose to invade the race track results.

At first glance, one would think the Mangione family were Vaudeville Headliners who had struck it rich and were determined to prove to the rest of Detroit that they indeed belonged in the upper crust and were perhaps merely entering a Police Station to report their missing monkey. However, those in this tight-knit Polish neighborhood monitoring their arrival knew this wasn't the case — and dangerously far from it.

Mr. Mangione eyed the soot stained precinct as he pulled a hand-rolled Cuban cigar out of his mouth. "Hold it down. I can't think!" The little troll angrily flung his cigar back into his hippo-like face where it stuck firmly between the spacing of his front teeth. His oversize lips wrapped around the cigar like an eager brat with a lollipop. He moved it back and forth at will as his mind raced with anticipation of what he was about to encounter inside the police station. He glanced up to see a Catholic Cross down the block and silently thanked God that his children's mother wasn't alive to witness this blindsided humiliation. God rest her soul. He crossed himself as three Hail Mary's galloped through his tormented mind.

"Maybe, I'll just rip his arms off," Lorenzo said, interrupting his father's dour thoughts. Bartolommeo's fat little hand jetted out from its sleeve and fly-swatted Lorenzo on the side of his head: slap number three thousand five hundred and thirty-three. Lorenzo had recorded each one since birth to memory. Someday, somehow, he planned to bump off the little stub. But not now… not right now.

"Just shut up like I told you. Or maybe you'd like to wait in the car with Walter?" Bartolommeo said.

Lorenzo rubbed his sore ear and answered anyway, "This guy's got it comin'."

Bartolommeo hippoed his way across the cracked sidewalk and up the short flight of steps toward the 6th Precinct entrance. He was not jolly. His three annoying sons were not jolly.

"Don't worry," Bartolommeo assured them, "The Polish Gang will never cross the Mangione family again."

Blood boiled behind Bartolommeo's eyes. His face flooded a deep olive, and his lungs searched for air in the tainted humidity, as he waited for Lorenzo to open the door. He followed his three sons after they rushed, barged and scooted past him across the nearly empty lobby until they reached the Sergeant's desk.

Gary McMahan sat rustling a stack of papers behind the desk pretending not to have been waiting impatiently for the Mangione act to arrive. He assessed the angry men from the corner of his eyes, which caused them to water slightly from the strain, as the three irate young Italian men jockeyed for position in front of his cluttered desk.

"Gentleman," McMahan asked in a thick Irish accent, looking past the three brothers, "may I be of any assistance?" Sweat dripped from his nostrils and stained the papers below. The sergeant rapidly blinked his eyes to clear his vision. From a movie starlet it might have been flirting, but with McMahan's oversized balding head and heavy hunched over shoulders, the effect seemed more like a medical problem.

"We're looking for Nicole," Lorenzo answered, moving out of Bartolommeo's reach.

McMahan fluttered at Bartolommeo, "Are you Mr. Mangione?"

Bartolommeo reached to remove the hand-rolled from his face. Caruso jumped in with, "That's right, baldy. Where's Nicole?"

"Do you speak English, Sir?" The Sergeant again addressed Bartolommeo.

Bartolommeo backhanded Caruso as the middle brother opened his mouth and smacked Lorenzo up the other side of his head, just to remind them who was running this show: smack number three thousand five hundred and thirty-four.

"When I get the chance!" Bartolommeo said.

McMahan came out from behind his desk. “Oh good, follow me. We’ll have a nice little chat with the Captain.” He rubbed his blue sleeve across his salty, wet face. Now he had sweat in his eyes. The fluttering got worse.

Caruso had bitten his tongue when his father backhanded him. He stuck out his throbbing taster and tried to assess the damage. Meanwhile, Lorenzo rubbed his stinging red ears, and Angelo’s eyes searched the fly stained ceiling as they got in line to follow McMahan.

In the Captain’s office behind drawn blinds and under a single twirling overhead fan, the Captain sat back in a squeaky chair with his heels on top of a worn, coffee-stained wood desk. He passively twiddled his long bony thumbs as he anticipated his sergeant’s customary thumping on the beveled glass door. Two thumps meant good news. Three meant bad. Four meant it’s your ex-wife, hide!

When the three thumps finally arrived, followed by four more, the Captain fought back the urge to draw his revolver. Instead, he gently removed his shoes from the desk, mindful not to exert the kind of energy that would cause him body odor in case he decided to crowd into his broker’s office for lunch and wager a little borrowing on the New York Stock Exchange. United Steel looked good as well as General Electric…

He fingered his shirt and remembered his tie was in the top drawer and adjusted his rolled up sleeves around his pointy elbows. He ran a hand over his receding black hair, tinged with gray, to insure it was neatly slicked back from the temples and forced a smile on his dried out, wrinkled, road atlas face. “Come in.”

He shifted a few financial reports to a desk drawer as McMahan entered. McMahan tried not to flutter, his eyes watered again. “Captain, Mr. Mangione is here,” he said.

“Bring him in, Sergeant.” Patiently, the Captain watched as the Mangione family trooped into his office.

First Bartolommeo entered puffing his cigar, followed by Lorenzo rubbing his ears, then Caruso stretching his tongue, and ultimately Angelo casing the joint. All that was missing, thought the Captain, was the calliope, an animal or two, and Lady Godiva who he already had locked up in back. The Captain let the thought pass and gave McMahan a dreary look to make sure there weren’t more outside.

The Sergeant shook his head and left, mindful to pull the door closed behind him.

Bartolommeo tugged the cigar from his face. The smoke mushroomed up to the ceiling, clouding the room.

"Have a seat, gentlemen." The Captain pushed an ashtray towards Bartolommeo.

Bartolommeo ignored the ashtray and let his ashes drift to the scuffed tiled floor while his groomed boys played musical chairs behind him.

"We'll stand. Where's my daughter?"

The two disappointed winners stood back up.

"She'll be here in a minute. Care for something to drink?"

The boys started to order.

"No." Bartolommeo answered.

The boys canceled.

"Very well, Mr. Mangione, let's not beat around the mulberry. Your daughter was found asleep early this morning in the backseat of a convertible automobile... in her Sunday suit a few days early, if you catch my drift."

The Captain's words crowbarred Bartolommeo between the eyes so hard the three brothers were struck dumb.

This would be more fun than the Captain had speculated. Suddenly, he was glad he hadn't mentioned the nakedness over the phone. Maybe if he were to press charges the little fat man would turn blue and keel over right there in his office. Wouldn't that be a trick?

Things were worse than anything Bartolommeo could have imagined. His options of covering up this delicate and sticky situation ping-ponged through his thick skull. Naked! Surely the whole Polish neighborhood knew, or worse, saw! A long pregnant moment passed before Bartolommeo's mind could return back to the room. He felt like such a sap his feet stuck to the floor. His boys didn't dare make a move. "This young hoodlum found with my daughter, is he back there behind bars as well?"

"I'm afraid not."

"And why not?"

Sweat beaded on the Captain's forehead. He rose, steadied himself and walked to the water dispenser. He filled a paper cup with water, not bothering to extend the hospitality this time.

The boys eyed the water. It didn't go unnoticed by Bartolommeo.

"Let's just say, we haven't located him as of yet," the Captain answered after his Adam's apple bobbed a second time.

"Locate him, Captain..."

The Captain gave Bartolommeo a sideways look, sank a fifteen-footer with the crumbled cup into a metal wastepaper basket, and yelled through the beveled glass door which read "CAPTAIN'S OFFICE" spelled backwards, "Gary!"

A choke hold silence began to pressure-cook the room until bubbles gurgled up inside the water tank when McMahan reentered.

"Yes, Captain?" He no longer fluttered.

"Send in O'Garrity. Have him bring Miss Mangione with him."

"Aye, ay, Captain." Gary left again and closed the door.

At the back of 6th Precinct, in a box-like room, Detective O'Garrity and Nicole Mangione were situated on opposite sides of a battered table. A matching chair protested under O'Garrity's excess weight as he unconsciously rocked back and forth.

O'Garrity's pale blue eyes, holding the pain of a major league blunder, were framed by the terrified knowledge of having to pay for it, as they scanned the room for a way out of the mess he'd gotten himself into. The small painted-shut window, the soot-covered lamp shade directly over the table, the hand prints, his prominent amongst them, from many long and dirty interrogations on the walls and door, revealed no simple solutions. He had to think of something fast. His options weren't good. Reasonably, he could catch a hail of bullets, end up a floater, or worse, become a split personality littered throughout every flower bed in the city for his stupid mistake. It was a cruel time he lived in, a time gone mad with drink, and Christ knows he had seen smarter men die for less.

Sweat trickled from Patrick O'Garrity's graying black hair and ran over his whisky bloated face to the open collar of his rumpled sky blue shirt and down his broad muscular back, leaving a wet stain the length of his spine, not too unlike the markings of a skunk. Last week's breakfast smudge on his gloomy tie caught his eye as he mopped his forehead with it. He cleverly tried to conceal the evidence with a broad police tie clip. He didn't need a drink; he needed a full bottle of rye.

The core of O'Garrity's mistake sat across from him still dressed in last night's lavender, low v-neck, backless and sleeveless evening dress, with lilac godets that hung about her ankles. Due to Nicole Mangione's mere sixteen years, she had a natural figure for the style, cut straight up and down, no breast, no waist, no hip, and somehow, though upset, disheveled and completely overdressed for the occasion, she managed to look significantly desirable. Unfortunately for O'Garrity however, her disposition was even less congenial this unbearable morning than the rest of her family's. But there was one jumbo difference: Nicole was quite unmistakably beautiful.

In a tone meant to calm Nicole down, O'Garrity asked, "You were under a blanket, how was I supposed to know?"

"Because you've been on my father's payroll for years, you nincompoop!" she answered as she plucked at a stray black strand of hair. It escaped her helmet-like hat that fit so tightly around her face and down to the nape of her neck that her profile showed hardly more than an eye, the nose, mouth, chin, and the lock of hair. The lock was meant to decorate her cheek but with the heat it managed only to irritate her.

"That is none of your business, little girl."

"Oh, isn't it? Well, don't expect a Christmas bonus this year, you louse."

McMahan knocked on the door and came in, affronted by the tension in the room. "Captain wants you two up front."

"We'll be right there," O'Garrity snapped back.

McMahan left the room and closed the door behind him.

"Daddy must be here." The fire in her purple eyes simmered.

"Nicole, don't be foolish. This Polish boy, Bronislaus Niemiec, he's nothing but a young gangster."

"We're just friends, O'Garrity. We celebrated his seventeenth birthday last night with his family and friends, and if you hadn't stumbled on to it and made such a fuss this morning, I would've been back at the lake before anyone knew I was gone.

"You were naked, damn it. How will you explain that?"

"I always sleep stark naked. I was drunk as a boiled owl. It was hot. I must have thought I was at home and taken off my clothes."

Nicole caught the doubtful expression in O'Garrity's eyes.

"I don't care if you believe me. Father will know. I always pulled off my night dress as a child. Even in the winter. I'm warm blooded; something I'm sure a dishonest snake like you would know nothing about."

O'Garrity began to see a glimmer of hope. If Bronislaus didn't actually touch Nicole, things didn't seem so malignant. But there was more to this. There was a matter of a very delicate telegram he'd luckily discovered. Had the little Polack read it? The shit wouldn't admit to being born. O'Garrity smiled to himself. He knew he'd have to beat it out of him. Perhaps he could even convince Mangione to pay him a token bonus to administer the work over.

"And you can make your father believe that whopper?"

"Of course." She stopped, and then added. "Bronislaus understands that I am to marry Robert Bunniti and so do I, so keep your big fat nose out of it from here on out. Understood?"

O'Garrity reached into his shirt pocket and pulled out a crumpled telegram. "Yeah, well, maybe he doesn't understand this."

Nicole's eyes widened.

"Or maybe he does," he continued, seeing Nicole had taken the hook. He held it just out of Nicole's reach. "I'm sure Mr. Mangione will. Maybe you'd, like to tell me who's read this before I give it to him?"

Nicole grabbed for it and missed.

"Not so fast. This means trouble with a capital P… for Polack."

She went through her purse. The fire returned to the purple passages behind her eyes. If looks could drive a truck…

"It's yours, little girl."

"Did you go through my purse?"

"What does it mean?"

"Nothing to me."

"Who sent it?"

"I haven't a clue, you Scottish thug."

"Yeah?"

"Fat head. Give it back."

"Did Bronislaus read it?"

"Not to my knowledge."

"Are you two lovers?"

"We're friends!"

"I found it in the back of Bronislaus' car. Very careless of you."

"Liar."

"Who do you think sent it?"

"I haven't given it a thought."

"Liar."

Nicole's eyes down shifted into first degree murder.

It was just dumb luck for the Polack Kid. Especially if he sent it, O'Garrity thought as he got up and moved to the door and opened it. And just might save his tush. "Shall we?"

Back in the captain's office, behind the closed blinds and under the sound of the single twirling ceiling fan, the Captain waited silently along with Bartolommeo Mangione and his three fidgeting sons. Where in the hell was O'Garrity!?

Neighborhood kids could be heard playing outside the window. Across McGraw at the high school a pickup game of stick ball had begun, despite the heat, amongst kids who dreamt at night of Ty Cobb and Babe Ruth. The air in the room by then had become as thick as bean soup. Someone had passed a blind cheezer, but no one in the room had owned up to it yet. Bartolommeo eyed his sons murderously; a lethal glance that ran in the family.

The Captain was thankful he didn't own a canary. He went back to the water cooler and filled another cup with water. On his way back to his desk he stopped in front of the window to suck in a bit of the Polish neighborhood and see if his son was playing in the ball game. He was.

O'Garrity pawed at the beveled glass door and pushed it open. Bartolommeo nearly gulped his smoldering cigar and the boy's mouths dropped open like a row of vacant garages.

Nicole stood in the doorway, a rumpled little princess, lakes welling up behind her lashes threatening to streak her war paint the length of her poetic face. She clutched her purse between her tintless nails and picked at the beads that formed a scarlet rose. She sniffed the foul air and eyed her brothers coolly. They feigned innocence. O'Garrity nervously amused himself with his tie clip, trying not to look Bartolommeo in the eye.

Less pressure was found in a tea kettle. Life from outside the window threatened to shatter the silent hostility that filled the office.

The Captain yearned for a stiff bit of gator sweat. From the looks of things, so did everyone else. Of course, he wasn't about to admit to having a private stash and waste it on these morbid clowns.

"Mr. Mangione," the Captain said, "this is Detective O'Garrity. He'll be in charge of this case." The hostility refused to ease as Bartolommeo's face threw bricks into the windows of O'Garrity's eyes.

"How do you do, sir?" the big Scot stupidly asked with cotton jamming his craw. He eyed the water cooler.

"I could eat steel. And you, young lady, look at yourself!"

"Nothing happened that you should be ashamed of… I… we…" The dams leaked and her war paint streaked.

"Oh sheesh, here comes the water faucets."

"Caruso, hold your tongue!"

Bartolommeo went to Nicole and tried to hold her gently in his arms but couldn't without pressing his nose against her sunny-side ups, so he patted her lower back instead. It was quite evident this show of affection between Bartolommeo and daddy's little girl wasn't going over well with the three physically and emotionally abused brothers.

They passed sneers amongst themselves. Angelo went as far as to stick his finger down his throat, what puke, until Bartolommeo caught him. He pretended to be picking a molar. The nerve, Nicole flashes the world her natural parts and they get beaten up for it.

"I'm sorry, Father… I…"

"We'll have a nice long talk when we get home."

"You should blister her bottom-side for disgracing our family's name," Lorenzo blurted not being able to contain himself any longer.

"And that's enough out of you, Lorenzo!" Bartolommeo said with a wave of his hand, then turned on the Captain and continued, "Captain, I want this Bronislaus Niemiec arrested. And if possible, I want the whole Niemiec family behind bars!"

"Father, please…" Nicole began but Bartolommeo held up his hand again to cut her off, too. She knew better than to press.

The Captain had seen, heard, and smelled just about enough. He didn't have anything on Bronislaus. But if he left him out in the street too long, someone might. The Captain looked over at O'Garrity. "All right, calm down. O'Garrity, bring Bronislaus in for questioning. And don't make a nuisance of yourself in the process."

"With pleasure, I mean, yes sir," O'Garrity answered.

The Captain went back to his desk, sat down and in an air of dismissal, put his feet back on the desk and began to re-twiddle his thumbs. "I want to speak to him before dinner, today. Fill out a warrant downtown. And I want this done by the books, got me."

"I'll personally take care of it," O'Garrity cunningly assured no one, except for himself. Things were looking great. A warrant! Five minutes ago he was dead and now…

"If you don't, I will," Bartolommeo said.

The Captain shifted his eyes past his thumbs to make sure the thick man knew he meant business. "Mr. Mangione, I'm afraid it was your daughter who was found a la Morocco, not the Niemiec boy. Though I don't wish to, if you provoke me, I will press indecent exposure charges against Nicole and resisting arrest. Now, unless she plans to press some kind of charges against Bronislaus, seeing the boy is a minor as well, there's nothing legally you or I may do to the boy or his family. Personally, I must admit, Michal Niemiec is a good friend of mine. We all attend the same church up the street. So, if I find you have stepped across the legal path to cause harm to the Niemiec family in any way, I'll have your carcass back in here and behind bars before you can whistle "My amigo the DA" So, do you, Miss Mangione, wish to press charges against Bronislaus Niemiec?"

"No," she barely answered.

"I'm sorry?"

"No, I don't wish to press charges. Father, nothing happened. May we go home, please?"

Bartolommeo studied his daughter's precious face. He wanted to believe. He wanted to believe this never happened. He wanted to believe he'd find this dirty rat punk and stomp the little Poski's plums so hard that all his future crummy generations would pay for what he'd done to his little angel. He wanted to rip Bronislaus' throat, poke his eyes, beat his brains, tear his arms, break his legs, and slit his guts! If Bartolommeo was half the man he used to be, he would. Only, now he was of a different world, a different time, and he could only use what power he had left that would keep his hands clean... money.

"Captain, I want to sweeten the pie. Add a five thousand dollar reward to that warrant. I'll bankroll it myself."

"That won't be necessary..."

"I happen to think it is. Where do I sign?"

Once again the room filled with the silent hostility that sucked the happy clamor from the children playing outside back into its void.

A boy yelled into it through the window. "Hey you... O'Garrity, you gave my sister crabs!" But he wasted the gut splitting laughter on the Captain's Office. It echoed down the alley with every step as the little smart-aleck and his friends stumbled away. The Captain's kid yelled the score from left field. It was one to nothing in the bottom of the first.

2 - DWA

Due to this 4th of July falling on a Thursday and the early morning excitement about an angry naked beauty on the front lawn, it was overly busy in Michal's for a Wednesday lunch. Mostly short sleeved older men crowded at the bar but younger women in the latest summer dresses packed the cane chairs and glossy red vinyl booths while polished hardwood ceiling fans just pushed the hot industrialized air and burnt tobacco from corner to corner. Somewhat stifling even though the thick red padded vinyl front door was propped open, apparently unguarded, allowing the jocularity from within to escaped out into the sun-dried streets.

Stashu, the second oldest Niemiec brother, covered his early shift behind the bar. It curled out from the back johns, and fifteen occupied stools later, ended at a pool table that took up most of the floor between the front door and two other doors leading upstairs and downstairs. He rang the cash register and broke a fin while trying his best to hear complete stories being told by the row of toothless old men with gray, unshaven, blotchy faces. They sipped sparingly from coffee cups trying to shed the blue johnnies, the woolies, the ork-orks, the uglies, the black dog and more than likely a wife or two with a house full of grandkids.

Manny, an old geezer was saying as he hoisted his cup to his cankerous lips, his sullied hand shaking, "Sure as I bleed when I rattle and hiss, my boy was shot down by one of them three Purple bastards." His breath labored between swallows. The heat, the booze, his tobacco heart and his murdered boy hung on his poor pack of bones as he leaned against the bar. His upper back was painfully curved with age. His white head bobbed as his clogged carburetor struggled to maintain a regular pulse inside his sunken chest. An unfiltered cigarette dropped ashes onto the bar from his other hand. He didn't know whether to laugh or cry, and didn't have the strength to do either.

"Who?" another old-fart asked.

Stashu ran a series of cups through the sinks, placed them upside down on a bar towel and ran his wet hands over his dark, sophisticated, slicked-back hair before the old geezer continued.

"The Purple Gang!" The old geezer poked his frail finger at the headlines of a paper held by the old-fart.

"Walked in on Harry or Ray, I don't know which, havin' some summer-cabbage with my boy's kippydope over in Hamtramck and either Harry or Ray shot him dead in the street."

"Who? The Purple?"

"No, my son, you dumb cluck. Shot my no-good boy three times in the belly. And plugged the girl accidentally to boot." Manny hoisted his cup again.

The old-fart probed his paper, squinting through a magnifying glass to read. He held the glass up to look at Manny, and then back at the paper, then back at Manny. His enlarged eye saddened. "This was your Billy?"

"Was, is right. A long time ago."

"Ought a give 'em the chair," said a pug-ugly bachelor near the end of the bar.

"Ain't no proof... but as sure as I bleed..."

"How un-American, wastin' swell kitty like your boy run with... shit," said a man with black glasses at the center of the bar who had savage acid scars covering his hands and most of his face.

"How would you know?" Manny asked.

"I got ears, well part of 'em anyway. And what I hear is them three been hijackin' every beer wagon from here to Chicago and back. The cutthroat bastards."

"Hey, Stashu, you havin' any problems with them Purples?" the old-fart asked.

"Pa's on friendly terms." Stashu wiped the sweat from his good-natured face. His hazel eyes straining to keep up with things, and a blond in particular, as she entered the joint. His eyes pursued her while she charmed her way across the restaurant to the bar. "If you catch my drift," he added, giving the blond a third once-over.

Molly Kiminsky smiled at the row of men and sat on the first stool as they shifted down to make room. A lot of beat up hats tipped. Her baby blue eyes landed back on Stashu as he poured her a stiff one. Not as stiff as he'd like, and not as personal, but stiff all the same.

"Yeah, how friendly of terms?" Manny asked.

"You're drinking it."

The old geezer spit out his beer. His cronies gave out a hoot. "Michal buys this stagger-soup from the Purples?"

"Enough… but I never said it."

A warm glow grew over Molly's smile so riddled with sex every hand on the bar reached to pay for her cup of strip-me-naked as it trickled down to her sensuous belly. Stashu waved them off. Molly blew him a kiss. "I hear they been murderin' for rum money from here to Chicago," Manny said.

"What?" the old-fart asked again, cupping his hand over his scabby, hair-filled ear.

"I said, 'murderin',' you dumb cluck. For rum money, the dollar bill, for Christ's sakes." His breath came in sharp spurts, nearly painful to watch, as he sucked in just enough to keep drinking.

"All right, all right, don't get your cobbler's in a knot."

"Hey, there's a lady present," Stashu said.

"Not in this dive," Molly said.

"Say, speaking of which, why you ain't out packin' a spade?" asked a man who had had kept his mouth shut until he got up to wave his pistol at Sir Harry.

"Huh?"

"Your son, ain't you ought to be plantin' him?"

"What the hell for? I didn't kill him." The old geezer gave his cronies a half cocked smile. "Let the county dump him. Probably knew him better than I did."

"Ke-rist!" the man said as he entered the john.

Hey, Stashu, another round of that Purple shit beer."

More sweat stained Stashu's open white shirt. He continued to squint at the money he shuffled from the bar to the cash register. He counted out the change to the special chippy with the mischievous grin. The squinting was giving Stashu's head labor pains, so he put on his round wire rimmed glasses. Molly took the change and sauntered over then placed the money on the pool table. She didn't play but her bigger than life husband did. Blondes, Stashu thought.

Stashu took a drink order from Emily, the eldest of the Niemiec siblings. She was the only waitress working the floor and didn't seem to give a half a knockwurst that most of the overflowing room hadn't been waited on yet. She pleasantly swung her hips to Rudy Vallee crooning over the airwaves as she made her way between the five square, red and white checker clothed table tops, taking orders and flirting openly with the men eating in the row of black leather booths. She wore her naturally brick-red hair long, though the in-look was short. It curled down to her shoulders and was combed to the right where a bright blue barrette held it out of her face. She was squeezed into a black and white waitress uniform that hid less than it was meant to hide.

At the pool table, two young men in street clothes were taking on two older men in baker's whites. Money lined the table. Coffee cups were held in the hands of the three men not shooting. One young man with a cigarette dangling from his mouth sank three solid colored balls on one bank shot. He laughed robustly at the icebound glances from the two older players as he stepped outside and flung a throat full of nasal scrap into the street. He looked around assuring himself that all was well and re-entered Michal's to finish his shot.

Molly table hopped her way back to the bar and checked her short blond hair in the beveled mirror that ran the length of the wall behind the bar. "When will I see my picture on the wall up here, Stashu?" She leaned way back on the stool, holding onto the bar, giving Stashu a suspenseful look.

Every head at the bar strained to look bar right. The blind man sensed them heaving. Blood ran where no plasma had run for years.

As Molly leaned back she pretended to examine the pictures on the facing of the lowered bar ceiling. They were new and old shots of good times in Michal's, Niemiec family outings at their lake cottage, fishing and hunting trips and shots taken in Kraków before the War. The faces in the pictures were filled with smiles, mustaches, smoke, drink and adventure as Michal and Stephania waved back from the deck of a steam ship.

The old men gulped from their cups.

Stashu studied her nasty smile and the teasing meow eyes. The girl didn't play honest. He poured her another drink.

"So, when?"

Sweat dripped down the bridge of Stashu's nose. He had to pick his words carefully. He looked down the bar. The old geezers feigned not to be hanging onto every word. It was hard to do. This wasn't just a trap-the-rat game between Stashu and Molly; this was life and death, and most likely Stashu's. "Whenever you let me." He smiled back. She was driving him silly, all full of promise, beckoning him to dig his own early grave, making him pour her free drinks for cheap peeks at what nature had bestowed upon her. It was a cruddy, homicidal game and he knew it, but the thought and smell of her had impregnated his spirit and wouldn't let go. Blonds, he thought again and tried to get comfortable but failed.

Across the room, in the middle vinyl booth, Whitey MacNeil sat stewing. Across from him was Molly's younger cousin, and Whitey's live-in girlfriend, Sally Korner. Whitey tugged his tattered white fedora further down over his towhead hair. He wiped his twice broken pug nose with the back of his left hand, being attentive not to brush against his blood encrusted, sliced upper lip. In obvious torment, he examined his usual lunch, pastrami on toasted rye, through the one eye not puffed shut behind three shades of swollen violet skin.

He ignored Sally across the table. Which wasn't easy, she was dressed in friendly white dance trunks, a shocking pink blouse tied at the midriff, burlesque stockings and glossy black leather tap shoes. She artistically balanced Whitey's full glass of milk stuck in her cleavage and barked like a sea lion trying to get his attention. No dice. The bombshell blond stuck two straws in her nose and blew Taps into the glass. Still nothing, what's a gal got to do? Like her cousin, Sally was smiled on by nature, but she wasn't just a bombshell, she had talent. Not too bright, but she had a booking agent, and made a living singing at special events and local nightclubs, waiting to be discovered.

Molly's skyscraper husband, Sky, stuffed into a starched white baker's uniform, came up behind Sally and patted his cousin-in-law on the back. The milk slipped from its perch and spilled across the table and onto Whitey's lap.

"Hey!"

"What the…!?"

Sally shot Sky a murderous look.

"Pardon me, Whitey, Sally," Sky said.

Through his marshmallow lips, Whitey shrugged it off as he stood up so he wouldn't get all of his milk in his lap.

"Don't mention it..."

Sky beat a path as fast as he could toward the bar and his troublesome wife.

Whitey eyed Sally who had already started to wipe up the mess. "This stinkin' joint is jumpin' like a stuck bullfrog," he said while wiping his soaked crotch with a wad of napkins.

"It's amazing ain't it?" Sally said, her voice innocently sounding nearly as baby doll as she looked. "Who was that girl anyway?"

Whitey sat back down and tried one more futile attempt to eat his lunch but his battered gums were annihilating him. "Bless me, I should've ordered soup." He eyed Sally a second time. She looked even more puzzled than normal. "What?"

"So, who was she?"

"Who?"

"That beautiful young girl this mornin'."

"What beautiful young girl? I thought I woke up with you."

"Not me, Mr. Romantic. I'm talkin' about the girl in Bronislaus' car."

"Who said it was any occupation of yours?"

"Nobody, I'm just curious."

Whitey threw his sandwich down in disgust. It skidded onto the damp table as he raised his voice. "What are ya writin', a gossip column?"

Just then, back across the room, Bronislaus apprehensively entered the bar from the stairs behind the pool table. He tried to circumvent what he expected would be regular dogfight. His handsome tanned face looked hung-over and sleepy-eyed though freshly showered and what he routinely passed off as shaved. He pulled at the dampness perforating his light blue, short sleeved, cotton shirt that stuck to his lean, muscular body. He gave the moisture more attention than it deserved, so that his chin hung down on his chest and the sparkle in his greenish-gray eyes could avoid his neighbor's all-knowing smart-alecky grins. Their belligerent comments fell upon obstinate ears. His short, dark brown, wavy hair was combed back tightly to his scalp with a natural part on the left that lead to an annoying cowlick in the back. His other hand was dug deep into his pocket, passing up hearty, outstretched hands as he made his way over to Whitey.

It was worse than he had feared. Of all the dumb things he had done in his seventeen years, this was by far the most embarrassing. Pa would whip his butt. A naked girl in his car's backseat and on Ma and Pa's front lawn? What was he thinking? Why wasn't he thinking? There was no way to lie out of this one. Everyone knew or would before the day was over. He'd be lucky if Nicole ever spoke to him again. He just wished he could remember what had happened. Why was Nicole naked? Had they…? Naaah, well maybe, naaah… damn if he could recollect.

Sally saw him first. "Sssssshhhh… here he comes."

"What are ya sssshhhh'n for? Yooo, Bronislaus, top of the mornin', sunshine."

"Good mornin', Sal," Bronislaus said as he slid in alongside her. She gave him a hiya, handsome, warm smile and a kiss. Whitey flashed her the eye. Bronislaus looked across the table and examined the creative beating someone had given Whitey's twenty-three-year-old face. "What happened to your mug this time?"

"Had it redecorated."

"The heel showed up and got me booted again," Sally said.

"Sal's a show girl, you goon. You want her to stay home, whistle a weddin' march, before you end up with an unnatural harelip.

"What? Are you kiddin'? I'd rather take the punches."

"I'll give you some punches…" Sally made a fist.

"Just eat, will ya…?"

Whitey focused his good eye. It bulged. "So…?"

Bronislaus plopped Whitey's soggy sandwich back on its plate. "So what?"

"Sew buttons… Was it worth it?"

Bronislaus rubbed his hands over his face trying to regain some fresh blood to his thoughts.

"Whitey, don't be so crude."

"Who's yappin' at you? My uncle found the bum this morn' out front with some twinkle filly in the back seat of his convertible. Without her wrappers on. And I wanna know how she rode. All this time I thought he was a farg."

"Mr. Romantic," Sally sighed, pantomiming bliss.

Whitey flung a pickle at the bombshell and it stuck artfully upright in her cleavage. She plucked it out and bit it in half.

"Quit beatin' up your gums, huh, Whitey."

Bronislaus caught Whitey with his mouth wide open.

"Sure, sure, don't scorch your soup."

"Yeah, look, have you seen Pa?"

"He's still at the market. Said he had some special business 'cause of what went down this mornin'."

Bronislaus got up. "Thanks. Keep your workin' eye on the door." He nudged Sally's shoulder, "Dump this bum, Sal."

"You available?"

"Always." Bronislaus gave her a wink and slugged Whitey's shoulder on the way by.

Whitey started to say something smart but Sally grabbed a thumb full of sandy hair on his forearm and yanked it. "Hold the phone, you lug-head!"

Jake, a narrow faced Jewish musician in his mid-twenties, slid in the booth beside Sally, pulling his hat off, revealing his fading hairline.

"Hey, I got the right to bust his chops. I'm his best friend, ain't I, Jake?" He rubbed the spot and quickly snatched his arm hair out of Sally's fingers and sprinkled it onto her tomatoes and vinegar.

"Say, you two are always so much fun," Jake said while picking up Whitey's sandwich. He cringed from its wetness and bit into it anyway. "You ought to have kids so you don't have to keep beating up on each other." He smiled as he chewed. "You through?" he asked indicating the sandwich.

"Ah shuddup... and no I ain't through, you sheep tick." Whitey grabbed for his sandwich but Jake took another bite before handing it over. Whitey eyed it. "Ah, keep it, I lost my appetite the moment you sat your clipped-dick down."

"So, Sal, I hear you're suddenly available on the fourth?"

"Thanks to Whitey I am. You got something nice?"

Jake's face lit up. He sure did.

Bronislaus entered the cracker box kitchen from the bar knowing he'd find his mother, Stephania Niemiec's, stocky frame bent over the stove trying to reach an over-boiling pot of red cabbage on the back burner. He thought he'd test the troubled waters to see how deep he was in it.

"Mornin', Ma."

Stephania didn't answer her youngest troublemaking son.

Bronislaus wandered over to the backdoor and looked out over the manicured garden with three colors of roses alongside the four car garage. Two kitchen fans hummed overhead. “Yep, it’s another one of those beautiful Detroit summer days.” He took in a meaningful breath of scented air, holding it in as he opened his shirt in hope of a breeze. Mother Nature wasn’t offering. He let his breath out slowly wishing the pounding behind his eyebrows would just kill him already.

Without looking Ma asked, “You feel funny today?”

“I feel like burnt kielbasa.”

Stephania looked at her pan of kielbasa and turned down the flame.

Bronislaus ran his fingers through his quickly drying, wavy black hair and rubbed his temples with his thumbs for a second. He stepped behind Ma and gave her a hug and a kiss on the cheek and snatched a slice of kielbasa from the frying pan on the front burner. Ma swung a wooden spoon with deadly aim at his hand, catching him square across the knuckles. “Yeeow… you still love me, or what?”

“I feed you, then you know.”

“Is he angry?”

“What do you think? He left early to the market so he could go talk to those men who sell us their stolen booze.”

“The Purples? It’s that serious?”

“He thinks enough to ask for help. You know how I feel about those men.”

“I meant to take her back, Ma. We just fell asleep. Guess we got carried away, or somethin’.”

“Who would know better?”

The phone rang. From the other room Stashu answered it at the register and yelled over the noise at the bar. His voice came through the door. “Hey, Romeo, it’s for you.” Laughter from the whole bar permeating the kitchen.

Bronislaus cringed, but plucked the phone off the wall before anyone else picked up. “Hello…?” He listened “Yeah, it’s me. Who’s this? He listened again. “Yeah, I got my ear glued to the phone.” He listened some more while scratching the hairs on his rippled stomach. “Alright, thanks… I will… thanks again. Ah, Nicole?” The phone clicked in his ear. He looked at Stephania who eyed him motherly as he hung up the phone.

“Trouble?”

He nodded. "Expect company."

Emily entered joyfully from the bar. "O'Garrity's out front."

Bronislaus rolled his eyes upward, "This ought to brighten my day."

Emily hung up an order ticket. "Two number threes with hash hold the Mayo on one. If Whitey asks for a new pickle, don't give it to him."

"Where's he at now?" Bronislaus asked his big sister.

Emily looked at her kid brother, shaking her head. "You really messed up this time. That girl's in big trouble 'cause of you."

"You think I don't know?"

"What did I tell you?"

"Not to bring her."

Ma looked at Emily. Then Bronislaus. "You like this girl?"

"What… I don't know, Ma… we've been friends since I was a tadpole out at the lake."

"How come you never told us about her?"

"What… she's just a girl… a friend, you met her, couple of times, she'd come by on her boat. I just asked her to come to be nice. I didn't expect her to say yes. You know, being neighborly."

"You want to be neighborly, there's plenty of girls around here."

"Thanks, Sis."

"So you picked her up?"

"Yeah, well she asked me to. She just wanted to see what our family life was like away from the lake. Just this one time, being friendly, we didn't plan on stayin' so late."

"Or gettin' so drunk."

"Yeah, that was my fault. She's a nice girl, honest."

"Not in the eyes of this neighborhood, thanks to a no-good bum like you," Emily told him.

"Remind me to use you as a business reference."

"That was her on the box?" Ma asked.

"Yeah, she called to warn me." Remembering suddenly. "Damn, where's Whitey?"

"Trying to look manly at the front door." Emily rechecked her orders. "One knock and cab, side of city. Two medium hams with."

Stephania took down the order and began to fix it. "If it's trouble, don't stay."

On his way out the backdoor Bronislaus grabbed two of his favorites — city chicken, veal and pork skewered, browned with cracker crumbs and spices, and then baked to a golden brown — dodging his mother's wild spoon. "Ouch, Ma! I'll be on the back stairs."

Out front, on the sidewalk, and in the shade of Michal's, stood a showered and shaved O'Garrity with three plain-clothes men. None of them pretended to be bright looking. O'Garrity was still humming from having his butt chewed. He rubbed his hands together, beginning to enjoy himself again. "I can't wait to see the look on the old man's puss when he gets a load of this warrant for his darling little boy's arrest," he said under a nasty chuckle.

"One of us will probably end up sitting on it," Bosko said, "permanently," he added with an air of doom.

O'Garrity gave Bosko a whack in the direction of the back door. "Go around and keep your eyes wide open and your mouth shut tight."

Whitey came out and stood on the stoop, picking at his wet crotch. "Well, well, well, if it ain't my dear old uncle, Detective O'Garrity, and his three merry flatfooted henchmen. Top of the mornin' to ya, gents."

"Don't hand us that, you little jab bag. I want to see the old man."

"And who might that be, Uncle O'Garrity?" Whitey asked with enough sweet sincerity to give hummingbirds diabetes.

O'Garrity signaled with a flick of his head to the bigger of the two remaining officers to grab Whitey. "We're not here for any of your backtalk you little snot-nosed piece of shit," O'Garrity said as the bigger officer threw Whitey's five-foot-five frame up against the padded open door.

"Just knowin' we were here scares the piss out of you, Whitey, or what?" the bigger officer said.

"I thought it was your sister comin' to finger me as the daddy."

The officer banged Whitey's head on the door for it.

The two young men playing pool came out to see who was knocking.

Whitey stopped them with a cocky-sure half smile. "I'll handle these mugs, boys."

They went back inside throwing nasty looks back at the big cop holding Whitey.

"Mr. Niemiec ain't here," Whitey said. "I'm sure he'll wet his own trousers when he hears you stopped by lookin' for him."

"Where is he?" O'Garrity asked.

"You're the snoop. But if you ask me..."

"I am!"

The officer bent Whitey's arm.

"Aaahhh! It's Wednesday, he's probably at the market like he's done for the past fifteen years. I don't recall him ever askin' your permission. Aaahhh!"

"Where's the boy?"

"Edju went fishin'."

"Do I have to make him beat you, Whitey?"

"Stashu's at the cash register."

O'Garrity nodded and the bigger officer pinned Whitey's welted face to the hot door and gave his arm another yank for good measure. Whitey stifled a complaint. No sense giving these lugs the pleasure or they'd make a habit of it. He smiled crookedly down at his uncle.

"I'll just have a look-see for myself." O'Garrity walked up the three steps. "Let's go, boys."

"Say, we ain't goin' in there, are we," the smaller officer said, knowing it wasn't a good idea.

"Why not? I got a warrant."

"We'd just be lookin' for trouble."

"You heard the Captain, before dinner. So what are you waitin' for? We got a personal invitation." O'Garrity grinned and headed for the door. The bigger officer pushed Whitey up front. The smaller officer reluctantly followed, making sure no one jumped him from behind the door.

Just inside the door of Michal's, O'Garrity stopped and cased the joint. A lot of gulping from coffee cups went on. The men at the pool table halted. The cue ball banked twice and rolled to a standstill against the eight ball. The place hadn't changed much since it had supposedly gone dry.

Every working eye, except Whitey's, watched O'Garrity walk through the crowded room with his two men pushing his nephew along. O'Garrity paused in front of Stashu and the cash register.

"Table for four?" Stashu asked neighborly.

"We came for a carry out," O'Garrity answered him.

"Friends of yours, Whitey?"

"Family, and a couple of pals."

"Shuddup! Where's Bronislaus?"

Sally started toward Whitey but he shot her a look to stay out of it so she turned up her nose and sat back down in a huff.

Stashu closed the register, the bell rang, "Gone fishin'."

O'Garrity slid his arm along the counter and knocked a box of toothpicks, a booklet of receipts and three stacks of pool table quarters with a clatter to the floor. Every guy at the bar stood up except the big palooka that spilled Sally's milk.

"I have a warrant for the arrest of Bronislaus Niemiec," O'Garrity shouted over the crowd noise and flagged the warrant over his head until the neighborhood shut up.

"What a bunch of hog...." Whitey quipped.

"Here it is in black and white."

Stashu reached for it, "Come on give."

O'Garrity held it open, but wouldn't let his prize possession go.

"Who's payin' you for this one?" Stashu continued.

"Your little pain in the butt brother should be mindful of whose daughter he gets happy with around this dump. A Mr. Mangione was quite unfriendly this mornin'."

"So that's it?"

"That's it. Your little brother has a five thousand dollar bull's-eye on the back of his head."

"Hell, he's worth twice that much," Whitey quipped in again.

"That's right, folks." O'Garrity raised his voice to the crowd again, "Five thousand dollars for information leading to the arrest of Bronislaus Niemiec."

"I'll give ya that much to get your sad sack out of here," Manny said.

O'Garrity turned to Manny and stared him down. The clock ticking behind the bar was heard across the room until Manny, the old geezer with the tobacco heart, hiccupped and started a violent wheeze and fell over backwards with the clatter of a dried sack of bones. No one said a word. Molly bent down over Manny and put her ear to his chest.

"He's dead," she whispered. "You killed, him you crumbs," Molly said to the cops.

"Let's get outta here," the smaller cop whispered.

"I've always said your breath was ugly enough to butcher a man, O'Garrity," the old-fart said.

"Shuddup." O'Garrity leaned back over the counter and asked Stashu, "So, where's the little shit?"

The skyscraping palooka slid off his stool and stooped to pick up Manny's lifeless form. He stood up at the bar gently holding the old man.

The look in his eyes was as deep as coal and as mean as a rattle snake at the dead end of a shovel. He massively towered over everyone and said in a low rumble that started somewhere in the secret getaway tunnel to the false wall in the garage down in cellar, "He's gone fishin', like Stashu told ya. Now haul ass out of here, and take the duet of spare pricks with ya. Before I plant you all in the cellar."

O'Garrity looked up at Sky and down to Manny as the old geezer wet his pants for the last time and it splattered to the tile floor.

"Ke-rist!" the blind man said, "Have respect for the dead, O'Garrity."

The room broke out in laughter.

O'Garrity waited for the room to quiet again. "We'll have a little look-see. Let's go, boys." They dragged Whitey through the parting crowd toward the kitchen. Sally stood up as they went by. Whitey gave her another look to stay out of it. This time she ignored the warning and gave the bigger officer a size six tap shoe in the backside as he went by. The officer did a slight hop-skip and pushed Whitey's head into the next table as they headed to the kitchen. Whitey let out a groan. The neighborhood burst into guffaws again, then settled back down to the thought of Manny's dead body in their midst.

"To Manny," Stashu said, holding up a shot glass.

"To Manny," the others in the room said. But all their cups were empty. They looked at each other and at Emily standing among the tables. Poor Manny.

Emily watched O'Garrity and his men go into the kitchen and the door close behind them. "A drink on the house," Emily called.

A cheer broke out as the crowd rushed for the bar.

In the kitchen, Ma was filling a basket full of sliced Polish Rye bread, and Bosko was perched on a security stool just inside the backdoor with a hot plate of kielbasa, fried potatoes, vinegar laden sliced home grown tomatoes and red cabbage in his lap.

"More pumpernickel?" Stephania plopped two slices on Bosko's plate.

"No, no please, Mrs. Niemiec, I gotta get back out by the..." The words disappeared into the wad of bread already crammed in his cheeks as he looked up to find O'Garrity glowering at him from across the kitchen.

"Real nice, Bosko."

The other two officers held Whitey off the floor.

"Hey, she offered for free."

"Of course she did, you potato head." O'Garrity turned to Stephania. "Where's Bronislaus?"

"Gone fishin'."

Whitey snickered.

"I ain't seen anybody," Bosko defended himself.

"I'm not surprised."

Stephania held out a full plate of the sizzling sausage and cabbage to O'Garrity. "Patrick, why pick on my boy so much, huh? Here, take a seat, boys, eat while we talk this out." she offered.

The officers eyed the heaping plate, breathing profoundly. Everyone loved Stephania's Polish cooking.

Outside, Bronislaus ran out from behind the garage and into the service street toward the bread factory.

"That's him," O'Garrity shrieked. "Out of the way, Stephania."

He pushed the plate aside and ran out the back door.

The three officers tried to follow, but Whitey grabbed the bigger officer knocking the hot plate of food out of Stephania's hand and onto Bosko's lap. The smaller officer slipped on the spilled cabbage going out the door. His fall jarred Bosko off the stool, causing the bigger officer, with Whitey on his back, to crash down on them both. Stephania reached for her heaviest wooden spoon, and despite Whitey's protest and the angry cursing from the three officers, started to beat them all silly about their flailing ankles for making such a mess of her kitchen.

Outside, in the middle of Pittsburg Street, under the burning sun, between the restaurant and the Tasties Bakery, Bronislaus rolled under a passing delivery truck and disappeared.

O'Garrity wandered around in the middle of the street cursing the little Polack under his breath. "Damn you, where'd you go?" Sweat coming on fast, standing out there in the street. He spun back toward the restaurant and yelled at the three officers still brawling in the cabbage. "All right, you numb heads, get out here! Stephania, don't make me put handcuffs on you!"

The three officers scurried out, dragging Whitey. They hustled to catch O'Garrity who was halfway down Tasties' shipping ramp. Stephania's Polish oaths faded in the background as she turned and smiled to herself. Surprisingly, she felt much better, relaxed even. Emily entered and put her hands to her cheeks, taking in the destruction.

Stephania looked around at her kitchen. What a mess. And poor Manny had finally passed.

It was somehow even miserably hotter down at the bottom of the ramp. O'Garrity glanced at the reflection off the ten-pane upper office windows, catching his eye in the violent glare, as he entered where the three young men in bakery whites who crossed Martin Avenue earlier that morning were working. Very little air from the street was getting down to where they were on the loading dock, filling a Tasties' truck with crates of bread. Their heated bodies moved slowly, and their voices were muted under the bedlam of the bakery's conveyor machinery and the added heat of the massive conveyor ovens. Lipinski, the high school graduate, who had driven the convertible off Michal's grass, held the full clipboard checking the route manifest. His tall lean body and crisp white baker's uniform, as usual wasn't nearly as stained as his two friend's, Ducky and Moe.

Tommy (Ducky) Duckowski used his ox-like muscles to lift a wood crate filled with fresh bread over his blond head and heaved it onto a half-filled truck while Moe Thompson used a dolly to roll a stack of full crates across the bed of the truck. He leaned his big-ox body backwards using his full three hundred pounds of human-beef and pushed hard with his thick legs to keep the handcart's squeaking metal wheels, slowly moving forward.

O'Garrity and the officer's with Whitey in tow came striding down the ramp, getting hit even harder by the heat of the bakery escaping up the ramp.

"Lipinski!" O'Garrity yelled, holding no illusions as to the reception he'd get from this bunch of wise guys. The only thing O'Garrity liked about these three dry humps was that they weren't Bronislaus. But because they all had grown-up together and still hung around with Whitey and Bronislaus, they only meant one sure thing: trouble with a capitol T.

Lipinski, who his friends called Lip, pretended to finish a few figures on the clipboard before acknowledging O'Garrity's ominous presence. O'Garrity was accustomed to this ballyhoo from Lip so he waited trying his best not to breathe in the overwhelming smell of bread too deeply, not because he didn't like it, but because he was sick of it and it reminded him of his lot in life, and all these punks living around this place.

Finally Lip looked up and seemed genuinely surprised that O'Garrity and his beat-pounders where still there. "My sister doesn't want to see your rumpus no more, O'Garrity. So don't waste the air." He went back to his clipboard.

"Lipinski, I'm not here over your dumb Dora of a sister."

"No? Then what do you want, handouts? Here," he tossed over a loaf. "Scram..."

The loaf bounced off O'Garrity's chest and fell at his feet. He stepped on it, wishing it was Lip's head. "You want to listen to what I've got to say here in front of these rum-bums, or over at the station alone where no one can hear you cryin'?"

Lipinski glanced at Moe and Ducky and then down to Whitey. "Alright, so what's your beef?"

"I'm looking for that dime store gangster of a friend of yours."

"What else is new?" Moe asked sarcastically, scratching lint from his sticky belly?"

"I wasn't talking to you, so keep your big mouth shut."

"I wonder how long they'd give a guy for killin' a cruddy flat foot prick like you."

"Probably a medal and a parade down Woodward," Whitey answered. "In fact I'd give ya a fiver right now."

"Shuddup." O'Garrity turned back to Lipinski. "You've got two seconds to answer me correctly, or I'm takin' your good-for-less-than-nothin' buddy here," he shook Whitey hard, "in on obstruction charges."

"As far as we know, he's fishin' as usual. As he does nearly every day of his life, rain, snow or shine, and you know it."

"I know damn well he just ran in here!"

"We get paid by the hour, O'Garrity." Lip shot Ducky a look.

Ducky jumped down to a second truck and climbed into its cab.

"Check out the trucks," O'Garrity ordered the officers.

Bosko held onto Whitey while the other two poked around.

"So what's the grumble this time?" Lip asked. "You been chasin' that poor kid since he was eight years old when you claimed he lit dog dung on your porch."

"He's got a chump warrant," Whitey said.

"What?" asked Moe, yelling over the revving truck.

"A warrant," Whitey yelled back. "With a five thousand dollar reward tagged on," he added.

"That's right, boys… I got the little smart mouth this time. So, if you're lookin' for extra summertime money…"

Ducky started to back the truck down the ramp.

"We ain't as crooked as you, O'Garrity, so why don't you just go and…!"

Ducky blew the truck horn and O'Garrity's face flushed with anger as he read Lipinski's lips. The truck nearly crushed him before he jumped out of the way.

The two officers came back.

"Anything?" O'Garrity yelled at them, keeping his eyes on Lipinski

"Nothin, he could be anywhere in the place." the bigger officer yelled."

"Book him," O'Garrity said, smacking his nephew upside the back of his head.

"Ma will have your butt!" Whitey struggled to get free.

"My kid sister will bake me an apple pie for pullin' your lazy butt off the streets."

Whitey stopped, knowing his uncle was right. He hung his head on his chest in mock shame, noting the whereabouts of Bosko's toes and jammed down hard on them with the back of his leather heel. Bosko let out a banshee wail, clutching his flat foot. Whitey took the moment of freedom and dove for the truck and slid underneath it as Ducky shifted back into first and moved the truck so the two less agile officers couldn't get by. Bosko hobbled around in bloated agony while O'Garrity gestured in disgust.

"You idiot, don't just hop around… go get him!"

Bosko gave O'Garrity a mutinous glance and loathingly limped out.

O'Garrity turned on Lip, "One of these days, Lipinski, one of these stinkin' days."

At the top of the ramp O'Garrity rushed out of the docks to find Bosko with his hat off, leaning on a patrol car, watching as Manny's body was lowered by Stashu and Sky into a late model Erskine, an American automobile built by The Studebaker Corporation, in South Bend, Indiana. O'Garrity removed his hat when he caught the pain in Stashu eyes. "Alright, Bosko you ain't plantin' him, which way?"

Bosko pointed and followed O'Garrity across the parking lot toward a row of white painted wood homes.

"If I had two more like you, I'd kill myself," O'Garrity said over his shoulder.

"I've got a brother and a sister at home with nothin' to do."

"What!?" O'Garrity wheeled around on Bosko and got up into his face.

"Nothin'."

Back down in the docks, Moe and Ducky lifted the top two crates off the stack Moe had rolled up into the truck. Bronislaus sat up in the bottom crate. "How much you wanna bet Uncle O'Garrity doesn't like me?"

"And he's such a dear lovable soul," Lip said, as he helped Bronislaus out from under the bread trying not to crush any of it.

"What in the world went on after we left you last night?" Moe jumped up and got comfy on the stack of wood crates. He wiped the grit from his palms on his paint legs, then reached up with his forearm and swabbed the sweat from his face. He eyed a loaf of bread, picked it up, tore off the wrapper and wadded it into a ball and bit into it. "Yuuummm." The others just watched him chew. "So what happened?" he asked.

"Nothin' happened... as far as I remember. Nicole and I just sat around chewin' the fat after leavin' the bar, tryin' to clear our heads before we got on the road back to the lake. The last thing I remember, she was in back and I was in front, lookin' up at the stars, and she started tellin' me some grand fairy story about her hopes at college, you know me and school, the big yawn, but she was very excited, though her father wanted her to marry some guy she told me about instead and have rug rats, or something, so she was upset at him. I don't know, it's fuzzy so I must've dosed off."

Bronislaus' friends gave him the 'oh, sure look'.

"I swear... the next thing I remembered was O'Garrity leanin' on my car horn."

"Sure you didn't do a little horn honkin' yourself?' Ducky asked from the cab.

"Stick it, Ducky. It's not like that with me and Nicole. We're just friends. I met her out at the lake when we were eight or nine, I don't know, a long time ago while Ma picked in her secret mushroom spots. We just kinda' kept things to ourselves. Talked a lot. Mostly her while I tied flies, but I liked to listen to her tell her big traveling stories. She's been all over the place, overseas mostly, nearly around the world and back. Some places I ain't ever heard of even, so I looked them up in the library."

"You was in a library over this dame?"

"Yeah, so? It's called readin' Moe."

"I read. Write too. I just never done it so I could talk to some filly."

"Never mind. What'd Pa say about all that racket at six this mornin'?" Lip asked.

"Something like, "If he wanted his son given horn lessons, he'd buy him a trombone."

"So what'd he do when O'Garrity tried to slap the cuffs on and you took it on the lam?" Ducky asked.

"Nothin', yet. I ain't seen him. But O'Garrity took Nicole in wrapped in a blanket and called her pa... and he must've come down and raised the big stink-eye."

"We saw his Caddy on our way to breakfast," Lip said.

"He must've laid it on ugly thick for them to put out a five thousand dollar reward," Moe said.

"Maybe bankrollin' it himself, even."

"Well, there's got to be more to it than what we already know," Ducky added, scratching his head over a big yawn.

"Yeah, somethin's got O'Garrity prancin' around like a tomcat at a quail convention. I wonder...?" Bronislaus stopped to think.

"Never mind wonderin' about O'Garrity," Moe said. He bit into the bread again. "If I was you, and I'm glad I ain't, I'd be wonderin' about that girl's family."

"What can they do? Kill me?"

The young men looked at each other somberly. Because the truth was yes they could, and probably will try.

Meanwhile, still on foot, Whitey cut down a dusty alley, climbed a low broken-down, moldy board fence and sprinted through a field full of abandoned cars that someone had used for target practice. Three weeks before, two bodies had been found there with holes not put in them by genetics. The bigger and smaller officers were slowly losing ground on Whitey, while even further behind, O'Garrity puffed along followed by a limping, not giving damn, Bosko.

Whitey vanished over another taller fence, catching his good shirt on a loose nail and ripping it useless. The officers stopped, refusing to climb anything ever again, and turned back.

Whitey cut down another alley that led to Warren Avenue. He made a right and sped up a sidewalk passing a bustling meat market, a nearly empty hardware, and a dimly lit tailor shop.

Outside the tailor's, a slender man stood smoking behind that morning's paper. The headlines read "ENTIRE FAMILY OF SIX KILLED IN HOME WITH AX," "MISS MARGARET BACHI IS QUEEN OF CHERRY FESTIVAL," "CITY'S FOURTH FIERY IS SAFE," "CABARET THUGS GIVEN TWENTY YEARS," and "BULL ENDS OWN LIFE BECAUSE OF FLIES."

As Whitey hit the next street he made for the other side and jumped on the back of a flatbed of coal that slowed down to let two ladies cross. He searched the street to make sure he had gotten away — then collapsed sick to his stomach and in need of a smoke.

An elderly couple exited the tailor's with three bundles of clothing and got into their Chevrolet and drove off. The thin man behind the paper let his cigarette drop and stepped on it. He lowered the paper over his hip as he laid foot inside the tailor shop, his free hand slipping into his black tuxedo.

The young Mr. Goldberg behind the counter looked up with a smile as he closed the cash register with a ring of profit. His smile melted away when he saw his next customer meant business. Bad business. He reached for a snub-nose under the counter. He didn't make it. Crazy Carlo Axler pumped three 38 Special shells through the headlines into the tailor's skinny chest, and made it halfway through the shop toward the back door by the time his target hit the tile. At the precise moment Mr. Goldberg's three little girls became fatherless and his wife an unnecessary widow, the assassin was back in his black sedan at a light, nearly a block away, smoking a nice refreshing cigarette.

The job was an easy four figures toward his retirement fund from the Dyers' War raging on for reasons that did not concern Crazy Carlo. He was only a paid killer. Just a man doing what he did best — murder.

3 - TRZY

Located on Jefferson Boulevard, at the very outer fringe of Grosse Pointe Park, a sprawling white brick building with green wood trim and a high red tile roof lay in the midst of a parking lot lined with thirty foot Italian Stone Pines. On the front door a small bronze plaque simply read, "MANGIONE'S." Waiters, bartenders, chefs, busboys and extra kitchen help began to arrive and depart, leaving their cars and bicycles parked at the farthest end of the virtually empty parking lot. A single valet sat with his coat off hunched over a chair smoking a hand rolled cigarette, while the traffic on Jefferson Boulevard buzzed, chugged and clanged past in the swelter of the setting sun… and the onslaught of evening bugs.

Having Lake St. Clair within walking distance was only weighed as a benefit if Bartolommeo Mangione considered a ten degree drop in temperature worth the ten percent increase in insects. But then, this was Grosse Pointe, within arm's reach of the industrial rich, their doctors and lawyers and the like, who lived in the intimidating, elegant homes that lined most of Lake St. Clair and could afford to keep the insects at bay and men like Bartolommeo Mangione handsomely in the nightclub entertainment, food and beverage business.

Old money was still the mainstay of Grosse Pointe in July of 1929, but this was the Roaring Twenties just before the stock market crash and new, more violent money had begun to ransom its way into the upper crust of Detroit — the Italians. They seeped in without warning, as men died and fixed wills were read… as uninvited as rats on a ship to civilization. But this night the whys and hows didn't concern Bartolommeo Mangione. He had much deeper thoughts heaped on his plate.

Just up Jefferson a Grosse Pointe Yacht Club, newly designed by Boston architect Guy Lowell as an 18th century Italian Renaissance-style clubhouse, shone prominently along the shoreline of St. Clair Lake, and sported a 187-foot bell tower to serve as a navigational aid for boaters on the lake. It was about to be dedicated the very next day on this very July 4th. Bartolommeo Mangione had greatly looked forward to participating in this celebration. This was his personal triumph of fully arriving, and he wasn't a bit surprised the clubhouse featured stucco and a red tile roof just like his night club, considering how much money and construction products he and his associates donated to the design of the project. He was the embodiment of new money, he knew this, so giving back to the Grosse Pointe community, and a lot of it, was his way into the high life he wanted his family to live in, the upper crust of the American apple pie. If only his beloved wife could see him now. She would've been so pleased to see the life he'd made for himself and their four children. She was the only woman to have ever truly loved him, including his mother — except for his beautiful daughter Nicole. Not even his own mother had the heart to show such devotion to him as had his wife and now his daughter. His heart was so empty since his wife had passed away, only Nicole, the light of his life, had kept it from shrinking to everlasting nothingness.

Thus, the immigrant Italians became vaguely accepted and even their nightclubs, such as Mangione's, became a favorite place for the old rich to spend their money. But one thing was always kept on the table, even though pushed off into the dimness of business deals and hidden in the dark rooms of politics, if the newly rich barbarians became too much of a pest, a quiet deportation could easily send them packing back to where they came from. And above all, any family to bring shame upon the holy Grosse Pointe community would be shunned and, heaven forbid, taken off important social Holiday lists.

Such were the fears of the Mangione and Bunniti families. So as this day grew to night, a decision had to be made. What was to be done about this Polish boy, Bronislaus Niemiec?

Inside Mangione's, the help was just beginning the clockwork process of setting up to open for another full night of reservations. Anthony Bunniti, a tall, slender, charming man, sat alone at a table in front of the waltz floor and mulled over the afternoon paper, making sure his money was adequately spent, and nothing of this morning's little naked problem was mentioned by any of the scandal-grubbing reporters who drooled over juicy situations such as this one, lying in wait to haul down a hefty pray to wallow on the ground and be the first to pick at their self respecting bones. His eyes flicked from headline to headline as he thumbed through the social pages, dreading the turn of each page, yet relieved every time the page proved fruitless. The tension made his shoulders ache, and his neck stiffen with pain. He was feeling much older than his age this night. The game had changed and the rules to his happiness were no longer of those he cared to play.

Much like a hippo from a river, Bartolommeo Mangione emerged from his office, weary of predators, and watchfully waddled past the bars over to the only occupied table. As Anthony lowered his paper to study the look on Bartolommeo's face for any encouraging sign, the frightful contrast between the two best friends became so apparent that even a time worn, Negro floor sweeper had to stop and scratch his head.

"So?" Anthony asked after Bartolommeo had finally squeaked and groaned himself into the booth.

Bartolommeo motioned the Negro to beat it. The old-timer sauntered off into the shadows of the stage with his push broom. Bartolommeo kept an eye on the sweeper to be sure what he was about to say was not overheard. "It's done. Carlo Axler, ten thousand."

"This is a Polish boy, not the Pope."

"Perhaps you prefer to have your son do it."

"The price of blood money, these men are vampires. I don't think we should go through with this, Bartolo." Anthony's face became so distraught he appeared to be a pale-skinned Englishman.

"This is my daughter found naked and your, soon to be, daughter-in-law."

Anthony retrieved a tattered telegram from his pocket and began to read aloud. "Nicole is mine, she was never yours. Your families' blood will never run pure." He studied the expression on Bartolommeo's face. It read nothing but trouble. "What kind of hogwash is this, Bartolo? Any bum could've sent it. It happens all the time for Christ's sake."

Bartolommeo took the telegram and crumpled it in his stubby hand. "Not to me. Don't you see, Anthony, they've fallen in love. They met at your God forsaken lake and now they're spending nights together. I say this Polish boy sent Nicole this telegram."

"We don't know that for sure. I say we hire a real detective."

"I say we end the problem right now and pay Carlo the money."

"I'd say you've gone mad."

"Then mad I've gone. But this Polack won't run off with my only daughter and destroy my family's name."

Anthony let the hard truth sink in. Nicole running off with this Polish boy, embarrassing his only son was hard venom to swallow. Reluctantly, "I don't trust reporters so don't get this in the papers. I can't afford a public scandal."

A broad, tough smile broke across Bartolommeo's face. "Relax, Mr. Big Shot District Attorney, no one will point their pencil-worn finger at us."

"What about O'Garrity? The fool, I don't like him. He couldn't find his way home from a daydream."

"That's why he's perfect for this. We've taken every legal step we can take. O'Garrity keeps the boy on the run. His family is, or perhaps could be, involved with illegal running of rum across the Detroit River. If the boy disappears or is brutally murdered, who would be the wiser? Certainly not O'Garrity."

"Still, this kind of thing makes me nervous. We're not little boys playing in Palermo any longer."

At this, Bartolommeo held up his glass. "Yes, we were troubled young men. To when days were different and we were different men."

Bartolommeo took a mouthful and swished it about his hippo teeth. "Salute," Anthony said and did the same, but with a lot more grace. "Not bad for a couple of old Guineas like you and I."

"You and your public life are old, Anthony. I am merely fermenting in the shade like fine wine waiting for my time to be cherished by others." Bartolommeo pulled two hand rolled cigars from his coat pocket. He rolled one between two of his stubby fingers and waited. He knew Anthony had tried to quit so he didn't offer. He merely clipped their ends. He knew Anthony well. Inevitably, Anthony extended his hand and Bartolommeo placed the cigar in it. The other one he threw at his own face and it lodged firmly in place between his stained teeth. He sucked on it like a newborn child. Anthony held up his lighter. Its flame leapt in front of Bartolommeo's face. Bartolommeo's eyes shifted away, hiding something as unfathomable as sinister from his best friend.

"What is it, Bartolommeo?"

"Nothing." Bartolommeo fought to hide any thought of his deep dark secret that was buried beyond the glow in his calculating eyes. As far as he knew, only two other people alive that night knew how much truth that telegram contained. And one of them was a poet.

"Are you sure?"

"Of course."

Anthony smoked a moment and dropped the mental strip search and sank into a familiar reflective mood. It was part of the reason why he tried to quit smoking. It reminded him of his dear departed wife. "Women," he said and sighed as he lit his own cigar again, "love them and they perish to the beyond, despise them, and they live to haunt you forever."

"Political power has made you cynical, my dear friend."

"Thank you. It has also made me a lonely man. I look forward to the pounding of little feet again."

"Perhaps you should remarry."

"Digamy? Never. A promise is a promise." Anthony swirled his cognac and held it up so that the work light from the stage shone through it. "How much of this have we brought across this month?"

Bartolommeo chuckled at his childhood friend and reached for the bottle that lay between them. He splashed another ounce in both glasses. "You, Anthony, would make love to the most beautiful woman in the world then ask yourself how much. I, on the other hand, would have to kill for such an opportunity and laugh at how little it cost me."

"I am a public figure. It's my nature to worry. I do worry, I promise you, Bartolo, I worry."

"Nature! The wind is the force of nature. The wind billows the sails of innocent men and launches the ships of reason. Nature doesn't worry where it blows our ship, and neither should you. So, relax, let the wind introduce us to whole new worlds."

"Screw Columbus, I don't want new worlds. I want money and power and a family to pass it onto. You understand me, don't you? Now, how much?"

"Trust me, my friend, we want the same things, me and you. Two more truck loads arrive at the lake tomorrow. For a total of just eight this month. I'll move it to Florida on the sixth and we'll be done for thirty days. Fast and simple." With this he drew contently on his cigar and blew out a cloud of boastful smoke, following it with his eyes toward the old timer who now somberly roamed further out onto the dance floor, locked in a silent romance with his mop. Bartolommeo leaned across the table, keeping his hands underneath, "Don't worry. I've got Albert and Johnny tracking the Niemiec family to see if they're stocking a warehouse. If Michal is running rum and is as careless as his boy, and we tip O'Garrity at the right moment, perhaps with a little luck, The Polish Gang will be out of the bootlegging business forever, maybe even deported on charges by my dear friend the DA. Charming enough?"

Anthony had to smile at the way his fat little friend's devious mind worked. "You always were a cruel bastard."

"True, I am to blame that bad things happen to those who wrong me. That is not being cruel in my eyes. That is just playing the game."

"And I'm fully aware I wouldn't be where I am today politically without a good man like you making things happen the way they're supposed to happen in this town." They toasted in agreement. "To Prohibition."

"May it, and all our generations live forever."

They drank deeply then smoked philosophically. A cloud formed above them before Bartolommeo continued, "You and I, Anthony, we should've been brothers."

"And now we shall be grandparents together, instead."

"At last."

"God bless America."

So the solution to the unfortunate circumstances that life had bestowed upon Bartolommeo and Anthony was simple — ten thousand dollars. The outcome, the Polish boy must die.

4 - CZTERY

The Mangione's sprawling ten thousand square foot family estate, in Grosse Pointe Farms, overlooked the waves of Lake St. Clair. Bartolommeo had virtually stolen the spectacular home for thousands under market value because the previous owners were found mysteriously dead on a yacht off the coast of Miami. Their five young children voted to put both the house and automobile McPherson Spring factory up for sale because none of them were out of high school yet and were gracefully offered to move to Oregon with their still single Aunt, Mary McPherson who taught grade school. So Bartolommeo, against minor protest from his new neighbors, snapped up his dream home without squabbling over the price. Even now, the death of the McPhersons remained a mystery. To some more than others.

Inside, towards the back of the home, Nicole thought over what had become of her life. She had one leg tucked under her exquisite little fanny while sitting in the middle of her spacious upstairs bedroom floor. In the window, the afternoon light faded into long shadows as she vigorously saddle soaped her riding boots until she threatened to wear the shine off.

Robert Bunniti came to stand at the door just out of sight and watched his young wife-to-be with angry, confused eyes. How could such a thing happen? Why did it happen? And what did it mean? This Polack, this dirt, with Nicole, why?

Things were so perfect. Their lives set, forever, established way before he could even remember. Soon he and Nicole would marry, joining their two families forever and they could do the intimate things that had filled his every dream, possessed his every wakened moment together. They would be man and woman, husband and wife, hand in hand, body and soul, blending two desires into one maddening climatic bliss only true lovers could share. The sensual touches, the enticing glances, the dream-like erotic moments they shared over the years growing up would soon finally become a reality. She would be his forevermore and nothing would stand in the way of them expanding the family name, passing his family genes and Nicole's family genes onto to their children and their children's children, forever.

Then this! It was degrading, unthinkable at the very best. How, how, how? He wanted to hurt someone, twist an arm, break a leg, and sever a head. His anger was so great it hurt deep down in his manhood. His heart cried out for pity, his soul screamed for revenge while his mind searched for basic answers. Did Nicole still love him, had she ever really loved him?

What could he do without putting distance between Nicole and himself forever? Had this Polack touched her, his hands, his body, his breath, his... his...? Nicole said no, not even his eyes. But she was found naked by O'Garrity and seen by God knows who else. Death had crossed his mind all day. But who's? His own, Nicole's, this Polack's?

Without looking up Nicole asked, "Lorenzo, would you..." She stopped when she discovered Robert instead of Lorenzo. She was taken aback by his troubled, twisted face. "Robert!"

Robert stepped into the room, trying to relax his tormented features into what might be considered a smile. It didn't work. He was a much stronger version of his father. Two hundred pounds of lean, mean meat. And like his father, he took to wearing dark suits. He held his coat in his clenched fist but his tie was up tight around his throat despite the heat. It was a formal calling. "Surprised, are we?" He wanted to be charming, but anger crept into his voice.

"Yes, I mean, I thought you'd be angry with me and wouldn't want to see me." She continued to rub the boot to Robert's annoyance.

"I am and I don't, but father insisted I come over and have a talk with you." Damn, he thought. Why couldn't he calm down? He wanted to smooth things out, not make it worse. But just looking at her, made his heart hurt, like a dagger to the chest and anger just bubbled out of its wound.

Nicole stood up and put her boots aside and sat at her pink marble vanity table beside her bed. She watched him through the mirror as she picked up her brush and began to stroke her long black hair. She had never seen him like this. It both excited and scared her. Sure she had seen him mad before, but never like this. Never had she felt afraid for herself, for him, for them both for their life together. "I'm sorry, if that means anything."

"Does it?"

"I suppose it does."

Robert crossed the room to the window and looked out back near the four car garage to where Nicole's three brothers worked on Lorenzo's car. Lorenzo was under the car groping about for a tool until Angelo treaded on his outstretched hand. A shouting match proceeded, until finally Caruso had heard enough and seized the tool in question and hurled it across Jefferson Avenue into about eight feet of Lake St. Clair.

"Your brother's filled me in with the details." Robert looked away from the window to study Nicole's reaction.

"Did they? How considerate of them." Obviously her brothers had ridden her all day. If she never spoke or saw any of them again it would be a miracle.

"I can't say I'm surprised."

"If you came here to be rude, you can leave right now."

Robert wasn't winning any points. "How do you expect me to feel? With all the other nights you've spent out at the lake cabin alone. And then you're found in the back seat of some hood's car. And his family owns the other half of the lake. Just how in hell do you expect me to feel?!"

"I don't expect anything."

Robert pounded his fist on the flowered wallpaper until the plaster and boards underneath gave away.

Nicole didn't say anything.

Robert sheepishly stood in front of the cracked plaster facing Nicole. "I'm damned teed-off if you really want to know! And I don't like the idea of this telegram either! Your father seems to think this dirt-bag Polack sent it."

"He is Polish, not a Polack. As much as I am an Italian, not a Dago."

This pushed a button. "What's he to you, anyway?!"

Nicole stopped brushing her hair and turned to face Robert. "Bronislaus and I are childhood friends. I've known him since his father first bought the other side of your lake. Is that what you need to hear?"

"Then why haven't I met him?!"

"You have. Remember the boy fishing?"

Robert searched his mind. "The skinny kid, with that fishing hat? The one always out in the rowboat?"

"He's grown. As have we."

Robert's eye's narrowed.

"It was his seventeenth birthday last night and his family threw a party for him at their bar and restaurant. I was mad at father over something silly that doesn't concern you, so I stupidly said yes, even though I know he didn't expect me to. But, I road in with him. We got a little tipsy and fell asleep in his car. No harm was meant by either of us. I'm sorry if I hurt you. This was the first and only time we left the lake together, the first time I ever spoke to him away from the lake. I swear. On my mother's grave."

"What about your clothing. I suppose you have a good explanation for that too."

"I do."

"Did he touch you?"

"You know me better."

"Did he see you then, or anyone else?"

"I don't know, I don't think so. I had a blanket over me. I covered as quickly as I could."

"Who gave you the blanket?"

"I don't know. I think O'Garrity."

"Someone must have seen you."

"Robert, I often end up sleeping naked. Even in the winter. I was drunk. I'm not saying it was wise or right. I'm just saying I must have taken off my clothing in my sleep."

"Do you expect me…?"

"Remember when I was fourteen and we camped out, and I woke up naked?"

"Of course, how could I forget?"

"Well?"

"And he never touched you?"

"Not once. Believe me, Robert. He was more surprised than I was. As for the telegram, I don't think Bronislaus," she stopped to think. "Well, it could've come from anyone. Your father is a public figure and both our families are well known, if not liked. It could've been someone from school, pulling a nasty prank. Maybe one of the many girls standing in line, I'm sure who would love to marry you."

This seemed to please him that she knew he was well desired by many women other than her. But it was Nichol he loved, and would make his wife because it was meant to be. "Please keep one thing in mind," he crossed to the door, pausing as he thought it over, choosing his words carefully, "your mother gave her life so you could be brought into the Mangione family to grow up to be my wife, and unite the Bunniti and Mangione families by giving birth to our child. I'm the last male Bunniti able to pass on our blood, and I intend to do whatever is needed to see our name is carried on in a manner befitting to the family. Do you understand that?"

"Yes I do."

"And?"

"We have no other choice other than to do what our fathers have planned. What we have planned."

She looked into his eyes, and he into hers. Both knew in their hearts that no matter how they felt about each other at that very moment neither had a choice in the matter. It was done. They would marry as planned.

In the backyard, now under a light, Lorenzo and his two younger brothers still fussed with his car. Angelo held the hood open as Lorenzo bent over the fender, trying his best to reach an errant sparkplug. Caruso leaned in from over the grill with the light.

Robert snuck up under the disguise of Lorenzo's and Caruso's mumble and grumble and goosed Angelo. Angelo yelped and grabbed for his backside letting go of the hood. It crashed down on Caruso's head and Lorenzo's back.

"What the hell's the matter with you, Caruso?!" Lorenzo hollered pinned under the hood.

"Don't yell at me, goddamn it. I'm under here with you!" Caruso yelled back.

Robert and Angelo opened the hood. Caruso and Lorenzo sprang out from under it. They grabbed their little brother by the throat. Robert pushed in between them and held them apart. "Relax, it was me. I didn't know he was holding the hood up."

Lorenzo rubbed his lower back. "Shit, you almost broke my friggin' back."

"To hell with your back, my head is bleeding real blood." Caruso held out the two remaining fingers on his left hand to show them the evidence.

"Don't blame me," Angelo told them. "Lady Face here stuck his thumb up my backside." Angelo went to thumb Robert's nose.

Robert pushed away the hand. "Never mind, you'll both live."

For the first time the three brothers had a chance to see the emotion in Robert's eyes. "Whoa, get a load of you," Lorenzo said.

"Have a chuckle and get over it."

"Careful, Lorenzo," advised Angelo, "he's got the eyes of a rabid dog."

Lorenzo stopped Caruso from adding in. "I see you've spoken to our darling little sister."

"If that's what you want to call it," Robert answered.

"So?" Lorenzo asked.

Robert looked up at Nicole's window to make sure she wasn't listening in. "I don't care what our fathers say. I say we nail the foolish bastard."

"To the bottom of the Detroit River," Caruso said.

"First chance we get," added Lorenzo.

Robert looked at each brother's face. When he couldn't take it any longer and felt satisfied that they meant it, he turned away and walked towards his car at the end of the drive. Halfway down it, he turned back to them. "Sleep on it. We'll talk it over tomorrow at the lake." As he walked away the three brothers went back to work on Lorenzo's car, in search of the errant spark plug.

5 - PIĘĆ

Later that night, when the last of the Sun faded away from the Detroit River, a quick flash of green light jetted out over the darkened water from a small island off Jefferson Avenue known as Belle Isle Park. In response, a faint roar from an inboard rotting wood powerboat came skidding out over the water, knifing through the darkness from Windsor, Canada, growing fiercer with no intentions of stopping until it hit shore.

Abruptly, just as it reached knee-deep water, the engine cut, and the ruby inboard skidded out of the night into the arms of three darkly clad figures that seemed to materialize from the bottom of the murky waters.

A trash truck driven by Lipinski backed out of the brush and up to the speedboat, and before the law could utter 'Rum Running on the Detroit River', the speedboat was emptied and the truck was loaded. The boat then sprang back to life again and roared back across the river with the Skyscraper behind its wheel. The trash truck pulled back onto the road with the original driver of the powerboat, Edju Niemiec, Bronislaus' oldest brother, now grinding its gears.

Later, Sky would bring Edju's car back over on the Halcyon Ferry out of Walkersville, and meet the truck just west of the soon to open Ambassador Bridge, at the Niemiec warehouse that was lost among rows of abandoned timber beamed warehouses.

The other two dark clad men could usually be found playing pool at Michal's or spitting tobacco out the door. And that was pretty much how The Polish Gang brought their share of liquor into the United States. Nothing fancy, nothing tricky, and nothing a hundred other outfits weren't doing at least three times a week; and nothing a dying man couldn't catch them in the act of if he felt like it.

Before Edju left Belle Isle Park, he stopped the truck twice and Lipinski picked up barrels of trash and dumped them into the back of the truck to make sure the liquor boxes weren't in plain sight.

Near the Belle Isle Bridge, where Grand Boulevard crossed Jefferson Avenue, Edju and Lipinski passed a gray Dodge Essex sedan parked just off the road under a stand of maple trees. Inside were Johnny and Albert, the two men Bartolommeo had put on the trail of Niemiec's warehouse.

Johnny lifted his head above the dash and tipped his cheap brim hat back to wipe away the city grime. He slid his glasses up to his mole eyes so that he could vaguely make the garbage truck's license number. "That's it, smooth as puddin' pie."

Albert sat up in the driver's seat and lit himself a cig, which Johnny promptly snatched; so he lit another. "Yeah, these Polacks ain't so bashful. For all we know they could be breezin' a load every night and go unnoticed like beef-hearts into the wind."

"Some slimy bastard ought to teach these sausage rolls not to be so clever." Johnny's dim mole eyes shone from the ash of the cig. He chuckled as he blew out the smoke and ebbed into a choke. "I'm dying," he said, gasping for air. His glasses slid down his nose and fell to his lap.

"Ain't we all." Albert started his car and shoved it into gear. "Let's go root up what Mr. Mangione's payin' us to unearth." He wiped a mosquito from his sticky face, leaving a streak of blood across a cucumber nose, and his chimp-like brow. He rolled the insect between his fingers and popped it between his fetid, tobacco-stained teeth. "Protein."

"Gees, you're disgusting," Johnny said, coming out of his fit, letting go of a wad out the window. "It's times like this when I love bein' a creep." He plucked his glasses off his crotch.

"Yeah, what would creeps like us do if it weren't for Prohibition?"

Johnny took a profound drag from the cig and burst out in another fit.

"Why don't you put that out?"

"I'm enjoyin' it, you mind?"

"Sounds like it."

They made a left on Jefferson and proceeded across downtown Detroit after Edju, Lipinski, and the garbage truck. At Woodward they cut north one block over to Fort Street, continued west towards Fort Wayne, and past the Woodmere Cemetery to the ancient, closed down warehouse district.

6 - SZEŚĆ

Most people arrived at Michal's on foot, so judging by the parking it wasn't obvious that illegal booze flowed like a Niagara spring flood. All the exterior doors were kept shut and guarded and little light came from the heavily curtained windows. The only sign that maybe something other than a family dinner took place was the faint sound of four Negroes earning cold cash making music, and an occasional woman's voice singing a ballad or two.

Once in awhile, just for kicks, the four man band would blast out a round of "Roll out the Barrels" to everyone's delight, and anyone not too inebriated to open their mouths or pound a fist on a table, could join in on the fun. Michal hated this because furniture always got broken. But, what could he do? It was a Polish tradition after all.

By ten o'clock the party inside was running full blast. At half past, Edju pulled up to let Lipinski and Skyscraper out before he put his black four door New Century Six Hupmobile into the garage. Lipinski went up the back stairs that led directly into the office and was let in by Ducky after giving the code. Skyscraper cut through the kitchen after seeing Edju safely out of the garage. He headed for the bar to suck down a tall cold one and to see what kind of trouble his slatternly wife had gotten herself into.

Instead of going directly up to the office, Edju walked with a slight limp around to the front. He removed his lucky red cap from his reddish-blond head and scratched the matching hair on his protruding belly. Like his younger brother, Stashu, he had slightly large ears, and an open, good-natured face. He smoked a Cuban, but flicked the soggy butt out into the middle of Pittsburg Street before approaching the front door. He looked around casually before knocking. One couldn't be too careful. A small slide window opened and closed before the door was unlocked by Skyscraper holding his second, well-earned, cold one.

Normally Edju would have gone up with Lipinski, but it had been a long, hot sticky day following what happened this morning between O'Garrity and Bronislaus. He needed a drink wondering what the outcome of that ruckus ended up costing Pa; and who knows, maybe his estranged wife had called. He tried not to turn bleak in the face thinking about her.

Once inside, Edju was greeted by a blast of smoke, full of stiff howdy doos and handshakes, until finally he was able to push his way to the bar where the skinny young night bartender, Jimmy Six-Toes Smith, had a coffee cup waiting for him. He picked up the drink as he questioned Jimmy about his wife, getting only a shake of the head before the bartender had to move on. Jimmy had lost half a foot working in a Ford smelting plant so once healing self-proclaimed Six-Toes had bartended at Michal's the past two years.

Edju took the full cup with him past a row of friendly boozed filled faces plastered to chairs and benches against the wall. The pool table was neatly pushed out of the way so that people could dance. The four piece band played in front of the drawn curtains on a shallow makeshift stage.

Edju nodded to them and headed up the front stairs which led to the family's three bedroom apartment and Michal's office. His wife had skidooed two weeks earlier with his kid, leaving him behind with just a hasty written note on a used deli bag and her mother's address in Miami. Since then he'd been staying above the bar or out at the lake. He put his house, which was down the block, up for sale. She wasn't coming back and he knew it. So he didn't want to live there alone.

He let himself in with a key and crossed the living room's thick maroon carpeting to the old bedroom that he once again shared with his two younger brothers. He kicked off his smelly streetwalkers and continued on through the yellow and white painted kitchen until he reached the locked inner office door. He downed the three shots of rum in the coffee cup, shook out its upshot on his nerves, and rapped a code on the door as he placed the empty cup on the sink's white tiled counter.

Ducky's voice came booming through the door. "Yeah, who's there?"

"A duos and an ace."

The door opened and Edju entered the office to find a lineup of long faces: Michal's, Stashu's, Moe's, Lip's and Ducky's. At least Michal tried to smile as he shifted his well-fed body in his chair behind his non-cluttered desk. His shirtsleeves were rolled up to his elbows and his tie was pulled down below his open collar, his coat hung by the door. His coal black hair hadn't a hint of gray. His kind blue eyes looked worried though and his face slightly drawn from the burden of the day. A cigar was stashed in the ashtray. Edju slid onto a stool at a portable bar while Moe, joined by Ducky, crushed a stylish wood framed maroon couch beside the two open windows, praying for a breeze. None came. Lip sat on the couch's arm, his meaty upper right limb braced on the window sill.

Edju glanced around. He got a bad feeling. "Trouble?" He asked.

"Plenty." Stashu, pour your brother a fresh one.

"Never mind, I had one." Edju eyed the rum bottle in Stashu's hand. "So, what's the problem? We get invites to a funeral?"

Stashu poured himself another drink. "Not yet," he answered.

"So why the sentimental faces?"

Michal held out his glass and Stashu put a splash of run in it. "It's your little brother."

"Bronislaus? What'd they get him for this time? Stealin' two cent whistles?" Edju changed his mind reached for a glass and some cubes out of the ice bucket on the coffee table. Stashu waved the bottle over his brother's glass. Edju added coke from a half filled bottle.

"He went and got himself in big trouble this time." Michal motioned for the boys to help themselves. Lip did the honors for Moe and Ducky.

"Like what?" Edju glanced at Lip who shrugged.

"Like a dame," Stashu answered.

"Sounds healthy to me."

"Not this me," Lip added.

"O'Garrity came touting a warrant around this morning while you were across the river. I told Lip not to spring it on you. I didn't want you worrying while you were working. By the way, how did it go? Anything look funny to you?"

"Dry as a rat's ass, like always. Why?"

"There's a five thousand dollar reward out along with that warrant." Michal played with his dead cigar. He was tempted to relight it but the room was hot and crowded enough as it was. He looked at Moe.

"My mama got a call from one of her cousins who cleans up over at Mangione's Nightclub on the east side. Claims he heard them mention Carlo Axler," Moe said.

"Yeah?"

"He didn't hear no more."

"Crazy Carlo, huh? Sounds like big tent money," Edju said.

"He said Bartolommeo Mangione was the one who mentioned the name. He was talkin' to Anthony Bunniti."

"The DA? Holy…! We're not talkin' about that little girl last night are we? She's the DA's little girl?" Edju took out his cigarettes and offered one to Stashu who turned it down. Edju lit up and offered his father a match.

Michal shook his head. "Put it out, it's stuffy in here."

"Sure." He took another drag and stubbed it out. "The one I saw sleeping in the back of the kid's car this mornin'?"

"That's the one, but not the DA's daughter, she's Nicole Mangione. Bartolommeo Mangione's little girl, and engaged to the DA's boy. And she was naked."

"Say, I don't get it. She wasn't unclothed when I put a blanket on her. And Bronislaus was out cold. I even put his hat on his face to block the light."

"Lip, fill him in on the details and get yourself something to eat. Meanwhile, Stashu, get on the horn and gather our people together. We got work to do. Now listen up, boys, from here on out, pad your coats. I'm betting there's big money already spent to keep this from splashing high society. There's a monster for hire in this town, and he's headed our way to make sure our boy is out of the limelight. Moe, that means you, too."

"Yes, sir, Mr. Niemiec, I'm with ya one hundred percent."

Edju moved over to the desk and picked up a letter addressed to him. He looked at his pop. "When?"

"I picked it up at your place this morning. Must'ave come yesterday."

Edju opened the letter and read it. The others watched. "Dames." He tossed the letter down.

Michal picked it off the desk. He read it.

"What's it say?" Stashu asked.

"She wants to live in Miami," Michal told him.

"Never should've brought her up here in the first place," Edju said, pouring another drink. "She likes it down there."

"Miami's not so bad," Michal said. "Wouldn't mind building a place down there someday."

"Yeah..." Edju downed his drink.

"But we got work to do first, right?"

"Right."

Lip began to fill Edju in on the day's activities.

Outside the office, about fifty yards down the alley, a black sedan waited. The only sign that someone was inside the car was a faint glow from a Camel cigarette. The smoker watched and waited. Up above, he could see the shadows of The Polish Gang bouncing on the walls and ceiling through the open windows. He watched as food arrived from down below, the smell of Ma's kitchen hitting him full frontal, fighting the hunger pangs of ordering to go for himself. He waited until Moe and Edju finally emerged from the backdoor and came down the stairs from the office. He had nothing against them. In fact he knew none of them and figured he wouldn't beyond this business transaction.

Edju and Moe walked around to the Bakery's side of the restaurant where the four car garage opened onto Pittsburg Street. They checked up and down the street to make sure the row of parked cars on either side of the street were empty. Edju stopped and looked back at the unfamiliar black sedan parked fifty yards down the alley.

"You got something?" Moe asked.

Edju kept his eye on the car. "Ah, it's probably just rickets. I'm gettin' too old for this game." He raked his nails over his bloated belly and unlocked the garage. He went in and backed his car out. He left it running as he held the door open for Moe.

Moe laid a great big basket of food in the passenger's side of the tan bench seat and squeezed his heavy frame in behind the wood steering wheel. He adjusted the plush seat back to his liking. "Ahhhh, stylin'."

"You tell that son-of-a-jack-rabbit, if he hits another deer with this thing, I'll tear his heart out."

"Sure thing, Boss." Moe adjusted the wing glass and throttled the engine. "She sounds real lively. Anything else?" Moe turned on the fat chrome headlights that were bolted across the shiny radiator. A single wiper blade hung down in front of his face.

"Yeah, watch the battery cable, it comes loose... and you guys be careful.

"Don't worry, Edju."

"This thing looks like a family bucket, but it's got a bored out eight-cylinder that'll out game any copper in this state."

"Woo wee, I can hear them horses a gallopin'." Moe gave Edju a big toothy smile.

Edju slammed the door shut.

"Just tell my mama like I asked ya. And don't worry none, we'll take real good care." Moe pulled Edju's car out of the driveway and pulverized the gears up the street. Edju looked after his car to find Moe's big white teeth grinning back at him out of the rearview mirror.

"Smart-aleck." Edju turned back toward the restaurant. He made his way to the back stairs and reached in for his gun on the way up. As he did, the black sedan sprang to life fifty yards down the alley and pulled around the backside of the garage, making a left after Moe. Edju ran back across the short yard to the gate, but by the time he made it to the street, the sedan was just a dull spot at the end of the short block. He didn't have to think hard on who it was. It was Carlo Axler.

Carlo Axler made another left at the end of Pittsburg after Moe. He knew he was the best hired killer money could buy; and his neat work was worth every penny of it. No one had proved him wrong... no one.

7 - SIEDEM

It was one of those isolated romantic Michigan lakes with rolling hills lined with old stand trees all around it. Though no more than twenty miles outside of Detroit, it might have been in another state for all one could tell from the highest point in the area — a quick short-winded climb at best in this humidity; just one small rolling hill slightly higher than the others at the far end of a dense stand of hard wood, split in two by a dusty gravel road. Little known by outsiders, the center of the wood, on either side of the lake was the dividing lines between the Niemiec family's and the Bunniti family's land. And the fish filled waters were as equitably divided by a silent hostility two distinctly different ethnic groups often foster towards one another despite both being as American as the other.

The slightly larger hill overlooked the Niemiec side of the naturally deep lake, where a frail one bedroom cabin was built some years back by Stashu Niemiec to provide lodging when he and his two brothers came to fish. Michal had won the land in a late night smoke filled crap game over ten years ago. He had given it to his sons to keep them out of trouble.

At first, the only real drawback about the lake, as far as Michal was concerned, started when the other half was acquired by the DA, who pulled strings to out-bid Michal for it in twenty-four. Over the first summer, Anthony Bunniti had workers add twenty-five horse stables to the two existing red hay barns, turning his side of the lake into a year round bustling equestrian club. A year later the DA had those same workers burn down the perfectly good century old, hand-honed hardwood log farmhouse to build a sprawling river stone faced ranch home with several matching guest cottages, all with painted white window frames, green trim and French doors, under clay roof tiles. New elaborate landscaping followed the next spring after a three slot boathouse with a hundred foot dock and a gazebo had seemed to materialize on its own. The result was that the innocence of the lake had been violated until nature grew back over the years to the white railed fences and the pain of the raping of its timber healed into a subtle erotic scar.

Since then, once a year a realtor secretly representing Mr. Bunniti would call with a new offer for the Niemiec land, which Michal politely declined. Michal had decided that having something a powerful man like Anthony Bunniti wanted was a trump card waiting to be played… until Bronislaus brought the girl home. Now the stakes had changed, and he wished to hell he'd played the card long ago.

If he had known that Bunniti built the place for the girl because of her love of horses and that she was always there, he would've been glad to sell the place. If he had known about the girl and Bronislaus' festering flirtatious relationship, he could've foreseen the results. But he hadn't, and now he was forced to hide his boy out there, under their noses.

But there was no hiding the boy from Carlo. Michal knew that. Out in the country would only make it easier for Carlo to do his job quietly. Michal felt he had to take the chance that Carlo wouldn't strike so close to the DA's country home. Maybe Michal was losing his mind on this chance, but he needed time to work things out. His hired hands had a lot of work to do. A violent storm was coming and he could feel the growing pressure at the back of his skull. Until he could figure something out, Bronislaus and his friends would have to be on their own, out in the open, and as close to Bunniti as he could keep them. Born killers had special work ethics. There was no telling if Carlo understood what Michal was betting on, or cared.

In fact, at that very moment, Carlo Axler sat roasting in his black sedan on that same slightly higher hill, hidden from sight by underbrush, watching the lake through binoculars while the boys, out in a rowboat, fished.

Over the sound of early morning calling birds, Whitey's outraged voice rang out, "I don't believe this, one of those stinkin' birds just dumped on me."

"You should be thankful," Bronislaus said.

"What the hell for?"

"Dagos don't fly."

The joyful sound of Bronislaus and Moe's laughter filled the air but was short lived, drowned by the not amused Whitey splashing lake water on them.

Later, after the morning mist had turned to full humidity and the hot noon sun approached, Bronislaus, Whitey and Moe still sat in Stashu's rowboat. The anchor hung deep and they each had a line out. Moe and Whitey had their pant legs rolled up below the knees and their shoes, socks, and jackets were off. Both wore short sleeve dress shirts unbuttoned so that sweat beaded up on Whitey's hairless chest, whereas, it tended to sludge down Moe's chest, swamping at the top of his protruding stomach.

In sober thought, Bronislaus was lucky enough to have had a clean pair of tan fishing Pants and a fresh A-shirt to slip into that was stashed in the cabin. He was barefoot as well.

Whitey, between cigs, kept a look out with his good eye through binoculars and his fidgeting kept the boat at a steady rock. Moe, on the other hand, stared motionless over the side of the boat. He dangled a worm from his massive mitt and dipped it into the water. As the seconds dragged by, the humidity increased. It was hard to tell who was the least miserable.

"I'm gettin' hungry," Moe said.

"You just ate the last two sandwiches, you big ox," Whitey answered.

"I know, but thinkin' of these fish fryin' in butter makes my mouth water up and wants to taste somethin' salty."

"What fish? We ain't had a stinkin' nibble all day."

"Then quit rockin' the boat, you're scarin' them away."

"How about you quit stickin' your big ugly mug over the side. You're givin' the fish growin' pains."

Moe heaved the wet worm and it splattered on the collapsed bridge of Whitey's nose and stayed there. "Yuuuuuccccckkkk," Whitey pulled the squirmer from his face and threw it overboard. "I ought 'a murder ya." He looked over at Bronislaus who hadn't seemed to notice a thing. "Yoo-hoo, Bronislaus, you still with the livin'?" Bronislaus ignored him. Whitey didn't catch the hint. "Hey Romeo, cheer up. It could've been worse, you know."

"Yeah, she could've been ugly," Moe added.

"Knock off the chatter, you dips, I'm tryin' to catch my lunch, here."

"So catch it. Who's stoppin' ya?" Whitey said.

Bronislaus looked up from under his fishing cap that had an array of his favorite lures attached. "The best thing about fish is they don't chatter so much."

"Unlike some dames we know."

Bronislaus gave Moe a hateful look.

"I'm fishin', I'm fishin'," Moe said while digging another worm out of the can and went back to dangling it overboard.

"You know what burns my butt? You've been comin' out here all this time and meetin' this Nicole dame and me and Moe are the last to know."

"Yeah, we bein' your best buddies and all."

"You weren't supposed to know. Keepin' it a private matter was half the fun."

"Yeah well," Whitey said, "this is a real noxious joy."

"Yep, me too, I'm hot, sticky and hungry. I'm havin' one hell of a time."

"You two are like fingernails on a chalkboard. She's just another dame, got that?"

"Sure, we got it, don't us, Whitey?"

"I don't know, Moe, they sure seemed palzy-walzy to me."

"Keep it up and I'll mop the deck with the both of ya."

"Woo-wee, Whitey, you scared?"

"Yeah, I'm dumping in my skivs right now."

Bronislaus ended the conversation by ducking his eyes back under his lure filled fishing cap. Whitey lit a cig and went back to the binoculars and Moe started counting the growls from his stomach. He had gotten to six before Bronislaus thought out loud.

"I promised her I'd get her back out here before her people knew she was gone." His somber mood flooded the boat to nearly sinking it. "I sure bungalowed that one."

"There she blows!" Whitey yelled.

"Who?" Moe asked

"Her, the dame, the girl on the horse, right there."

Bronislaus reached for the glasses. "Where?"

"Just to the left of the second red barn, from right to left, with the two trucks parked in front."

"You better not be…. May a pickerel dump caviar in my shorts. I must be goin' blind. I can't seem to make her out from here. Let's move in closer."

Moe took the glasses and looked.

"Have you gone numb in the lobe?" Whitey asked. "We shouldn't even be out here. The place is probably swarmin' with mean little guys with black curly hair and mobster mustaches."

"I ain't takin' no slug 'cause of no dame. And I sure ain't rowin' way the hell over there in this heat," Moe said.

Bronislaus began to reel in his line. "Come on, I'll lend ya a hand."

"I don't care if you lend two hands and a foot. I ain't goin' near that place."

"Yeah, it's a crummy idea," Whitey agreed.

"That dame's been nothin' but a thorn in the rumpus. And in case you ain't noticed lately, everyone ain't exactly pushin' around full wheelbarrows these days."

"Look, guys," Bronislaus tried to reason, "I know if you give me half a chance, I can fix this whole mess."

"Or get us killed." Moe and Whitey looked at each other.

"Okay," Bronislaus said agreeably, "I'll drop you at the shore."

"Oh sure," Whitey said, "and we'll swing by later and fish you out of the drink. Do us a favor, ol'-buddy, ol'-pal, and send this dame a dozen smelly ones."

"Mr. Niemiec said to stay out of sight until he irons things out," Moe said.

"You guys comin' or goin'?"

Whitey and Moe just looked at each other.

Just then a bird that had been hovering over the boat opened its bay doors and bombed Whitey again. "That's it!" Whitey went to shoot it but Bronislaus grabbed his arm and Whitey's gun fell into the drink.

"You'll wake up the whole neighborhood."

"Stinkin' birds, what do I look like, Grant's Tomb?!"

8 - ÓSEMKA

"Stroke, stroke, stroke." The row boat hit the mud shore and lodged into the shoulder high marsh grass.

"Thanks for the help, pal," Moe said.

Bronislaus hopped out and held the boat for Whitey. "Don't mention it. Stay with the boat."

"With pleasure."

Whitey jumped out of the boat beside Bronislaus with his shoes on and promptly sank to his rolled up pant legs in the mud. "Bein' your best friend ain't easy."

Bronislaus pulled Whitey onto dry land. "Who got you your first job, your first car and your first girl?"

Whitey bent to excavate his lost shoe. "The same creep who gave me my first broken nose, my first night in jail and the worst case of chicken pox in recent history." He found the shoe and pulled it out with a low sucking noise. Thick mud clung to it.

Bronislaus took the shoe and dipped it into the water. "So, we're even." He handed Whitey back his soggy shoe. "Let's go." Bronislaus kicked the boat back out into the water.

Moe tossed out a line. "Tell Nicole I said hello. And bring me back some of whatever they're cookin'. Maybe some potato salad…" he sniffed the air. "Smell that barbecue sauce? Man, I'm playin' for the wrong team. Hurry up, I'm starvin'. Hey, Whitey, leave that shoe. Maybe I'll cook it in this Sun and eat it."

"Shuddup."

Bronislaus and Whitey were still about one hundred yards from the barns. Hidden by the marsh grass, they made their way down along the shoreline until the sounds of two horses jumping were just beyond a trimmed hedgerow.

Whitey crawled through the hedge poking his face out to find that Nicole and her best friend Barbara Licavoli were on the two horses jumping log fences. Barbara's parents repeatedly claimed to have no relations to Yonnie Licavoli, one of the most powerful gangsters in Detroit, who later in life would be convicted for the murder of John Kennedy, Sr. But that didn't stop the rumors. Barbara and Nicole's horses were large strong muscular bay Quarter Horses that might have been sisters. Despite the heat both girls sported the same English riding outfits, tall black boots, cream jodhpurs and red riding coats with black bow ties and caps. Barbara was an olive-skinned Italian and had a slightly hooked nose that pointed down toward a hint of a mustache. Her thick black hair was braided into one long rope and swung freely on her back. The contrast between the two girls, Nicole's skin being so fair, was almost distracting to Whitey watching them.

Robert Bunniti sat on a shaded portion of the fence clapping his hands after each jump. He wasn't nearly as dark skinned as Barbara but they could've been cousins they looked so much alike. He wore a white summer suit. The coat hung on the fence, but his tie was up around his neck.

"That looks like her, over there, the light one. It must be hot in that getup, she's startin' to burn out here in all this fancy glare," Whitey said back towards the thrashing sound Bronislaus was making trying to find a hole in the hedge.

"Get your butt out of the way and let me look."

Whitey pulled back and Bronislaus appeared. "That's her all right. Swank, huh?"

Whitey poked around the hedge looking for another way through. "A dame like that would look swank in a gunny sack. Especially if it's floatin' down the D-river." He found a small hole finally and stuck his head through about two feet left of Bronislaus' prone body. "Who's the stiff sweatin' it out along the fence, the competition? He looks kinda bulky, no wonder ya been sneakin' around like a hedgehog in heat."

"How would you like a poke in the eye?"

"If you're not interested in this dame, I'm a cocker spaniel."

"Then roll over, Spot, and play dead, 'cause Nicole plans to marry this stiff and that suits me plenty."

"Yeah, well anyway she's pretty good."

"Yeah, she's pretty good all right."

Bronislaus and Whitey watched as Robert stopped clapping and jumped down from the fence. He called out to Nicole. "I can't handle this heat much longer. Why don't you take a break for lemonade?"

"I'm almost finished, save me a glass," Nicole answered while trotting her bay near enough to throw dirt on Bronislaus and Whitey.

"Barbara?" Robert asked, trying not to show any overt temperament toward Nicole.

Barbara seized the moment to get off her horse and handed the reins over to a tall, wiry ranch hand that had been lingering in the shadow of the stable like a reptile on a rock. "I feel like a poached egg. I'll join you," she answered, taking Robert's arm, and walking off with him. Barbara giggled at something Robert said and turned to look at Nicole over her shoulder. Nicole watched the two of them walk off before turning her horse towards the tallest fence and jumping the entire circuit.

Bronislaus and Whitey still watched. Under the sound of pounding hooves Whitey said, "It's your funeral, but if you want my opinion…"

"I don't," Bronislaus interrupted, "so don't get hurt thinkin'."

"Well, listen up friend, I've taken more than my share of punches over my silly dame and I ain't about to start takin' lead over yours. So if I see one Guinea with hardware, the next thing you'll hear is my size nines walking on water."

Bronislaus took his handgun out of his pants. It was a pearl-handled Colt 45. He looked at it, then at Whitey and with great reluctance, handed it over to his best friend. "Here, take this. And don't lose it. It's Pa's."

Whitey took the gun, checked to see if it was loaded and laid still next to Bronislaus who seemed to have put his entire attention back on Nicole.

"You see anything funny about them other two?"

"Yeah, Barbara's been pining after Robert for years. Nicole couldn't care less. They're like third cousins or somethin'. She's been a pain in the ass but harmless though, tryin' to hide our friendship from her."

"Sneakin' around the ranch like hot cats, huh?"

"Zamknij się."

"I'm just sayin'."

Nicole got off her horse and let the ranch hand take it. She hesitated in thinking of following Robert, and then changed her mind and headed towards the sprawling, new one-story ranch house that sat up on the manicured hill where five large shade trees encircled it.

As she walked up the hill, she turned toward the sound of the riding club members who grouped around an open fire pit between a row of guest cabins and two barns behind the stables. Another group was on horseback underneath the trees out behind the house. The smell of barbecuing chicken and steaks thickened the air as another ranch hand in a white chef's hat and stained apron turned the sizzling meat.

Walter's voice could be heard over those of Caruso's, and Angelo's. "What do I look like, a waiter? Grab your own damn meat." And so the fourth annual Bunniti/Mangione riding club Fourth of July barbecue went on. As usual, it was for the kids so neither Bartolommeo nor Anthony attended.

Whitey broke away from Bronislaus and made his way to one of the old red hay barns where two trucks were parked on the other side. If need be, he'd draw a diversion away from Moe. With all the burning meat in the air, he couldn't help thinking that any swell broiler was worth a few lumps over but taking scrap lead from jealous boyfriends and crazy family members was out of his league. Out of Bronislaus', too, if he woke up in time.

Bronislaus headed the other way, in a roundabout fashion, towards the ranch house where unbeknown to him Nicole had already entered the bedroom and started to undress. Bronislaus made it to the house unseen, waited for a small group of riders to pass, and looked into windows for Nicole. By the time he located her in the master bedroom she had already backed behind a partition and thrown her riding clothes over the top. Bronislaus left the window disappointed. Everyone in the world got to see her naked but him. He slipped into the house through the back kitchen door. From the kitchen window Bronislaus could see Robert at the barbecue helping the ranch hand rotate the meat on the grill while the flames leapt back at them from the juicy meat. As far as Bronislaus could tell, no one else was inside the house.

At the back barn door, Whitey listened for a moment, before squeezing inside. Sunlight came through the cracks between wood planks throwing beams and shadows across the dusty barn, and pigeons fluttered up in the rafters as phantom war bombers in disguise, giving Whitey the spooks.

He walked cautiously through the loose straw, hay and dirt, following a heavily used path, mindful not to get dumped on again, until a rooster fluttered up from a fresh stack of hay. His pumper leaped up around his tonsils. The bird brushed against his chest and face, feathers flying, knocking Whitey flat on his rump. He aimed the pearl handle and fought back the urge to blast the damn bird. After his heart fell back into place, he picked himself up to brush himself off. Hay, grain dust and feathers clung to his sticky body like it would if tarred. A dollar size clod of something brown and smelly was plastered to his tender side. He flicked it off wiping his stinky fingers on the wall.

"I'll murder ya, Bronislaus, I swear I will."

Whitey examined the barn from where he stood; newly built storage rooms behind locked sliding doors were to either side. Fresh hay went nearly to the rafters on both sides from the lofts. Directly above him was open space up to dried mold stains on the leaky roof. In front of him at the center of the barn a rusted 1917 Model F Fordson Tractor tilted to one side from a broken front steel wheel and a knockout dented front grill and radiator cover as though something flat and heavy, like a large flatbed truck, had stupidly backed into it. Whitey moved away from the fumes of its fuel. Beyond that were two vast sliding barn doors where the paths forked in the dust and loose hay leading past both sides of the tractor towards the new storage rooms. Whitey chose the path to the right and followed it to the barn doors and peeked out through a crack with his bad eye, then switched to his good one.

Five feet from his eye stood Johnny, Albert and Lorenzo. Behind them, the crumpled tail gate to an empty large flatbed truck stood with its gate permanently open. A set of handcarts rested against it. Apparently they had just emptied something from the truck into the barn or worse were about to pick something up. They headed toward Whitey. Whitey pulled his eye back out of the crack and looked around in a panic. To the left of the barn doors he found an old peg ladder leading up to the dusty hay loft and scampered up it like a rat under attack from a pitchfork.

"Well, we thank you, boys," Lorenzo said. He slapped Johnny on the back just outside the door, causing Johnny to slip into another fit of coughing. He ralphed up a throat full of phlegm and spat it out at a chicken playing tug-of-war with a worm, as Albert reached up and slammed but failed to shut the tailgate. "Nice. Sorry about the truck, Albert."

"Forget it, that piece of shit tractor got the worse of it."

"Might want to empty that gas tank, though," Johnny said.

"We'll get it done. Just send us the bill," Lorenzo added.

"Nah, we lifted the truck from a guy doin' ten to life anyway."

"We good then?"

"Nothing makes me happier than a taxless fast buck," Albert said. "Sort of holiday pay, ain't it."

"Exceptin' a taxless fast dame, that is, which is a holiday any day," Johnny added, at which they all laughed.

"How about a beer, we got steaks on?" Lorenzo offered expecting them to decline and beat it as usual.

Albert looked at his watch, "Well..."

"Why not, it's a holiday, ain't it?" Johnny answered for them and the three men walked back around the hay barn toward the barbecue area.

As they neared the others, Robert broke away from the pit. The ranch hand who had attended to the horses had just informed him of Nicole's whereabouts. Barbara watched after Robert. Lorenzo slid under the umbrella beside her.

"Help yourself boys," Lorenzo said.

"You didn't invite them, did you?" Barbara asked.

"Don't worry about it."

"They're hoods, aren't they?"

"Of course not, they're hay brokers.

"Hey?"

"Your horse has to eat doesn't it?"

"Of course."

"Well, so do they."

"What's taking Nicole so long?" Barbara asked looking up to the house.

"Who cares... you want something to drink?" Lorenzo asked, getting back up and moving toward an ice chest.

"Sure... my throat feels scratchy"

"In this heat?"

"This hay, my allergies are killing me."

Back up the hill at the ranch house, Nicole was almost done with her shower. Bronislaus still waited in the living room listening for the water to stop, while behind him, unbeknownst to him, Robert approached with intentions of finding Nicole alone and hopefully still undressed. Her being naked had been on his mind. Bronislaus backed out of view as Nicole shut off the water and stepped out of the shower. The water glistened off her body like a beached white-coat harp seal. She looked over her slender form in the mirror. Nature was taking its time. Barbara's breasts were nearly twice the size of hers already. Then again so was her nose. She smiled to herself at her mean little joke and wrapped her precious body with a towel.

A sense of not being alone washed over her, sending goose bumps down to her unpainted toes. "Barbara? Who's there? Robert?" She plucked a shotgun from a wall rack. "I can see your shadow, whoever you are. I've got a loaded twelve-gauge, and I'm not afraid to use it."

Bronislaus held out his white hanky in the open door. "Careful, Princess, I'm a bleeder." He stepped into the room.

Nicole held the shotgun on him. "Bronislaus?!"

Bronislaus scratched himself about the ear. "Little girls with hardware gets me allergic."

"Are you insane?"

"No more than the next guy. How about puttin' down the artillery, you're givin' me a rash?"

"They'll hurt you, you know…" she lowered the gun.

Bronislaus took it from her and checked to see if it was loaded. It wasn't.

"Thanks." He smiled.

"What's so darn funny?"

"You are, I am, this whole charmin' situation is."

Nicole remembered that she was standing there Harry Starkers with nothing on but a towel. She flushed from head to heel and quickly moved behind the partition to dress.

"Please, Bronislaus, I don't need any more trouble."

"That makes two of us."

"You've got a lot of nerve showing up around here after running off like that, leaving me to face all those people… alone."

"O'Garrity would give his first born to put me behind bars, so I wasn't about to hang around and make it easy for him. By the way, thanks for calling me yesterday."

"Well, you're not welcome. Do you realize the kind of embarrassment we've caused my family? My brothers won't even be civil to me. And Robert will kill you if he finds you here."

"Yeah, yeah, I know, I'm sorry. Life ain't been so swell around my place either. We're still friends though, ain't we?"

"Boy you make me so mad." She poked her head around the partition to see the little boy's hopeful smile on Bronislaus' face. She frowned back at him. "I guess."

"Good, now if you'll just finish gettin' dressed, we can straighten this whole mess out by havin' a little friendly chat with your father."

"Seeing my father is out the question."

"Okay, then we'll just call him on the phone."

"Do you honestly think my father wants to talk to you at all?"

Just outside the kitchen door, Robert stopped when he heard Nicole raise her voice. When he heard Bronislaus answer, he drew his gun from the back of his trousers and eased the backdoor open. The nerve of this guy showing up here.

"You don't seem to understand what's goin' on, do you?"

Nicole apparently was having trouble getting dressed. She looked around the partition toward a chair where her clean panties lay. Bronislaus followed her glance. She gave him "Will you help me eyes," and he scooped the panties up with the barrel of the shotgun and handed them over. "Thank you. No, I don't fully understand, Bronislaus, so will you please leave."

"Look, your father isn't playing around with a bunch of polka drunk idiots here. My family is mostly nice people at heart but they are as dangerous as any other family in this city. My pop has some pretty violent friends he does business with, people your family doesn't want to know. Here in Detroit, Chicago, Philly and in Europe. My pop grew up with some of these people in Kraków. I know Pop wouldn't want it, and will try to end this in-house, but things would happen and domino very fast with just a few phone calls into a citywide war if your father makes a move on any of us."

"If you just leave now, nothing will happen."

"It's not that easy, Nicole. We know damn well your father put a contract out on me. And don't give me those eyes."

"I know, I know, The Polish Gang, I danced with them, remember? Like you said, they seemed like polite people for the most part."

"They are for the most part, but if anything should happen to me or any of us, Pop would be forced to retaliate to save face if nothin' else, and who knows where this would end? Do you remember those Valentine Day Murders in Chicago? One of those men was Pop's second cousin. It was a massacre."

"Are you saying your family would hurt mine like that?"

"Yes. Maybe, I hope not. Pop keeps a very low profile here in Detroit. For good reasons. We don't want any trouble like what's going around this town and others. It's our credo. We just want to make a modest living by servicing our neighborhood and friends. But if anything should happen to me, I can't say things wouldn't change.

Nicole went back to dressing.

"Have you ever heard of Carlo Axler?"

"No. Should I?"

"He's a for hire cold-blooded killer. A hitman, who's taken out a dozen men and women in this town and others."

"So?"

"So, that warrant your father's got O'Garrity wavin' around is nothin' but smoke to make things look legit. Your father hired this guy to outright gun me down."

"Now I know you're insane. Get out, Bronislaus, now!

"Somehow I knew you would say that. I'll leave as soon as you get on that phone and tell your father to cancel that contract on me."

"My father wouldn't do such a thing. I don't know who you think he is, but my father is a well respected businessman running a first class nightclub in Grosse Point. He has friends with high level political ties to this town. He'd never stoop down to your family's cultural level of violence. But if Robert finds you here, I don't know what he'd do. So please, Bronislaus, I'll talk to my father about the warrant when I get home, but you've got to promise never to send me another silly telegram."

A puzzled look washed over Bronislaus' face.

Nicole saw the truth in his eyes. But she had to ask, "You did send me a telegram, didn't you?"

"Now who's runnin' the fever? I don't know why, but would you mind runnin' that one by me again?"

"Someone sent me a telegram two days ago stating in a roundabout way that I am not a true Mangione. My father seems to think it's you trying to interfere with my marriage to Robert."

"Whoa, wait a minute here, Nicole, your father's knockin' on the wrong cabin, 'cause I haven't sent anything anywhere in years. And who you marry is your business. Shoot, I thought we based our friendship on both knowin' that."

They studied each other's face. It was true that they were both fully aware of Nicole's pending marriage, but the subject never seemed to come up often enough to get in the way of their friendship. She was just seven when they had met and he just eight. She came across Bronislaus one morning while on horseback. He was resting on a rock after just swimming across the entire lake, which she watch in amazement from up in the barn, but never told him. She gave him a ride home on the back of her horse as far as she could go because of a barbwire fence. She never laughed so hard in her life until she found this funny boy from the other side of town, this cute boy from the other side of the lake. He hadn't wanted his friends to see him playing with a girl, and she didn't want her brothers to beat him up, so they had made a pact to be secret friends. Who would've thought he'd grow into such a handsome lug, with such deep penetrating eyes, dark wavy hair and hard rippling muscle? Bronislaus knew all along what Nicole would grow into, a beautiful, classy, out of his reach, and pain in his side if he allowed it to get to him.

"Then who sent it?" She glanced at the sound of approaching horses and laughter outside the closed windows.

Bronislaus tore his eyes away from hers. "It's probably just some dumb prank. But I can tell you one thing, your father ain't seen the last of The Polish Gang if he tries to payout on that contract, so talk to him. I'll talk to Pop about the telegram and see what. But, I swear I didn't send it. I better go." With that he turned toward the door only to receive a cool reception from business end of Robert's Smith & Wesson 38 Special.

Bronislaus held the shotgun on Robert. They both evaluated the situation. Bronislaus knew one thing for sure… the shotgun wasn't loaded.

"You should've listened to the lady, Polack."

Without taking his eyes off Robert, Bronislaus asked, "Nicole, would you mind opening that window?"

Nicole wasn't sure what to do, "But..."

"Just open it, that one, it's stuffy."

"Stay away from the window." Robert cocked his gun. "So, we finally meet again. You and I, Nicole and you, Nicole and the two of us. Sort of cozy isn't it, Polack?"

"If you like crowds... Dago."

Robert remained cool. Bronislaus waited him out. "All right," Robert said, "make your move."

Bronislaus didn't move. What chance did he have if Robert actually practiced with that heater? The shotgun wasn't loaded and all three of them knew it. The thing that puzzled Bronislaus most was that the window was closed. Why? It had to be 90 degrees outside. To get to the window he had to run past Nicole. If Robert waited for him to get past her, Bronislaus knew he had a chance. If Robert didn't wait and fired early and missed, chances are Nicole would get it. The light from the window was still partially blocked by Nicole. That meant she was practically behind him. All Bronislaus needed was a step. Robert glanced past Bronislaus at Nicole, and Bronislaus made his move. He tossed the shotgun at Robert and headed for the window. Robert sidestepped the shotgun as Bronislaus sped past Nicole, making Robert hesitate. Bronislaus dove and crashed through the window, Nicole ducked and Robert sent two bullets into the wall three and four inches away from the window sill.

Outside, glass went flying along with Bronislaus who landed at the hoofs of seven horses. Bronislaus rolled under the belly of a big gray Appaloosa. The big gray didn't take much of a liking to that, and even less to the shattering glass or the gunshots, and reared up, throwing its rider back over its tail and onto the ground. The other horses reacted very much the same way as Bronislaus continued to roll on the ground until he was just outside the stampede and up against one of the big shade trees.

As riders started dropping to the ground, Robert stuck his head out the window and tried to take aim at Bronislaus while fighting off Nicole, who pulled on his other arm. He managed to take three more shots before Bronislaus disappeared around the west corner of the house.

Out by the barbecue pit, Lorenzo and the others were all on their feet. Johnny sucked down the remainder of his third beer and stuck another in his pocket for the ride home. "What class," he said, stopping to pick beef from his teeth, "fireworks and everything."

Caruso looked at his two brothers, they shrugged. "What fireworks?" They shrugged again. "That sounded like gunshots to me."

Lorenzo took off towards the house. "Me, too. Walter, Johnny, Albert, cover the barn," he yelled over his shoulder. "Caruso, Angelo, follow me." The other horse club members remained by the pit. They were not sure what was going on, but very sure they wanted nothing to do with whatever was.

From inside the barn, Whitey heard the unmistakable shooting, knowing he had Pop's gun, and frantically looked for a spot to put out the cigarette he knew he shouldn't have lit. But straw and dust were everywhere waiting to burst into flames so he stuck it back in his mouth and headed down the ladder. Once on the ground, he found himself standing next to the leaky Fordson Tractor, patting himself down looking for the pearl handled gun. It wasn't on him. "Why me, Lord?" He looked back up to see where he left it on a support beam.

The sound of running steps brought his eyes to the two vast barn doors. Doors quickly opened and slammed on the truck cab just outside. Before Whitey could take a single step, the two barn doors where flung open, and Walter, Johnny, and Albert filled the opening, standing in the shadow of the barn, now fully armed. Johnny made a move to raise his gun, and Whitey went for the tractor's gas cap, holding his cig over the opening. "One move and I blow us all to Hamtramck."

"Take him, Johnny," Walter, Mangione's driver said, his deep stuffed alligator-eyes calculating the odds as he stared Whitey down.

Johnny lowered his gun. "Forget you, Walt. I ain't endin' up no toasted weenie over this." He started coughing again.

"Shut up!" Walter yelled at him.

"He can't help it..."

"Now," Whitey dug in his pocket for his cig pack, "just back your tail ends out of this barn."

Albert pounded Johnny's back. "All right, buddy," he said, "just..."

"I didn't ask for a dance recital, I said back it up, now! Or maybe you want your shirts turned inside out with you still in 'em?"

They put their feet into reverse as Whitey fumbled to light another cig off the first. He needed time. He held his breath so that his hands wouldn't shake. All he got instead was a red face and a cramping in his stomach. Sweat poured down his back, face, and hands as he fought not to get the cigs wet. His temples began to pound from the heat and dust, and not breathing. Come on, Whitey, breath, he thought, don't pass out on me man. Please God, get me out of this jam and I'll stop living in sin. I'll marry Sally, or at least make her move back home. I swear, no more punches from crowdin' her professional life.

His swollen eye and lip ached from his rising blood pressure. Finally, he managed to light the second cig. He took a long hit to ensure that it was lit well. It made him dizzy and he accidentally nudged the lit tip off the first cigarette into the gas tank. A huge moment of panic big enough to drive a bus through filled the barn. But nothing happened after it passed. Whitey looked at the three men and their guns. A slow sheepish grin spread across his face while theirs all stayed drawn and ashen.

The three men suddenly realized that they were not blown to bits, and took steps towards Whitey with every intention of painfully hurting him.

The little Scot stopped smiling as they approached.

When all three where in the barn Whitey took one last urgent drag from the fresh cig and sent it down into the tank before diving at the door behind him, the one he had entered from. The other three men dove backwards. There was a slight hesitation before the tractor detonated with a concussion of three sticks of dynamite, hitting and sending all four men rocketing out of the barn in several directions.

Whitey magic-carpeted out the back atop the barn door propelled by the blast until he collided with something hard about ten feet away from the barn that slowed his flight. With a sickening thud, the shattered old door stopped but Whitey traveled beyond and over Bronislaus, who had been pinned to the ground, and was about to be plugged by Robert until the door hit Robert square in the shoulders, pinning him underneath.

Another violent blast of smoke and fire followed Whitey out of the barn as Robert sprang back up, throwing the door off him, and immediately knocked him back down. His clothes and hair were smoldering, but not nearly as bad as Whitey's, who had practically lost the entire back of his shirt and pants, and whose sweat was rapidly turning into steam from the heat. Soot rained down out of the smoke. Robert raised his hand to shoot Bronislaus before he realized that he no longer held his gun.

Bronislaus seized the moment to scramble through the flock of crazed chickens gathering their chicks and ran for Whitey who was artfully disguised as a pile of smoldering rags. Bronislaus scooped his best pal up on the way by. Before Robert could regain his senses enough to find his gun, the two young men were at full stride alongside the new stables heading toward a fresh mound of horse manure.

Nicole's three brothers came staggering toward Robert with their faces and hands covered with soot and ash. They began to fire after the two fleeing boys.

Bronislaus and Whitey dove for the manure pile. Whitey made it halfway up with bullets sinking in around him. Bronislaus reached over the clumpy damp mound and dragged him to safety, digging Whitey's face into the horse extract.

"Uuuuggggguckkk, what is this stuff?" Whitey yelled.

"Move it," Bronislaus yelled back at him. And they took off running again.

The Mangione brothers emptied their guns. Angelo's smoldering felt hat burst into flames so Lorenzo grabbed it off his little brother's head and stomped it out as they reloaded their guns.

The three brothers found Robert fumbling around in the smoke and chickens looking for his gun. "Oh boy," Lorenzo said adding a low whistle, "get a load of you." He led Robert out of the smoke. Caruso found Robert's gun and gave it back to him.

Robert looked Lorenzo over. "You don't look so dandy yourself. What the hell happened?" Robert breathed deeply to clear his head.

The three brothers hadn't a clue as to what just happened. Walter, Albert and Johnny came around the corner, decorated like the others, but much worse. Johnny had a deep gash above his left mole eye from his broken glasses, his blood streaking the soot, war-painting his face like a mad Indian. Albert was naked from the waist up. One side of his monkey-brow head was virtually bald including all his facial hair. Walter was the worse of the three. He stood in his shoes, socks and smoldering boxers. Only the rim of his hat remained around his neck and now his prematurely balding head gleamed naked to the ears and his deep stuffed alligator-eyes were jammed nearly shut with soot. His hands and face were painfully red from the heat, bubbled as though with an evil sunburn and his alligator-peepers were yellowed from the soot and smoke.

"What the hell did you guys do, Walter!?" Lorenzo shouted.

"Huh!? We didn't do nothin'. That little punk threw a cig into the tractor's gas tank." Walter blinked and his eyelashes fell out.

The barn began to explode again. Everyone hit the ground from the sheer force of the blast.

"The booze!" Lorenzo yelled, "Let's get out of here."

They picked themselves up as the barn burst again sending the top of the barn, and huge chunks of old timber raining down into the lake.

Robert reloaded his gun. "Stay with the men and put it out. I'm going after them."

"I'm comin' with you," Lorenzo said.

"Alright," Robert agreed. "Caruso, call Mr. Mangione and ask him to contact my father. The rest of you, try to put this fire out the best you can. But stay clear of the barn. There's apt to be more explosions. No cops, understand?"

Ranch hands and the men and women from the equestrian club began to line up with buckets of water but Caruso shooed them away from the exploded barn as Robert and Lorenzo headed after Bronislaus and Whitey. Lorenzo stopped at his car and took out a Thompson submachine gun from under the backseat. Robert nodded his head in approval. They cut back around the new stalls and headed past the manure pile, where Whitey had lunched, toward the marsh, a hunting they would go.

9 - DZIEWIĄTKA

Deep into the marsh, Bronislaus and Whitey plugged along in the mushy earth. The marsh grass that cut at their arms and legs made the going even tougher. Whitey managed to say between painful breaths, "Damn it, Bronislaus, if that dame gets us killed, I'll never speak to you again."

"Just head for the woods'"

"What about Moe?"

"We'll be sittin' ducks in that boat." Bronislaus suddenly stopped to listen.

"What?"

"Shhh… over there."

"What is it?"

"Deer."

"I can't believe this."

"Come on, let's follow." Bronislaus moved faster through the grass.

"Am I goin' out of my noggin?

"Shut up, will ya? I want to see where they go."

"In the middle of all this ballyhoo, you want to hunt deer?"

"Why don't you wake up, Whitey? Deer know the best way to and through the woods." Bronislaus entered an open area where the deer had been resting in the tall grass. The grass was flattened. Bronislaus paused in the center, searching for the deer path out. Whitey flopped down. "Ahhh, heaven." He looked up to find himself alone. "Bronislaus?"

"This way."

Whitey got up and scampered after Bronislaus' voice.

At the beginning of the marsh, Robert and Lorenzo cautiously hunted Bronislaus and Whitey. To their left, a voice rose up from out in the lake.

"I got one, I got one!"

"Did you hear that?" Robert whispered.

"Yeah, over there," Lorenzo whispered back.

"Let's take him."

They worked through the marsh toward the voice until they were inches from the water's edge. They carefully separated the tall marsh grass. Out about ten yards, Moe sat in Stashu's boat fighting with a large fish. "Damn, boy," he mumbled to himself, "you went and got yourself flat in a mess now. All these crazy ball face folks shootin' at one another, blowin' up the world and you go and hook the largest damn carp you ever laid your black-eyed peas on."

Moe slowly became aware of a reflection in the water. He blinked hoping it would go away. When it didn't, he followed the reflection to the shore, over to Lorenzo's and Robert's mud-caked feet, up their tattered pant legs to their singed upper bodies, to their angry raccoon eyes. He gulped out of having nothing else to do about it.

"What are you doing out here, boy?" Robert asked. He wasn't expecting to find a Negro fishing on his father's side of the lake.

"Fishin'." Moe pretended to be just some dumb angler and continued to fight the fish. He glanced down to find his gun in the bottom of the boat.

"Beat it, this is a private lake," Robert told him.

"Yes, sir, I'll just row my buttocks right out, just as soon as I..."

"Hey, I've seen you before?" Lorenzo said. "Yeah, yesterday mornin', outside that Polack dive. Are you waitin' for somebody, boy?"

"Who me? Just our Lord Jesus, like everybody else. And I suspect he'll be callin' on me soon," Moe said with genuine surprise. "Sir," he added.

"You sure?"

"You must be thinkin' of some other person 'cause..." Moe let go of the pole and the carp pulled it down into the water. He picked up the oars and started to row.

Robert didn't like it either. "Take him."

Moe quickened his stroke. Lorenzo sprayed the boat and cut it in half as Moe dove into the water and began to swim toward the bottom and as far away as he could from the onslaught of bullets cutting through the water all around him.

Lorenzo and Robert rocked back and forth on their toes, waiting for him to come up.

"What're the odds?" asked Robert.

"Fifty-fifty, these things scatter pretty quickly."

At the edge of the woods the thick marsh grass turned into a cluster of dry sumac. The deer were already about fifty yards into the trees by the time Bronislaus and Whitey, out of breath but still running, came upon a barbed wire fence not far from the spot Nicole had once dropped him.

Bronislaus climbed through but Whitey drooped down on a pile of rocks and hung his head between his knees, gasping for air. He kept spitting trying to get the taste of manure out of his gums. He looked up at the woods. From their looks, Whitey wanted nothing to do them. For one, they were gloomy and spooky looking. The underbrush was also thick and certainly prickly, and who knows what lived in a place like that.

"Maybe we should go back and help Moe? Maybe they got 'im."

"Get up, keep movin'. Moe can take care of himself."

"I don't like this, there's liable to be a bear in there or somethin'."

"Listen, Whitey, I promise, there are no bears around here, so quit your bellyachin'."

"Bellyachin'? You've made me do a lot of things in my life, Bronislaus, but I never thought I'd have to bite horseradish because of you. So I ain't goin' in those woods. I ain't a fan of Mother Nature and she don't take much of a shine to me, so forget it, I'm sittin' right here until the cops show up."

"Fine, stay here then."

"Thanks, I will."

"Good, because you're sittin' on fire ants."

"Fire ants! In Michigan?" Whitey jumped up and started slapping them off himself. "Help me! Ouch! They're, ouch! Eatin' me!"

"Relax, they're just carpenter ants."

In the distance, Lorenzo's Tommy-Gun blasted the water again. Whitey looked in that direction then back at the woods. He took a deep breath and climbed the fence, getting what was left of a tattered pant leg caught in the barbed wire. Bronislaus had to rip the pant leg off to get

Whitey loose. Whitey picked himself up and brushed two more ants off his arm and back.

"You bastard, I'll probably get sprayed by a skunk and die of loneliness or somethin'." He looked up to find that Bronislaus had disappeared into the woods so he ran after him.

Robert and Lorenzo came out from the water into the higher ground and marsh grass. Walter ran up from behind them and Lorenzo spun around and opened up on him with the Tommy-Gun. Walter dove down into the marsh grass.

"Damn it, Lorenzo. It's me, Walter!"

"What is it?" Lorenzo was angrier for being surprised than sorry.

Walter picked himself up. "Your father, he wants you on the phone, now." He looked down at himself. "Damn it, would you look at me?! I just changed." His knees and arms were covered with mud and decayed leaves.

"What did he say about the booze?" Lorenzo asked.

"Hell, I don't know. I didn't talk to him, Caruso did," Lorenzo said.

"Go ahead, I'll keep after them," Robert said.

"Let me talk to him first. They're headed toward their cabin anyway. We can take the car around and probably beat them there."

Robert paused to think. He wanted that Polack now. He looked toward the woods.

"Don't do it, Robert," Lorenzo said. "They could be in there waiting to bushwhack us."

Just about the center of the woods, where the prickly underbrush was at its thickest, Bronislaus and Whitey fought to get through it, headed for the cabin. To Whitey, entering these woods was one of the worst ideas he could have ever imagined. Thorny brush slapped at his face as he fought off mosquitoes vying for his blood.

"What are these, vampire bees?

"Keep movin', they're just mosquitoes."

Whitey pulled up to look down into the front of his pants. "Damn."

Bronislaus doubled back. "What now?"

"Just checkin' my dipstick. I'm down a quart"

Bronislaus grabbed him by the arm and dragged him along.

On the dirt road leading around the lake, a cloud of dust tailed Lorenzo's 1929 Marmon Model 68 four door eight cylinder sedan as it barreled down the unnamed lakeside road. It made a left on another bumpier dirt road apply called Sumac that lead to the Niemiec cabin. The two young men inside hung on for dear life as Lorenzo braked to slow the car down.

Back inside the woods, Bronislaus was nearly dragging Whitey along until Whitey gave up and doubled over with stomach cramps. "I can't run no more. My head is poundin' again, and I'm feelin' chills. I think I'm gonna heave."

"Come on, the cabin's right up here."

"I can't, not another step." Whitey took out his cigs. "The wind's all out of me."

Bronislaus looked behind them. "They're liable to be…"

Before Bronislaus could finish, a big hulking figure jumped out and tackled them both. Bronislaus and Whitey started to beat it about its wet back.

"It's me, it's me, muffle up you guys, they'll hear you."

Bronislaus quit, but Whitey swung away at the air with both his good and bad eye closed. Moe held Whitey off with a thick paw on his forehead.

"Knock off, Whitey, it's Moe."

Whitey opened his eyes. "You, lummox," he said. "I knew it all along."

Moe clamped his hand on Whitey's mouth. "Sssshhh! O'Garrity."

Whitey stifled a scream of agony from Moe sweaty palm touching his busted lip.

Moe let go. When the pain subsided, Whitey punched Bronislaus in the arm. "Wake me when this is over, will ya?"

Bronislaus hit Whitey back. "Don't push your luck, or I'll fatten your other lip."

"What happened back there?" Moe whispered.

"Nothin'," Bronislaus answered. He shot Whitey a look as the pain in his arm peaked.

"Yeah, nothin'," Whitey said sarcastically. "I just got blown up, shot at, force-fed horse droppin's, attacked by cannibal ants, scandalized by barbed wire, and involuntarily donated blood to the flying needy. Other than that, nothin'…"

Moe studied the look on Bronislaus' face. "Just another pleasant day at the lake?"

"Exactly, minus all the bellyachin'. Have they found Edju's car yet?" Bronislaus crept closer to the edge of the woods.

"I don't think so. But O'Garrity's got three car loads of flatfoots with him, and those two Dagos who tried to write my obituary on a Chicago Typewriter just pulled up a few seconds ago."

Bronislaus mumbled, "Dames."

"You can say that again," Moe said.

"And a hell-of-a-lot louder," Whitey added.

"You still got Pa's gun, by the way?"

Whitey shook his head. "Sorry."

Bronislaus looked at Moe. "Mine went down with the boat. But I saved the binoculars."

"The car's full of the stuff anyway," Whitey said.

Bronislaus stretched out on his belly again and the others did likewise as they crept together to the edge of the woods. Bronislaus said, "A lot of good that will do us if we get bushwhacked between here and there. Let's have a look."

Each in turn spread apart the underbrush just enough to see what was taking place in the front yard of Stashu's cabin. Whitey made sure there weren't any fire ants lurking about. The little buggers, he thought.

10 - DZIESIĘĆ

Out front of Stashu's cabin, a red-faced O'Garrity tried to calm down Robert and Lorenzo. Both had attempted to wipe their faces, but not very hard. The three not-so-bright dicks were there with seven other uniformed cops. Two of the squad cars had overshot the drive and dug into the new sod on Stashu's front yard. Bosko found an out of the way bush at the far side of the cabin and urinated.

A fairly new blue Dodge pulled up, packed with fishing gear. It was Stashu and Tommy Duckowski. They sat in the car to take in the view. O'Garrity headed toward the car, followed by Robert and Lorenzo. Stashu and Ducky stepped out of the Dodge and slammed the doors to emphasize how unhappy they were not to be alone.

"What is this, a picnic?" Stashu asked.

"And the bugs just showed up," O'Garrity answered.

"Your damn automobiles are tearin' up my lawn. So get them back on the road where they belong."

"You own this cabin?" Robert asked.

Stashu took a good look at Robert and Lorenzo's still singed and smoke smeared faces. "What did you do? Bust these two for cat burglary?"

Robert grabbed at Stashu, but O'Garrity moved in between them. "All right, girls, cut the chatter. What brings you two clowns out here, Stashu?"

"It's a holiday. We're out here to kill a few fish," Stashu answered.

Ducky spoke up, "Yeah, who'd you come out to murderize?"

"A stinkin' Polack..." Lorenzo blurted out leaving O'Garrity wishing he could shoot him.

"More friends of yours, O'Garrity?"

"Don't be a wise guy. I know damn well what you're doin' out here."

"Ah, O'Garrity, quit spittin' tobacco out your backside. We just came to fish," Ducky said.

Behind O'Garrity and his men, Bronislaus and the boys cut across the dirt road, hidden by the settling dust. They made their way to Edju's car where they had stashed it under Staghorn sumac, cut from the growth, which lined the dirt road, directly across from the cabin.

O'Garrity pushed past Stashu on his way back to the cabin. Bosko, having finished relieving himself, and the other two dicks, followed after O'Garrity. "Have a look-see, boys. And, Bosko, don't get lost."

The uniformed cops started to poke about. Robert and Lorenzo headed for the cabin. Ducky reached into his pocket and pressed his gun to Robert's ribs. "You ain't invited."

Robert tried to stare him down.

"I'm gettin' real itchy. I ain't killed a daddy's boy in days."

Robert backed off but kept a hateful watch on both Stashu and Ducky.

Lorenzo kept his eye on the cabin where he could see O'Garrity on the horn in the back room through the window. O'Garrity stood under the arch of the door in front of a large bay window that overlooked Stashu's dock and most of the lake. The dicks poked around inside and took turns in the restroom flushing the pull chain toilet to O'Garrity's annoyance. The seven uniformed cops checked around in the surrounding bush for any hiding Polacks. There weren't any.

Just then, the powerboat crossing the lake, with Walter in it, pulled up to Stashu's dock. He had changed again. The uniforms detained him, frisking him over good, until Robert and Lorenzo went out back to have a word with them about it. Satisfied they were all doing their jobs, they all came back around to the front of the cabin as O'Garrity let the screen door slap behind him. The three dicks followed behind, each in turn letting the screen door slap. O'Garrity gave them a good hard look.

"What?" Bosko asked.

O'Garrity fought down a few choice words.

"Satisfied, Copper?"

"Shut up, Stashu. All right, boys, pack it in." O'Garrity removed his brown felt hat and wiped the sweat from his brow with a new yellow hanky. His light blue shirt was twice as damp as it was when he went in to make the call. He glanced toward the top of the hill overlooking the lake, the one where Carlo Axler sat patiently in his car behind underbrush just off the road. O'Garrity waited until his men were all packed back in their cars. "Listen up, Stashu, you tell your old man that Bronislaus is tiptoein' on eggs. A little bird just told me he's now facin' B&E plus arson. If you know where he's at right now you better send him over before someone gets hurt." O'Garrity's eyes looked different, the fire had gone out.

Stashu saw it, so did Ducky. "Yeah, yeah, sure, O'Garrity, I'll run home right now."

O'Garrity marched to his car and got in. He glanced again at the hill then back at Stashu. He wanted to say something. He wanted to put a stop to what was about to happen, but he couldn't, he was in too deep. Suddenly it wasn't fun anymore. "Go home, Stashu. Just remember I warned you. You two, boys, I'll see you both back on your side of the lake. Take him with you." He looked Robert and Lorenzo over with a cold stare. He didn't like it, damn, he didn't like it. He drove off followed by the two car loads of flunkies.

Stashu looked down at his lawn. Four deep tire tracks were dug into it. Stashu steamed to the cabin, flung the screen door open and went in to pour himself a drink from a flask in his desk. He watched out the bay window as Walter made his way across the lake in the speedboat. He noticed that his row boat was gone. He picked up his twelve-gauge and went back out the front door to find Robert and Lorenzo still facing down Ducky. Stashu fired the shotgun up into the trees scattering birds. Lorenzo and Robert hit the ground.

"Get off my land."

"You ain't heard the last of us, Polack," Robert said as the two young men got back up.

Stashu aimed the gun at Lorenzo's sedan and blew out one of the back passenger windows. "I've heard all I'm gonna hear from you today. Now get."

Robert and Lorenzo backed off to his car and got in. Stashu reloaded the shotgun, and pointed it back at the car as it leaped into motion and disappeared into the copper's dust, multiplying it by one.

Ducky and Stashu now stood there alone dumbfounded, looking into the trees and brush, watching the dust settled across the road.

"I don't get it." Ducky said, scratching the back of his neck where a mosquito had just lunched. "Did you see the look on O'Garrity's face, something's up? But I don't get it."

"Yeah, neither do I, Ducky. Neither do I."

Edju's New Century Six Hupmobile was still fully hidden under the cut thatch of sumac. The dust from the road drifted down through the young birch overhead and settled onto the drying sumac leaves. Bronislaus held a hanky over his mouth as he spoke. "Remind me not to hide out here again," he said holding binoculars to his eyes with his other hand. He watched across the road to see if anyone planned to double back.

"Remind me not to know you from now," said Whitey, standing in fresh briefs as he rummaged under the back seat for a clean shirt. "Figures, I lost my cigs."

Moe wiggled into a pair of striped boxers. He wore garters to hold up his wet brown socks. He still had his soggy shoes on. He checked to make sure the Thompson submachine gun he held was loaded. The Hupmobile was indeed full of the stuff. There were enough guns and ammo to go around and some.

But no cigs. Whitey tried on a shirt that was too big for him. "Guys, you could've at least had the decency to stop by my joint and pick up some clothes that fit me."

"Mr. Niemiec thought they'd be watchin, your dump.

You ever use one of these?" Moe indicated the Thompson.

Whitey reached way underneath the backseat for a pair of clean socks. "Sure," he said from inside the car, "the last time I knocked off your momma's candy store." Whitey snickered. So Moe grabbed a mitt full of Whitey's oversized shirt and pulled him out of the car until his neck was even with the door latch.

"Hey!" Whitey tried to straighten up, but before he could, Moe had the door closed on his neck. Whitey's muffled choking sounds from inside the car and the thrashing of his arms and legs finally aroused Bronislaus, attention. Bronislaus looked away and let Moe choke Whitey a little while longer, and didn't look back until he felt Whitey had got what he had coming. "Do I have to nursemaid you two slugs?"

Moe opened the car door. Whitey plopped to the ground and clutched his throat. He gasped for air. His good eye looked distant. "You creep," he said coming back around, "I ought to murder ya."

Moe put the tip of the Thompson to the end of Whitey's battered nose. "Don't be sayin' nothin' sassy about Momma."

Bronislaus came over and gave Whitey the binoculars. "I'm goin' across the road. Put some clothes on, the two of ya, and try not to kill each other while I'm gone." He hiked up his fishing pants and headed across the road toward the cabin. Whitey and Moe resumed dressing. Whitey kept his mouth shut, stewing, devising devious plans on how to get even with Moe.

"I don't know, Pop. It don't look good." Stashu used the phone, "Just left… a bunch of them… yeah, my boat's gone, too. I don't see it out on the lake," Stashu continued into the phone. He sat on his desk in front of the bay window, listening as Michal gave him instructions on what to do next, when Bronislaus appeared outside the window. "Wait a minute, Pop. The knucklehead just showed up"

"I got bad news about your boat," Bronislaus said.

"Just get in here."

Bronislaus climbed in the window and across Stashu's desk. Stashu went back to the phone. "Pop? Just a minute." He looked at Bronislaus. "Where's Whitey and Moe?"

"Beatin' each other up across the road, in Edju's car. They're fine. You wouldn't believe what just went down."

"Bet we would." Stashu handed Bronislaus the phone. "He wants to yell at you."

"Lucky me." Bronislaus took the phone. "Pop?" he said into the receiver, holding it back as a barrage of yelling came back at him, he cleared his ear with a finger. When it was safe he replaced his finger with the phone. "Just fine, they're across the road." He listened to Michal. "The place went up… let's just say it's the best Fourth of July celebration I ever saw, or anyone else for that matter. Sky rockets and everything. It sent the old barn's whole roof nearly a hundred yards into the lake. Whitey thinks at least two truckloads of booze, if not more."

Stashu cringed.

Bronislaus listened. "I think so. Hell, with all the heavies hangin' around, what else could it have been?" He listened again. "Sure did, I'm tellin' ya sky rockets! Must've been some ripe stuff."

Michal started to laugh over the phone. Bronislaus tried not to join in.

"Yeah, two big beautiful truck loads of hard stuff, at least."

Louder laughter came over the phone.

Bronislaus looked at Stashu. "He thinks it's funny.

"Listen."

"I can hear."

Bronislaus spoke into the phone again, "Whitey threw a cig in a tractor's gas tank." Bellowing laughter this time. "Nah, just singed his ass a little." More laughter. "No offense, but it really wasn't all that funny, Pop. Someone could've been hurt. Those Dagos tried to rub us out. I know, I know, but I just went over to square things with Nicole. Pop, we're friends, I thought we could have a talk with her father. Maybe you should talk to him while I lay low. Alusia? What Alusia? Oh that Alusia. That should put a smile on the boys' exteriors. I'll give her a jingle to let her know when we're on our way. By the by, Nicole mentioned something about a telegram her father thinks I sent. Beats me. I think it's worth lookin' into though. We'll call first. See ya. Bronislaus hung up.

Across the road Whitey looked through the binoculars toward the cabin while Moe sat beside him in Edju's car cleaning his nails. "So, what's goin' on now?"

Whitey answered without putting down the binoculars. "How should I know? They just got off the horn."

"What's takin' them so long?"

"Ah, milk a duck, will ya, Moe. I don't know. I'm sick of this whole mess already." Whitey took a swipe at Moe's arm.

Moe hit Whitey back. "Quit your bellyachin', Whitey, you're breakin' my heart."

Whitey struck back. Then Moe took a turn, then Whitey, then Moe, then Whitey, and so on.

Back at the cabin, Ducky entered with a bag of groceries. He placed it next to two others on the counter that divided the front door from the box-like kitchen that also acted as a breakfast bar.

Stashu sat at one of three stools and stretched his feet out toward the dwarfish living room. Bronislaus leaned over the counter from the kitchen side.

Ducky said, "That's the last of it," and picked up the drink Bronislaus had poured him. He downed it and his eyes instantly turned glassy, stifling a low croak deep in his throat. "What the hell was that?"

"Moonshine."

"Stashu keeps the good stuff in his desk."

"Jesus, how can you two drink this stuff? It makes your toes tingle."

Stashu reached into the last bag, "Wait until the little hairs fall out," and pulled out a Polish Daily News. "Here," he handed the paper to Bronislaus, "get a load of this. You're a celeb."

Bronislaus took the paper and looked over the front page and read the Polish words about him. "What, no picture?"

"Priced us three grand out just to get your name mentioned." Stashu said. "Someone put a clamp on the story in the Detroit Press and News. Take a good look, no mention of the girl's name. Even though they said they would."

Bronislaus slowly read through the article, this time checking for mention of Nicole. Not even a hint of her in the article. "Have you guys gone balmy? I'll have every Polish joe able to read this on the road looking to gun me down."

"Pop wants to keep this out in the open for now. That way they may still think twice about hittin' you."

"Somehow I don't feel comforted." Bronislaus folded up the paper and put it down. He poured another round. The two brothers downed theirs but Ducky threw his over his shoulder. Bronislaus and Stashu looked at Ducky and the mess he had made.

"Missed."

"Cut him off."

Up on the hill, overlooking the ethnically divided lake, Carlo Axler sat in his black Super Six sedan, its paint purposely dimmed from neglect, designed not to attract attention. The air around him was as thick from tobacco smoke as the hill was with blue spruce and wild blackberry bushes. Despite the heat, he kept his windows up, the coat of his tuxedo buttoned and his red bow tie up around his neck. Obviously, he had slept in spurts that way. The car's torn interior temperature had peaked over a hundred and ten for an hour now. But he could take the torture. He could bear the pain, the heat, the sweat, the stink, the hell… because he knew that's where he should end up, or down. Hell, if it existed. Home if he had one. But to him, he knew in his heart there was no God, no Heaven no Hell, for if there were, men like him would never walk free on Earth. They would be born still in the womb sent directly to Hell, struck dead by arch angels before gasp, and not given the chance to soil the Earth's air with a single cry to live, not given a chance to wreak havoc on good innocent souls, the souls he had taken. The soul he was about to take again this day, the soul of Bronislaus Niemiec.

He looked out over the land below through binoculars. Occasionally he reach out and picked a berry from a cup on the dash and squished it in his fingers, then licked his fingers clean, visualizing licking a victim's blood from his demonic fingers, a job well done. He watched down below as Stashu and Ducky left the cabin, shook hands with Bronislaus at the door, got into Stashu's blue Dodge and drove off in a swirl of dust. He followed Stashu's car until it was around the bend and out of sight. In a normal life he'd probably like these people. They had spunk, hung together and actually cared for one another with a brotherly love he never personally felt for anyone, having grown up in a beat-down orphanage, and later two different reform schools, after being abandoned at birth by his nameless prostitute mother. No one came for him. No one had ever wanted him. And at sixteen after setting a match to his past, he hit the streets doing what came natural to him. Killing people. In a normal life, if he had one where he knew his real name or ethnic makeup, he'd stop by and lift a pint or three at Michal's, maybe grab lunch, he ate Polish food at times, he'd make a friend, meet his sister even, but there was nothing normal about this dark lonely life, this hot day or this evil spirit.

Carlo pointed the field glasses toward Edju's car to find Whitey and Moe still striking each other's arms. Their movements were slow and painful by now as each took his turn trying to make the other say uncle. It was almost time to make his move. The pray was in place, the game was in play. Another life was about to stand still.

The hitman swung the binoculars back to the cabin. Through the large picture window, he could just make out Bronislaus' feet dangling from Stashu's desk. He assumed Bronislaus was back on the phone. He could kill them all. But that would ruin the art of what he did. Besides, he killed for money. The pleasure was in the money he held afterwards. The killing was just a byproduct. The end was prosperity. It didn't matter why someone paid for another's death. Frankly, he didn't care to know. Just that the bills were real, unmarked, and in small denominations so that they were easy to put in any of the fifty accounts he owned in twenty-five cities. At first he kept his money in a box buried in the ground, then a safety deposit box, but it just sat there unless he touched it. In his accounts he could watch them grow like bastard children, give them names, see the results of a hard day's work. Soon he would have enough to fulfill his dreams, hobnob with rich babes, sail the open seas, and live the life that should have been his if his parent weren't the nameless scum they were. He'd never work again. He'd spend his last dime to cremate himself and have his ashes dropped from a plane over a volcano by someone who owed him. Then he hoped it would be like this: hot, unbearable and everlasting. But he knew even in death he wouldn't get what he deserved. There was no eye-for-an-eye that could see fit to even the visions of what he'd done to so many others, and their loved ones.

He put down the glasses, eased off the brake and let it roll through the blackberry bushes, squashing them onto the road under the tires and silently coasted his death-wagon down the hill toward the cabin. Halfway there, he opened a violin case on the seat, revealing a Thompson submachine gun. Switching the engine key to on, as the car reached the beginning of Stashu's new lawn. He put the car in second and popped the clutch. The sedan jumped to life. Carlo calmly picked up the Thompson, opened his door, stepped out onto his Super Six's running board, sporting the full tuxedo and proceeded to pepper Stashu's cabin as he went by.

Inside, glass shattered and wood splintered, but it couldn't be heard under the rattle of the Chicago Typewriter. Obituary lines seemed to magically appear on the walls, pictures and cabinets. The three bags of groceries ripped and spilled onto the floor as the Typewriter clacked away, pickles, bread, meat, eggs, exploding into shreds of garbage, a meaningless jumble of wasted lead filled words. The curtains on both the front and back-bay windows danced a deadly hula as the bluish-gray drops of mortality passed through them and the glass behind them fell from their frames. What seemed like minutes only took seconds before crazy Carlo reached the far side of Stashu's lawn, sat back in his death wagon, and calmly set his foot to the gas pedal and sped off, leaving a mixture of dust and gun smoke behind.

From the front seat of Edju's car, Moe and Whitey could only watch and listen with horror. They scrambled out of the car as fast as they could and sprinted through the sumac into the middle of the dust-filled road where Whitey, despite the intense throbbing in his right arm, sprayed the Thompson into the dust trailing Carlo's sedan until his arms involuntarily fell back to his side.

"Did you get the number?!" Whitey yelled as he ran toward the cabin after Moe.

"Just the first two, F U," Moe yelled back over his shoulder.

They made it to the front of the cabin and put on the skids, not really believing what they knew was all too real. The windows were shattered, the screen door was torn to shreds and inside the walls where spattered with little round holes. Whitey went in first. Moe followed. The broken pickle jar rocked back and forth on the hardwood floor and filled the room full of the scent of sour dill. Whitey looked at the kitchen cabinets. They were opened and splintered, their remnants, glasses, cups and plates, lay scattered all over the counters and breadbox below. Whitey looked over the bar to the living room floor. No Bronislaus. "Bronislaus?" No answer.

Moe went first into the miniature living room where the walls and two small walnut and glass cabinets were full of sharp round voids. Pictures of the Niemiec family lay sprawled out on the mocha colored throw-rug with their frames broken, the photos torn. Feathers from three pillows and stuffing from the tropical auburn and chartreuse print couch still drifted down from the ceiling. "Bronislaus, you in here?" Again, no answer.

Whitey brushed past Moe through the archway to where the desk sat in front of what was left of the bay windows. Glass, fragments of wood and plaster were spread out on the lawn toward the dock. The old outhouse had three new peep holes. The phone had taken a direct hit and lay in pieces on a small cot to the left. The walls around the desk and windows were polka dotted like Swiss cheese. But no Bronislaus.

Moe followed behind Whitey. He examined a pickle making sure there weren't any glass shards in it. He found some. Whitey looked out the vacant bay window to the outhouse, to the docks, and the ground below the window. Still no Bronislaus.

"What a mess," Moe whispered, tossing the pickle out the window. His belly growled in disappointment.

"Where the hell is he?"

It hit them both at the same time. Stashu's new bathroom! They headed for the door as a flushing came from beyond. They waited. Water ran in the sink, and then shut off. Bronislaus opened the door and came out doing up the fly on a clean pair of trousers, cradling the newspaper under his arm, and appeared freshly showered and shaved.

"What, a guy can't take a peaceful dump around here?" Bronislaus looked around the shredded room and at the smoking Thompson Whitey still held in his hands. "What the hell did you go and do this for?"

"Bite yourself, it wasn't us," Whitey said. "Some stiff in a tux sprayed the joint from his chariot out front."

"What'd you do, watch him?" Bronislaus tossed the paper aside.

"Yeah. Well, sort of."

"Sure as hell didn't miss much."

"Except what he was aiming for."

"When Stashu sees this place, we'll wish the stiff bull's-eyed us."

Moe asked, "What kind of mug goes around wavin' a violin dressed in an all-day suit, anyway?"

Bronislaus glanced back out to the dirt road. "Sounds like Crazy Carlo's M.O. So let's empty this place before he comes back to admire his handiwork." Bronislaus picked up his fishing cap from behind the desk, shook the glass out of it, examined the life-ending hole through it and put it on his head. He grabbed up his shoes and shook out his shirt.

The boys didn't need to be told twice. Led by Moe, they hustled across the lawn and the road, ignoring the sumac to get into Edju's four door. Bronislaus got in shoeless behind the wheel, Whitey claimed shotgun, so Moe climbed in the backseat. The bored out eights jumped to life and the Hupmobile sprang from its hiding place and out onto the road, leaving a trail of sumac and a flood of gravel and dust behind it. "To the devil, man, slow down," Whitey yelled from behind his hands covering his face.

Bronislaus put his foot further toward the floor, there being only one way out to the main road. The souped-up engine roared louder and gained fifteen miles per hour as it zoomed past the intersection that led around the woods to the equestrian.

From the back, Moe turned around to see O'Garrity reach the corner on the road leading to the other side of the lake just before Bronislaus' dust began to settle. "Step on it, we got company."

"Not for long." Bronislaus down shifted, nearly throwing the transmission out into the road and put his foot to the floor again. Whitey groaned and lowered his head between his knees. The car let out a slight shudder step and blasted off down the hardwood-lined dirt and gravel road.

O'Garrity and his three flunkies pulled out into Bronislaus' dust, followed by the two carloads of bluecoats.

Bronislaus swerved into a bend in the road. At the top of the turn a black Model T was dead ahead. Its driver, a hunched over Rabbi, barely peeked over its dash, smack dab in the middle of the road. Bronislaus slammed on the brakes.

Whitey and Moe let out screams as Whitey bounced off the dash, cracking the windshield with help from Moe careening his bulky weight into the back of the front seat.

Bronislaus down shifted again, grinding the gears badly, and swerved at the last moment cutting the wheels to the far right as the Rabbi cut to the left. Their running boards scraped, shooting sparks into the dust.

The blow jarred the wheel from Bronislaus' hands, and before he knew it, he was fighting his way through three and a half 190 degree spins as the Hupmobile passed through the bend in the road.

In the middle of the second spin the right backdoor swung open, sling-shooting Moe into a clumsy swan dive, resulting in a chomp of gravel and a nose full of dirt, with Edju's car stalled facing into its own dust.

The Rabbi went straight through the wall of dust and plowed into O'Garrity and the other two carloads of cops who hadn't a clue as to what had just happened. Sounds of crumpling and folding metal, broken glass and popping tires burst through the dust, followed by rolling pieces and tinkling bits of the Model T wandering toward Bronislaus and the boys.

Moe opened his eyes to find he not only lay out in the middle of the dusty road but also under the middle of Edju's car, which leaked hot oil onto his back and painfully scraped face.

Bronislaus was coming back around after twice butting heads with Whitey, a trickle of blood seeping from his nose, when Whitey finally blew his lunch into his hands between his legs.

"Billllaaaaaa!" Was all that came out of Whitey.

Bronislaus looked away. "Ah, damn, Whitey."

"Screw off, Bronislaus," Whitey replied.

Moe climbed back into the backseat. "Screw both you guys, let's get out of here!" He slammed the door shut.

Outside the car the air had begun to clear. Dim shapes of bewildered men could be seen beyond the tangled pile of junked cars.

Bronislaus tried the ignition. Nothing. Moe sprang back out of the car and threw open the engine hood. Bronislaus tried again with the same results. Whitey kept his face between his legs. Bronislaus hung his head out the window to avoid the stink. More dust settled. It seemed that no one laid mortally wounded, just a few broken spirits and heads.

The Rabbi yelled in Yiddish at O'Garrity from the epicenter of the pile. O'Garrity just pushed him aside. Bosko held the old man back and received a kick in the knee for it. The Rabbi continued after O'Garrity, who by then had his sights on Edju's car and was headed towards it fast.

Bronislaus tried the key again, nothing. "What does it look like?" He hung his head further out the window. He eyed Whitey's uncle.

"Like a car that don't work," Moe answered from under the hood.

"Edju's been havin' trouble with the battery cable," Whitey mumbled from between his legs.

Bronislaus told Moe to try it.

"This better work," Moe said and wiggled the cable as O'Garrity and his men picked up their pace toward them.

Bronislaus locked eyes with O'Garrity's. "It's got to."

The hood slammed down as the Hupmobile jumped to life. Bronislaus shoved the car into gear and drove directly at O'Garrity, spinning around in front of him, throwing dust all over the coppers again, and headed back towards Moe who was already at full sprint in the same direction. Bronislaus yelled for Moe to get in and Moe dove for the open backdoor and latched onto it. The car dragged him down the road while he fought to climb in.

O'Garrity's men choked on the dust. Some pulled their guns, but O'Garrity prevented them. "My idiot nephew's in there."

The Rabbi came up beside O'Garrity and in between Yiddish curses promised to sue them all.

"If I'm alive tomorrow, it'll be my pleasure." O'Garrity replied. He scratched his cheek and smeared a trickle of blood that dripped down from just above his left eyebrow. He examined the blood as it mixed with the dirt on his finger tips. So Carlo had failed. Deep down inside he was glad the punk was still alive… so he could get Bronislaus for this, and for all the other reasons he hated the little nickel-and-dime gangster. One of these days, Bronislaus, one of these stinking days.

11- JEDENAŚCIE

Reaching the end of the winding dirt road leading from the shared lake, Bronislaus turned the car left onto a paved straight two-lane and headed back toward Detroit City, hauling tail to reach Alusia's place before nightfall. All the windows were rolled down and Bronislaus and Whitey covered their noses with their shirt tails, while Moe hung his head out the rear passenger window.

"Pull over, Bronislaus, I'm chewin' wings out here, and I can't take Whitey's stench much longer."

"Let me find a safe place to hide."

"Pull over, I'm dyin', I'm tellin' ya."

"Shuddup, Moe," Whitey said from under his shirt.

"Please, pull over right now," Moe pleaded again.

"They're liable to be on our tail," Bronislaus told him.

Moe came back into the car and seized Bronislaus by the back of his shirt. "I said I can't take it no more, so pull this car over now. Or you're gonna have this angry dog on your tail. You hear me!"

"Back it off, Moe! What's wrong with ya?" Whitey yelled.

Moe clasped Whitey with his other hand and half pulled him into the backseat. "Listen to me, you. I'm tired of bein' fired at by crazy peckerwoods and I sure as hell ain't sittin' in this car another second suckin' up your peckerwood stink. You got that?"

Bronislaus pulled the car over into a freshly plowed open field. Moe got out and dragged Whitey out of the car.

"Don't make me pound ya one!" Whitey screamed at Moe.

"Then clean it up," Moe screamed back louder.

Bronislaus got out of the car and looked around to see if anyone was coming. "Come on, Moe, cut the liver-works. We got to stick together out here."

"I'll cut it. I'll stick it back together, as soon as he cleans up his slop."

Whitey stuck his face up to Moe. "With what, my looks?"

Moe clutched the front of Whitey's oversized shirt and ripped it off his body and handed it back to him. "Here, use this."

"Why you," Whitey took a swing that caught Moe on the left ear. Moe picked Whitey up and held him over his head. Bronislaus tackled Moe and the three of them tumbled down a small ragweed slope throwing punches, scratching and biting, working their way to the edge of the plowed field, like three crazed immigrant farm workers fighting over the farmer's daughter.

Crazy Carlo's faded black Super Six sedan rolled up silently and parked behind Edju's New Century Six Hupmobile that Edju had just bought and modified from the Hupp Motor Company, located at 345 Bellevue Avenue in Detroit, Michigan the day after his wife left him and took his other souped up ride down to Florida for good. Crazy Carlo couldn't have cared less if he knew the sentimentally of the moment. He got out and walked to the top of the slope and watched the violent stupidity unfold. Not liking the sun in his face, he adjusted his black Fedora that smartly sported a shinny grosgrain ribbon band. The scrappy little one was holding his own with the big one, and his pray kept catching punches from both. He didn't want to interrupt a good tumble, but he had a job to finish. The dark one was strong, he thought. Maybe he'd have to kill him first, free. What a shame. The little one would die as well if he became difficult and started mouthing off about staying alive. They'd see his face… be able to point him out. Maybe this wasn't the time. But the ditch… and the unusual open field for this time of year struck him as a perfect place to shoot down all three with no place for them to run and hide. Shot, murdered in a ditch. Three Men Found Dead In A Ditch. That's how the headlines would read. No suspects. All single shots to the hearts. The ditch was so poetic. Maybe he'd let one live to tell his story. Give him his name. Crazy Carlo was here. Murder by Carlo. It'd look good on a business card.

Whitey noticed first and froze, catching a fat left jab from Moe and toppled backwards over Bronislaus. Moe looked past his jab and recognized the distinct black of Carlo's all-day suit. He let go of Bronislaus with his other hand and Bronislaus flopped back down in the dry plowed soil.

"Oh, oh," is all Moe could muster.

"Get up," Carlo said.

Moe picked Bronislaus up and helped brush him off.

Whitey struggled up from his knees. Now both his eyes looked puffy.

Carlo pointed his gun at Moe and Whitey. "You two, start running."

Whitey couldn't believe his luck. "What?" He looked at Moe to see if he had heard the same words.

"You heard me, just turn around and head that way." He motioned his chin toward the woods across the plowed field, keeping his eyes locked on the boys." He and I got unfinished biz."

Whitey turned to Bronislaus. Bronislaus gave him a nudge toward Moe.

"You heard the man, scram."

"But...."

"Beat it, Whitey. Moe, get him outta here." Bronislaus kept his eyes on Carlo's face the best he could, seeing just behind Carlo's Fedora the sun blistered off Edju's car. The sun was directly on Carlo's face, making him dip the snap of the brim more than he probably wanted.

Moe took Whitey and pulled him away from Bronislaus, dragging him, kicking up dust, out into the plowed field.

Whitey pulled away from Moe and turned back to Carlo and yelled across the ditch. "Hey, slicker, you ain't worth the spit on my pal's shoes." Tears welled up in his eyes.

Carlo raised his gun and leveled it on Whitey. He pulled back the hammer. Whitey took the hint. He turned around and raced Moe across the furrows towards the sun hanging at the top of the distant woods.

Bronislaus watched them till they were out of sight. He thought of running for it, but Carlo would drop him for sure before he got two steps. His only chance, he thought, was to take his last sidestep directly into the sun and crouch as he turned back toward Carlo.

Carlo squinted into the glare of the sun, his barrel following as he aimed for Bronislaus' heart and coolly pulled the trigger.

Bronislaus spun from the blow and dropped sideways to the edge of the ditch, rolled to the bottom, landing halfway into the cracked earth of the drainage ditch. He stayed motionless, partly concealed by ragweed, dead corn stocks and scorched wild grass. Just another lifeless body.

Carlo wasn't sure. The punk had dipped on him. He moved to check on Bronislaus, liked to see the bodies just in case, but the roar from an oncoming Drant Star, less than a quarter mile up the paved road, made him think twice. He hesitated, took a second step towards the ditch, then changed his mind knowing he didn't have time, and calmly strolled back to his Super Six and sped off.

The oncoming Durant Star slowed as it approached Edju's car. It was Barbara and Nicole with Walter driving Nicole's car. He didn't stop. Nicole searched the open Hupmobile and the shadows in the field. Not knowing what had just taken place, in her heart, she feared the worse. She yelled for Walter to pull over, tried to get the door open but Barbara held her back while Walter sped away fast from the plowed field, ignoring her verbal and physical protests.

As Nicole's car rounded the bend and disappeared, Moe and Whitey reappeared from the shadows and came bounding back across the field. They stopped at the far side of the ditch in time to witness Bronislaus bleeding profusely from an upper body wound. He was trying to crawl out from the other side with his one good arm. Before they could reach him, his fingers let go of the dirt, and he collapsed with a gasp, rolling back, face down into a thatch of ragweed.

12 - DWANAŚCIE

Michal Niemiec sat across his desk from two heavy-set hired hands. One of them had a scar across his throat from ear to ear that smiled while his eye chased after a fly and frowned again when his eyes came back to rest on Michal. He spun the cylinder of his six-shooter absent-mindedly as Michal counted from a stack of one hundred dollar bills, and then steadily dealt them out in four even piles like gin rummy on his desk. The other hired-hand sat still in his chair, almost catatonic, as he counted along on his fingers with Michal to himself. Once in a while he would twitch and give an eerie sigh. Rumor had it that he had taken a bullet to the back of the head just above the base of the spine and it was still there. Michal didn't like having to do business with these sorts, but at times like this it was unavoidable. In harsh matters like these it was important to have men around with experience; men who were willing to be expendable for a price; men who knew the score, understood the consequences, and were willing to pay them as long as they got theirs up front… cash on the coffin.

Stashu and Ducky let themselves in with a key. The two hired hands didn't look away from the money. Michal did.

"How'd it go?"

Stashu motioned to the two men.

"We're dobra."

"Just like you said. They had a man on each side of the ferry."

Michal looked back at the two hired hands. "Tonight's on then boys." He handed them both two stacks of bills. They put the money in their coat pockets and got up without a word and were let out the door by Stashu.

Ducky moved to the corner, looking down below through the window at the parking lot. The two hired hands approached a dark sedan with its motor running, where two other men waited. The four of them got in and drove off. Ducky turned back to Michal and nodded. “Nice quiet gents.”

“Real ghosts from Christmas past.” Michal got up and took a painting down from the wall. He opened an unlocked safe. He put the remaining stack of bills back in it, closed it and gave the tumbler three quick spins.

“We should’ve squashed those two rats at the ferry,” Stashu said.

Michal sat back at his desk. “Who were they?”

“Johnny Wisser and Albert Ducheneaux. Stinkin’ rats.

“The world would be better off without them,” Ducky said.

“Don’t worry, those two rats are about to introduce the hungry cat to an angry dog holdin’ an empty cheese box. I need everyone ready by ten. He checked the clock on the wall. That gives you three hours,” Michal said.

“Have you heard from Bronislaus?” Stashu asked.

Michal eased himself down in his chair. He tried not to look worried. “I talked to Whitey about an hour ago. Bronislaus took a slug — he’ll live.” He wiped sweat from his forehead with a hanky and blew his nose in it.

Stashu and Ducky waited on their feet. Stashu eyed the bar. Michal nodded his head and Ducky did the honors, giving Michal his share.

“Now listen up. Mangione and his friends mean business on this one. It looks like he’s planning to get even and take the warehouse after all. I hope he does. Meanwhile, he’ll be watching this place, so we’ll need business as usual. He’s got a big surprise coming his way. No one pushes around The Polish Gang.”

“Yeah,” Ducky added.

“Edju and Lipinski have any problems on the way over?” Michal asked.

“No, the two rats made Edju plain as day, stopped long enough for a phone call and caught the next ferry home,” Stashu said, pulling up a chair.

“Good.”

“To think this whole plan depends on O’Garrity makes my knees knock,” Ducky said. He sat on the window ledge until Michal gave him a look to stay away from the windows. He moved over to the maroon couch.

"Don't worry, I know O'Garrity like gum on the bottom of my shoe."

"I can't wait to see the look on his puss," Stashu said.

"Let's just make sure the yoke doesn't end up on ours," Ducky said.

"O'Garrity's had this comin' since he was too short to spit. Just make sure he gets the word on time."

Stashu got up and went to the door. Ducky followed. Stashu patted his pocket and pulled out a telegram. "He'll get it. What about Bronislaus?"

"I told Whitey and Moe to stay put. They're holdin' up at Alusia's. She's had the house doctor in to look at them. They've had a rough day."

"Let's hope they don't do anything stupid again, Stashu said, heading for the door. He stopped. "Maybe we should send someone over there to sit on 'em."

"I'm gonna need everyone at the warehouse. Bronislaus is down for the night anyway. I had the doctor give him something."

"I'd like to give him something," Stashu went out the door after Duckowski. He closed the door behind him.

Michal smiled, "Wait until you get a load of your cabin," he thought. He chuckled out loud at the thought of the fights between his three boys. He shook his head thinking how the world had changed since he had opened this place. He just wanted to make a living. Something he could pass on, and now look what's happened. Emily was still single from working way too many hours running food and drink. Edju's wife had run back home to Miami with his kid. Stashu won't stop mooning over the Skyscraper's wife, which could only get him beaten. And now his youngest son lay in bed in a whorehouse owned by his wife's childhood girlfriend, with one bullet already in him, and another still out there somewhere with his initials on it.

And O'Garrity, the son-of-a-dog for a neighborhood cop, he hated Bronislaus so much he was running around town waving a five thousand dollar invitation to his funeral. To make matters worse, if it were possible, a crazed Dago family with heavy DA connections wanted them all behind bars, or dead, and surely out of business, if not out of the country. All this violence coming The Polish Gang's way, just because some Dago's daughter was found hung-over and naked in the back seat of his son's car on the front lawn of his establishment. Didn't anyone have a sense of humor these days? And the implications of this telegram. People could be so touchy. But to top it off, his own wife wanted him out of the bar business. It was all this damn killing. Just last week Stephania dove out of his moving automobile thinking they were being bombed when the radiator blew up in this damn heat. What was he to do? It wasn't him, it wasn't even his family. It was just the times brought on by Prohibition. For this, he lived away from God. What was a good man to do, except to protect his family? He picked his used cigar out of the ashtray and lit it. He had things to do. But first things first. He reached for the phone and dialed a number he knew by heart. He let it ring.

"It's Michal. Someone will pick you up just like I told you. It's all set, Alusia, don't be afraid. I'll see ya there." He hung up, and this time looked up another number and dialed with a heavy hand. This call would get expensive.

Bartolommeo Mangione sat at his desk in his office eating from a plate still half full of extra-creamy linguine, just how he loved it, exactly how his wife used to make it, and how his own mother had taught her. A white stained cloth napkin was tucked under both of his chins and hung over his shirt. Unfortunately the napkin didn't protect his shirt sleeves. What the hell, his coat would cover it. Damn heat, if it didn't cool off he'd start to stink like a buffalo and have to go home and change his shirt anyway. Maybe he'd send Lorenzo. Mouthy kid. If he gave Bartolommeo any more backtalk, he'd make him his official food taster. He'd lost three in the last five years. After losing two good chefs he got wise and started hiring expendable dishwashers. Who'd give a damn if a couple of nobodies died from this crap? Good chefs were hard to come by these days with so many joints opening up vying for their talents. He had to buy and close a place to get the kitchen staff he had now. And this one could follow his mother's recipes as though she was pinching the spices herself. Handsome fellow, too, the guest liked him. But some fool was trying to kill him, was it him, poisoning him in his own food establishment. What was this world coming to? A man couldn't even eat in peace for God's sake. It had gotten so bad he was losing weight.

He used a spoon against his fork to scoop his dinner into his face — scoop, three chomps, a little bread, two chomps, a swallow, and then repeat. Occasionally he would gulp straight from an overly expensive bottle of Merlo from Chateau Gazin Pomerol, something his friend Anthony had been pushing him to broaden his pallet with and include on his wine list, so that Anthony and his visiting political friends could having something other than Italian grapes to choose from when they dined at Mangione's. As much as Bartolommeo appreciated his best friend's input into his gentrification, he resented even more that his friend's suggestions primarily benefited Anthony's tolerance of him, as though he wasn't good enough as he was and would never, no matter how much he tried, be as good an American gentleman as Anthony and his powerful family. This thought, true or imaginary, made the French wine bitter as he rested it on his fat tongue, seeking the hints of mint, plum, chocolate, coffee or liquorice, a bouquet of almond, toast, tobacco or vanilla that Anthony spoke so handsomely of when he sold him on it. But all he could taste was red wine as he swallowed. As much as he loved his best friend, the thought of not having been born under the umbrella of an influential family like him made Bartolommeo envy his silver spoon and yet even hate Anthony a little just the same, and this shamed him a bit, boarding on self-loathing because he couldn't help himself. But his bright light, this pending marriage, between daughter and son, the commingling of their ancient Roman bloods, as far as Anthony knew, would even the playing field forever and at least his grandchildren wouldn't be looked down upon by anyone, not even the great and powerful District Attorney, Anthony Bunniti and his far reaching kin. Bartolommeo Mangione and his family will finally have arrived and truly be part of the tastiest upper crust, the noblemen of Detroit and he, Bartolommeo, would wine and dine, perhaps even be able to taste the very essence within his glass with the finest of fine around the world.

His thoughts came back to what was at hand. He impatiently glanced at the door every time someone passed outside on their way to the restroom. He would have checked his watch again, except that was how the first stain got on his sleeve. Goddamn it, where were they?

Finally, just before Bartolommeo finished eating, Albert and Johnny were let in by Lorenzo. Lorenzo remained in the room and shut the door behind them. Bartolommeo looked up and motioned for him to beat it. Lorenzo left with murder in his eyes.

Bartolommeo cleaned his plate, wiped his face, poured the cabernet into a glass this time, sat back in his chair, and belched. He wiped his hippo face again and plopped the napkin onto the plate. He sipped the wine. If he noticed the bandages on Johnny's face and hands, or the bandages under Albert's new hat, he didn't let on. "Che cosa hai preso per me, ragazzi?"

Albert and Johnny looked at their boss with blank faces.

"What'd you get for me, boys?" He thumbed his cigar.

"Oh, the same guy," Albert said, "Edju Niemiec went back across the river tonight. Only this time he took a friend. It was the same guy who brought the truck to Belle Isle the other night. His name's Dale Lipinski. His sister used to go around with some thick cop named O'Garrity. This sister works for sanitation which accounts for the use of the truck. We spread a little dough around and found out that they sometimes used a bread truck, sometimes an ice truck. Looks like business as usual with a little extra expected muscle."

Albert checked his pocket watch. "At eleven-thirty, three guys and a truck driver will meet them back on this side of the river. Could be any of the three trucks, we don't know. Last time they brought sixteen cases across. Two of the men on this side will take the speedboat back across and drive Edju's car back over on either the Hayne or Halcyon Ferry out of Walkerville. Our reliable source says they've pulled that once a night for a month and delivery arrives four hours later each time and rotates back to stay at night. That info cost us two extra bills."

Bartolommeo didn't make an offer to reimburse anyone.

Albert waited.

So did Bartolommeo.

"Of course we'll take it out of petty cash," Albert added, knowing this was a package deal. "Now followin' the same schedule and we ain't got a reason to believe they won't, tonight's shipment should arrive at the warehouse at exactly midnight. Depending on how much they've been able to move, they may have as much as 500 to 600 cases at the address we mentioned. We spent the night there last night. It's real shady and quiet. You could murder your own sister and nobody'd even notice. Plus, there's no security bell on the building inside or out. Oh yeah, they drove a white convertible coupe this time, it's registered to a Bronislaus Niemiec, that Polack kid from the lake." Albert eyed the wine.

Bartolommeo didn't offer.

Albert looked at Johnny who stifled a choke. "I don't think they expect a thing. Unless the car and truck change means anything to you. It don't to us. If they didn't muscle up, we'd worry."

Bartolommeo looked at Johnny.

"Nothin' yet on the boy," Johnny said, "but Carlo ain't the type to screw up. We should know within the hour if someone found his body." His eyes watered.

"You sure this Carlo character knows his business?" Bartolommeo asked.

"I'd stake my life on him," Johnny said.

"Of course you have. Important dignitaries will be here tonight dinning before the Yacht Club opening gala, to which I will be attending and slipping away to take care of this mess, and I don't need a body floating around town with bullets in it that leads to me."

Johnny and Albert looked at each other. "Trust us," Albert said, "Carlo could find and kill a snowman in hell."

"He'd better. We move tonight, bring your trucks. We'll have to replace what we lost this afternoon to fill our orders." He slid an envelope across the desk. "Here's the address I want it delivered to. It's out of state, so you'll get your cash as planned before, plus a bonus for travel time."

"How far out of state?"

"Eventually Florida."

"Florida?"

"Yeah, Florida, you want me to get somebody else?"

"No, no, it's just that Johnny's wanted in Alabama and Florida."

"No one will recognize him like that. Besides, we'll be dividing the loads up in Ohio. You'll leave your trucks there. I got men in Toledo who will help and family in Miami already expecting you. There's new ID in there for the both of you. You'll get further instructions once you reach Ohio. So, no slip-ups this time, or it will be your last."

"That wasn't our…" Johnny started to say.

Bartolommeo stopped him with his fat stubby hand. "If I was blamin' you, you wouldn't be here now."

"But why all this hocus pocus?

"We're dealing with a very delicate matter here. I can't afford any loose ends. That's why I'm givin' you a chance for the paid vacations."

"Yeah, but…" Johnny said.

Bartolommeo reached down to his lap and pulled out a snub nosed and placed it on the table. "It's either that… or I kill you both right now and have my boys drag you across the street and dump you out in the lake."

"I hear Florida ain't so crowded this time of year."

"Yup, and there's fishin' right off your cracker-house porch, I hear."

"The Polish Gang will never forget this Fourth of July celebration," Bartolommeo said, as he went back to his wine with an air of dismissal.

Johnny and Albert didn't wait for good-byes; they just got up and left.

Bartolommeo held the wine glass under his nose as he pictured himself getting even with the Niemiec family. He liked what he smelled despite what the French Merlo meant to him and his lack of pallet for fine wines. "Even if I have to kill them all myself." He looked at the door. "Lorenzo!"

The door opened. "What?"

"Go home and get me a clean shirt."

"What am I, your errand boy?"

"No, you're my smart mouthed son, now get. I'm waitin'."

Lorenzo slammed the door. One day, he thought, that fat little hippo will get his, and I'll run things my way. But not now, not right now.

13 - TRZYNAŚCIE

Just inside Hamtramck city limits, two blocks off Conant, men with their hats pulled shamefully low came in and out of Alusia's large three-story brown brick house. Despite the night heat, two other men wearing neckties and coats hung in the shadows of a dying elm tree that did its best to hide the house from the street lights. They weren't customers, but they meant business just the same. An evenly trimmed hedge lined the perimeter of the front lawn stopping at a shiny black Cadillac parked alongside the house, where a gimpy black chauffeur, with a metal leg brace, sat on a milk crate reading a law book. He didn't pay much attention to the music, the drink, the women, or the men coming in and out of the house because minding his own business kept food on the table for his wife and children and him in school.

His uncle, a much larger black man opened the front door for the entering and exiting clientele. He had on a tailored butler uniform fitted with a slight bulge under his left arm. He said neither hello nor good-bye, or looked anyone in the eyes. He just opened and shut the door, a human hinge, the size of a door, with a gun.

Upstairs, in one of the bedrooms on the second floor, Bronislaus lay asleep in a canopy bed — alone. Rhythmic thumping came from the room up above but the band wasn't playing this beat of bedpost on wall. Titanic floral arrangements lined the three bureau cabinets. An oak ceiling fan whirled under the noise from above.

There were open windows on each side of the bed, but heavy silk curtains with an orchid print blocked most of the street light and all of the air. A single oval framed picture of a little black-haired girl sat on a night stand beside the bed.

Whitey slept fitfully in an overstuffed green upholstered armchair, surrounded by fifteen or more identical children's teddy bears, all won on the same romantic night at a carnival some years ago. He had Alusia's trench coat pulled up around his ears. A ten ounce porterhouse round lay flat over the bridge of his nose. Its blood dripped down his cheek and pooled at the hollow of his throat.

Bronislaus startled awake. He sat up in pain. He wore a clean A-Shirt soaked with sweat and a fresh pair of boxer shorts. He moved his left shoulder and found it had a professionally wrapped clean bandage. He took a look around trying to remember where he was. Alusia's, I'm in Alusia's room, he thought.

Bronislaus brushed back the lace with his good arm and found Whitey in the corner surrounded by all his new friends, fitfully sucking air from under the porterhouse. "Whitey," Bronislaus said in a dry sticky voice. Whitey didn't stir. Bronislaus mustered up a little energy, "Whitey."

This time Whitey murmured something inaudible in his slumber.

"Whitey, wake up."

Whitey murmured something again that sounded like "Grab butt," in a tortured whimper.

Bronislaus reached over and painfully picked up an embroidered pillow. He bounced it off Whitey's chest.

Whitey laughed, puckered up his sore lips and tossed out a few smooches. "You little dickens," he murmured.

Bronislaus carefully got out of bed, managing not to knock anything over as he came toward Whitey and kicked him in the foot. Whitey jolted up sending teddy bears in flight and the blood down his chest to gather at his navel, but he didn't wake.

"Wake up, numb head. I need to talk to you." Bronislaus kicked Whitey's foot again.

Whitey woke up this time with a start. "You little bit…," he said. His face was half covered with dried beef blood. "What the…," he stood up dropping the steak to the floor. "Oh, it's only you, I must'ave fallen off."

"Fallen off? Hell, I thought you dropped dead."

"You ain't gettin' rid of me that easy. Give me something to wipe this up."

Bronislaus poured water from a porcelain pitcher and dropped a wet towel to the floor. "What's with the rain coat?"

"I showered. Didn't want this drippin' all over me. And from the feelin' I got in my shorts, it didn't work." He picked the steak up, cleaned the blood spot off the wood flooring, and eased it back on his face. "Aaahhh."

"Where is Moe?"

Whitey pointed a teddy bear toward the ceiling.

Bronislaus tried to ignore it. "How long has he been up there?"

"Since the doc left. Two or three hours. He's with two of them. How's the shoulder?" Whitey slipped his shoe off and rubbed his foot.

"It's givin' me the business. How're you feelin'?"

"I feel great, except my foot feels like someone's been dancin' on my toes. Look, my eyes are almost normal."

"Get his fat ass down here."

"Relax, Alusia said it was on the house. She didn't want him wandering off, so she put a couple of her gals on him to keep him put."

Bronislaus went over and pulled on a shirt that was laid out neatly on the bed, it hurt. He eased on a pair of pants also folded there. That hurt, too. The sweat gave him a chill despite the hot night air beginning to blow in behind the closed curtains.

"Don't let it creep up on ya," Whitey continued. "You'll start yourself bleedin' again."

Bronislaus threw Whitey a look.

"You're darn lucky anyway."

"Yeah, I'm feelin' real fortunate all over." Bronislaus went to the door. He yanked it open. "Moses!" he yelled into Moe's face, who had just reached for the doorknob when it opened.

Moe moved away. "Wooo… when was the last time you brushed your teeth?"

"Just after my two pals fed me a knuckle sandwich."

"At least you ain't hungry." Moe came in and paraded around the room like a cock in a hen house.

"Don't you look pleased as puddin'," Whitey said.

"Ain't every day I gets to bed down two white women for free without someone threatenin' to hang me in the woods for it."

"Yeah, well," Bronislaus said, "if you can keep yourself in your shorts long enough, I'd like to eat somethin' other than your two's bullshit."

Whitey's ears perked up. He pulled the steak from his face. "That goes for me, too. I'm starved."

"Count me in. Where to?" Moe went and looked out the window to see if he could see anything lit up close. "Don't see a thing from here. Maybe we can have something delivered from close around. There's a driver, too who could maybe pick up for us. But we better hurry. The radio says it's gonna finally rain."

"Tonight?" Whitey asked hopefully.

"No, next year…"

"Aaahhhh, shuddup."

Bronislaus pulled on a pair of clean socks and tried the shoes. "How do you girls feel about some good pasta?"

Moe and Whitey looked at each other. Pasta, in Hamtramck?

"What kind of pasta?" Whitey asked suspiciously.

"Expensive. I know a swell place on the eastside. I'm buying."

"Say, I don't like the sound of this," Whitey said.

"Hell," Moe said excitedly, "Pasta sounds just like the ticket for me. I love that squirmy Dago stuff. They deliver all this way, though?"

Whitey went over and helped Bronislaus on with his shoes. Bronislaus lay back on the bed exhausted as Whitey tied them. "This wouldn't be a classy joint called Mangione's, would it?"

"Coincidentally, of course.

Whitey let go of Bronislaus' foot. It landed heavily on the mahogany stained floor. Bronislaus let out a groan.

"I ain't ever been that hungry and I sure as hell ain't ever been that crazy," Moe said.

Bronislaus groaned again as he sat up.

"Are you out of your swollen mind, genius? These loose marbles are tryin' to turn you into worm-bait, and you want us to parade right up like six pins in a bowlin' alley." Whitey went back over and sat, slapping the steak, with punctuated finality, back on his face.

Moe went to the mirror to straighten his hat. One of the girls must have sat on it. "Besides," he said into the mirror, "Mr. Niemiec said to stay put, and I can't think of a better place to put it than right here, right now."

Bronislaus got up. His legs felt wobbly. "I got it all figured out," he said.

Moe turned to look at Whitey who was peeking out from under the juicy.

Bronislaus stood in front of the dresser looking over a row of carved wood heads without faces capped with very expensive wigs. He reached out and fingered the wavy bleached blond one. "There's a slug in my shoulder," he said as he stepped over and opened a mahogany-stained, elegantly hand-carved armoire to find it full of beautiful evening gowns, "that says maybe they think I'm dead."

"Yeah, and you're sure killin' me," Whitey said.

Bronislaus went to the window and looked out to see what it would take to climb out. Down below Alusia's Caddy was still there with its driver. "Just hear me out on this. It came to me when I was asleep…" He turned around to find Whitey and Moe with their fingers in their ears. "I knew you guys would understand."

14 - CZTERNAŚCIE

The Fyfe Building stood 14 floors tall at 10 W. Adams Avenue, on the corner of Adams and Woodward in downtown Detroit. It loomed above Central United Methodist Church, and Grand Circus Park. The high-rise building was constructed in 1916, and was one of Detroit's first; finished in 1919, and constructed in the neo-gothic architectural style, and designed by architect Sheldon Smith who established his firm in Detroit in 1853. The SmithGroup was one of the first operating architecture and engineering firms in the United States.

The Fyfe Building had 65 residential units, just large enough to make it possible to come and go without drawing attention. A plus was The Fyfe Shoe Store at the retail street level where Carlos Axler bought himself new shoes after every kill in case anyone thought to trace his footsteps, perhaps more of a superstition than a personal pleasantry. There were offices in the upper stories where he had never ventured. He had moved in because, even though the building was mainly used as a residential building, it had a lively bar at street level where no one ever asked his name. Better yet, The Fyfe Building management didn't seem to care who their clientele were as long as they paid their bills on time and didn't drag their dirt back home with them. Management never noticed that he had taken over the apartment after disposing of the body he killed there, a person he knew would not be missed.

No one came to visit him, and the only way to reach him was by private number that he changed once a month and only handed out to those who owed him money. He knew he was owed money, so when the phone on the time-tattered table between the two open windows looking down on Grand Circus Park rang, it didn't surprise Carlo. The wind had picked up considerably, but it did nothing to cool the air. Carlo let it ring four more times before he reluctantly reached over from the bed, snatched up the receiver and held it to his ear.

"Yeah? What do ya want? I'm a busy man, Albert, you expect me to be hangin' around the phone waitin' for you to call me? Yeah, I did the job. No, I didn't stick around to sign no autographs, if that's what you mean. There were two others there. I scared them off. A short punk and a big dark one. I'll give them both to you for five grand if it matters so much. I make deals when it benefits me. Well, too bad then, nothin's for nothin'. A car was comin'. Maybe they picked the body up. I'm tellin' ya, he's dead in a ditch. No, I told ya, I ain't got the body. You don't pay me to take bodies. You ain't the only one I got business with tonight ya know, Albert, so what do you want from me? I don't give refunds, palsy, so you better pay up like planned. I don't care who dies over this. Me or you. You threatenin' me? I didn't think so. Tonight? I don't know. Let me check my social itinerary. I get invites to all the swell places you know and there's a nightly fee to have me baby sit." He didn't move. He waited for a few seconds. "You still there? Tell you what, I'll have to cancel a very heavy date, but if you add a meal on the house, I'll fit you in, say ten, ten-thirty. I got business. The Fourth of July is always a big night for murder. Don't worry, I'll be there. Somewhere outside. Send out the food, I'll find it."

He hung up and put his arm over his eyes. What a country, he thought. Whatever happened to the good old days when a man's word was as good as death? He rolled over and went back to sleep.

15 - PIĘTNAŚCIE

Alusia's Caddy pulled into the drive out front of Mangione's and waited its turn to stop at the entrance. The place was packed with a large crowd of gamely dressed couples who came to celebrate the Fourth of July with a superb Dago special dinner, a little dancing, and a little live show, and maybe a glimpse at a celebrity or two. Music from the orchestra already drifted out to the street.

Walter waited outside the front door, siphoning oxygen through a Lucky. His deep stuffed alligator eyes gave all the dames the blinkless once over. His face sported that certain after glow from the barn fire and his new hat tried to cover up the evidence of his recent hair deficiency. The new lack of eyebrows and eyelashes only strengthened his belly scraping reptilian charm.

In Alusia's Caddy, Moe was dressed in the college kid's chauffeur getup. It didn't fit well and kept riding his boxers up his backside. He sat behind the wheel fidgeting with his hat pulled down, and black leather gloved hands sweating profusely on the driver's wheels. He inched the car forward eagerly waiting his turn to unload his passengers and hopefully at least score a plate of Dago food before Bronislaus got them all killed.

In the backseat, Whitey piled make-up over the fading black and blue knuckle marks peppering his face. He applied another coat of lipstick to his puffy lower lip, stinging the cracks in them. He sported a thick expensive blond wig done up in a permanent wave that splashed down around his earrings to the nape of his neck. He also wore one of Alusia's girl's stylish purple and pink floral chiffon frocks with a long v-neck that hugged his hips and flared with ruffles at his thigh. He batted his long false eyelashes into his hand mirror. He took a deep breath and reached down and adjusted his two thirty-eights found hanging behind the dresses, not knowing they weren't in style. The truth was, in an awkward sort of uptown classy hooker way, he looked good and it sort of scared him.

Bronislaus sat quietly by the window in a black tuxedo and top hat. He wore white gloves, a graying mustache and dark horn-rimmed glasses that threatened to give him a permanent headache. He wasn't sure what was about to happen. All he knew was he and Whitey were going in and Nicole was coming out with them, however it went down. His hair was now receding and graying thanks to a straight razor found in the bathroom. From his left knee down to under his shoe he wore Alusia's chauffeur's metal leg brace to give him an artificial limp. He looked like a handsome book worm.

Whitey looked at Bronislaus as the Caddy approached the door. "Sometimes, Bronislaus, you live one draft away from reality." Whitey wiped lipstick from his chipped and stained front teeth.

"What are ya complainin' about? You never looked better," Bronislaus told him, not taking his eyes off what he could see of the front door.

"You busy tomorrow night?" Moe asked over his shoulder. "I'm gettin' a taste for you young lily dames."

"Keep it up, wise guy."

"That's what all you girls say."

"Bronislaus."

"Knock it off, Moe."

"Shit." Moe stretched it out under his breath as he pulled the car to a stop in front of the red carpet.

"Here we are," Bronislaus said. "Remember your cues and we'll be out in five minutes."

"Yeah, feet first and in a box," Whitey muttered.

Moe opened his door. "You sure Jake's here?"

"He got us reservations, didn't he?"

"What a pal," Whitey said. He slipped on a pair of shoes. "Oh my achin' corns."

Moe rolled out and skipped around the back of the car and opened Whitey's door. Whitey slid out with Moe's help.

Bronislaus stepped out favoring the stiff leg and shoulder. The warm air blew at their backs. Moe helped Bronislaus steady himself.

"Thank you, James. Make sure you get something to eat."

"You're welcome, sir, and thank you."

"Not at all." Bronislaus pulled Whitey near and pretended to give him a kiss on the cheek.

"Back off," Whitey said through clenched teeth.

Moe tried his best not to run around the car to get back in, and drove off around to the parking lot.

Whitey looked up to find Walter's eyes giving him a double take. Walter smiled. Whitey wasn't sure what to do, so he batted his eyes, and smiled back, grasping Bronislaus off guard and crushing his bad shoulder to his loaded bosom with a hug.

"You're killin' me."

They walked past Walter who removed his hat to fan his face while he ran his hairless hand over his hairless head.

"Don't turn around. The guy flirtin' at the door is one of the bad eggs I poached out at the lake."

Bronislaus held Whitey back. "Ah, don't worry you look great, doll face." Bronislaus glanced over his shoulder to get a better look at Walter.

Walter kept his eyes on Whitey.

"He likes you, just act natural."

As they went through the door Whitey looked over his shoulder. Walter had his eyes glued on him. Whitey winked. Walter straightened his tie and hiked up his slacks. He was thrilled at the thought of a fancy escort dame giving him the time of night.

Bronislaus escorted Whitey through the plush entrance to the reception desk. The brace made him walk with a slight sideways swing to his right stiff knee.

A tall gaunt faced Maitre d' with slicked-back thinning hair greeted Bronislaus with Dracula teeth. Bronislaus gave him his assumed name. The Maitre d' went down his reservation list.

"Ah yes, your table, Dr. Tolzdorf." He picked up two menus. "Right this way." He headed toward the dining room. "Congratulations."

Whitey looked at Bronislaus. "What?"

"Thank you. You're pregnant." Whitey held back. Bronislaus pushed him forward into the wide open smoke-filled night club. "After you."

The spooky Maitre d' accompanied them down three tier levels into the crowded, noisy dining room to a small booth just in front of the dance floor. He handed them two party hats, a set of horns, tweeters, and a handful of other colorful, obnoxious noise makers. Bronislaus handed the Maitre d' a hundred dollar bill. The Maitre d' looked it over. "I dried it myself," Bronislaus said.

"You're too kind, Doctor." The Maitre d' turned the table out allowing Whitey to slide into his side of the booth and did the same for Bronislaus.

"Such a gentleman," Whitey said. The Maitre d' flashed his fangs politely and walked off.

They watched him go. "Clam up, Whitey."

"Clam what up? I can't believe I'm even doin' this stinky dame routine." Whitey raised his voice. "And now I'm pregnant?" The drunken couples from three or four tables around them clapped their hands. Whitey looked around, dying from embarrassment.

Bronislaus nodded to them. "It's our first."

"And our last," Whitey said under his breath.

"Just remember why you and Moe are doing this."

"I know, I know, 'cause you took a shell because of us."

"No, because you two clowns can't keep your hands off each other."

"Fine, but we're even after this. We walk out, I'm goin' straight home to pack. I'm gettin' the hell out of this town."

"We'll be on the road before your water breaks."

"I get to shoot you next time."

A waiter came to the table. "Can I get you something to drink perhaps?"

Whitey looked through his menu. "I'll take a glass of chocolate cow juice… to go."

"Chocolate cow…?"

"She means milk," Bronislaus looked at Whitey.

"Heat it, would ya."

"Please. Make it two, put a shot of something in mine." Bronislaus nodded to the man at the next table using his hand to signify the baby in Whitey's tummy.

"Very well," the waiter said and left.

Bronislaus kicked Whitey under the table, "Milk?"

"What? You know I can't drink in my condition."

"I'll give you a condition." Bronislaus removed his glasses and pretended to clean them and squinted as he surveyed the room, fighting off the dizzies.

Between tall slender windows, murals of Italy were majestically painted on the rough cream plaster walls that gave way to accents of hand-shaped kilned bricks. The top row of seats in the club were six sections up and ran along the back wall, and each table was equipped with a lamp and a phone. Ceiling fans were bolted to chocolate painted wood beams spanning the room positioned to ensure every table got its share. But mostly they just spun the smoke and heat around, and did little else.

The bar was in three sections to the far side of the room. Short broad steps ran down from each row of booths into piles of chattering guests lining up three deep and elbowing each other to get at the bars. Those that had nabbed the eye of an overworked bartender drank some of the finest booze this side of the border, and paid one of the highest prices this side of town.

At the back of the furthest bar section, a short hall ran to the restrooms, Bartolommeo's office, and an exit to the back parking area.

To the left of the dining room, behind the back row of booths, was the kitchen. Double swinging doors were hidden by a partition that enclosed a waiter's station where white and red uniforms zoomed in and out with full trays balanced over their heads.

Nicole unknowingly caught Bronislaus' attention as she made her way across the fifth dining tier where all the tables, unlike the other tiers, were connected banquet style. In the center of this large dinner party was Bartolommeo, Anthony, several upscale-model Grosse Pointe fashionables, and two other important-looking men who worked with Anthony. One of them, Bronislaus recognized from the papers as Bill Fisher, who was gunning for Governor.

The tier that lined the wall behind Bartolommeo's party was filled by the Mangione brothers and friends from the riding club. Caruso the middle brother and Lorenzo the eldest seemed no worse from the fire, but Angelo the youngest, who had his left hand wrapped in gauze and a bandage over his left ear, was obviously already drunk.

Over all, the place was jammed and jumping with maybe three hundred guests. From which an elderly flower lady was making a killing. No one seemed to care that it was hot and sticky, except Whitey who kept fidgeting with the garter that was constantly bunching up his own boxer shorts.

"I told ya both to take them off."

"Shuddup."

Couples danced in front of Whitey and Bronislaus' table. The dance floor was a complete mob. A twenty piece orchestra played on stage behind a natural blond with a classic set of hood ornaments. She stepped up to the microphone and began, in a soothing voice, a whispering tune meant to quite the crowd. She was cloaked in a glistening black satin handkerchief dress, a chiffon top with a loose fitting low V waistline. The back of the dress followed the same V neckline as she eyed the bandleader. Turning to the crowd a silver and cut-glass princess tiara jumped in the spotlight, throwing rainbow sparkles across the musicians dressed in snow white top hats, tails and patent leather shoes. The effect was classy, daring and promised a grand Fourth of July celebration. A stage exit was stage left behind emerald green curtains. Before the blond sang three cords, Bronislaus and Whitey were facing her way.

"I'll murder ya, Bronislaus."

"Relax, Sally will never know it's you."

"She will if we end shootin' up the joint. And I suppose Jake failed to mention that my girl was headlinin' here tonight."

"Actually he mentioned it, but it must've slipped my mind."

"I'll slip your mind. That's it, the deals off."

"It's too late for cold feet. This table almost cost me a grand."

"It's going to cost us our…" Whitey stopped, "I think your little canary just flew in."

"I see her. Okay," Bronislaus said, putting back on the glasses, "Here's the plan again."

Whitey waved him off. "I know, I know, you nab her, she screams, I get raped when they grab for me, and you get us both killed. Don't worry, I got it mesmerized."

Bronislaus got up, adjusting his limp. "Just meet me at the stage door." Bronislaus fought his way toward the restrooms back behind where Nicole and her father where sitting.

He only had to test the hardness of the leg brace once on a man who obviously didn't understand that "excuse me" meant "get the hell out of the way."

The waiter brought the two glasses of chocolate milk and Whitey downed his, leaving a coco mustache under his nose. He pulled out his cigs and lit one from the candle. He took a deep drag and looked up to find the waiter still looking at him real close. "Scram," Whitey said in his own voice, knowing it was a mistake as soon as he said it. He started looking for Bronislaus to warn him that he had been made.

The waiter left and went over to the Maitre d' who got on the phone. The phone rang on Lorenzo's table. He picked it up and listened. He hung up and dialed the office where Robert sat brooding over a fresh fight with Nicole.

Meanwhile, Bronislaus had made his move to Nicole's table. Nicole did a pivot when she first saw him. Is that? It couldn't be. It is! Bronislaus! He's alive! She'd kill him for showing up here. The men at the table followed her eyes to Bronislaus and started to get up. "It's okay, gentlemen, Father. It's a friend from school. Ah, a teacher. Math class." She picked up her purse and met Bronislaus among the tables. He led her by the elbow down through the bar crowd toward the dance floor.

"May I ask you a straightforward question?" She said through clenched teeth.

"No. Just keep smilin'."

Nicole forced herself to smile back at the friendly faces.

Bronislaus was bumped hard by a thug and stumbled into a chair. "Excuse me," he said to the feathered hat in it. He removed the glasses to stable himself. They reached the dance floor with a few more steps.

Nicole glanced around to see if anyone suspected anything funny. "What are you up to, Bronislaus?"

Bronislaus kept his eyes on the office door. "Just dance." They danced in front of Whitey who sipped Bronislaus' milk.

Nicole spotted the puzzling familiar, odd looking woman at the table with the chocolate milk mustache and blond wig. Whitey sneered back and blew out smoke. Nicole examined Whitey closer. She looked back at Bronislaus, then again at Whitey. "Oh my, your girl is quite the looker."

"Shuddup," Whitey mouthed.

Robert came storming out of the office and was met in the lobby, first by Lorenzo, then Caruso, and finally a drunken Angelo. Caruso went out the front door and came back in with Walter. Robert pointed a finger at Whitey and Walter did a slow burn under his already red face for being had. Robert sent Lorenzo and Walter toward Whitey. Robert's eyes found

Bronislaus and Nicole on the dance floor. Bronislaus patted his pocket to let Robert know he was carrying.

Nicole tried to follow everything until she felt something dripping on her toes. She looked down to see blood drop from Bronislaus' coat. Nicole looked back up at Bronislaus' face trying, but not succeeding, to mask the concern in her eyes. Bronislaus shrugged his good shoulder and gave her a slight told-you-so smirk.

Walter and Lorenzo arrived at Whitey's table and slid in the booth, one on each side of him. Whitey played up the game. He downed Bronislaus' milk, and fluttered his eyes. "Fancy meetin' you two blokes in a dive like this. Who's your barber? Sitting Bull?"

"Who would've known?" Walter said ignoring Whitey's taunt and pinched his cheek.

Lorenzo leaned in close and put his hand on Whitey's knee. "You look good, doll face, you alone?"

Whitey picked up a tweeter and tweeted Lorenzo under his nose hairs. Lorenzo snatched up the tweeter and crumpled it up and stuffed it in Bronislaus' empty milk glass.

The men and women sitting next to Whitey's table looked on in annoyance.

"Go back to your drink," Lorenzo said. "She's our long lost sister."

Whitey grabbed a hold of Walter's arm affectionately and played it up. Walter gave him a murderous look and tried to shake Whitey off. Whitey held on tight, and ended up being jerked violently back and forth, until he stamped out his cigarette on Walter' other wrist.

"Hey, she's pregnant. Get your hands off her," the young gent at the table next to them demanded.

"Shut your pie hole or I'll have your butt thrown out of here."

"Why, I never. Do something, Harold."

As Harold stood up, Walter pulled his gun. "Sit down."

Whitey grabbed a hold of Walter's face, squeezing his sore skin with all his might, making him pucker up, and planted a great big juicy kiss on his smackers.

Walter pulled away, spitting in disgust, to the enjoyment of the tables around him.

Whitey was making a spectacle of himself, "What's the matter, you don't like a gal who chews tobacco?" The laughter from the surrounding tables rose out from under the cover of the music.

Bartolommeo and Anthony became aware of what was happening below them. They didn't move to do anything about it. Instead, they did their best to keep their guest's attention away from the dance floor.

Bartolommeo looked over at Robert's confused, angry face. Both were wondering the same thing. Was Nicole in on this intrusion?

Robert and Angelo remained at the door. Caruso made his way to Bartolommeo's table. Bartolommeo flagged him away.

Tiny blood droplets continued to drip from under Bronislaus' coat to the dance floor where they splashed onto both of Nicole's new white open toe shoes. Bronislaus noted by squeezing her arm that Nicole kept wiping them on his trousers. She didn't care what he thought, they were expensive. He managed to keep half an eye on the service door, looking for Moe.

"Podziękowania."

"You're welcome."

Finally Moe emerged out from behind the waiter's station with a mug of Joe. He nodded to Bronislaus and patted his full belly. Bronislaus nodded back. Nicole looked up and Moe was gone.

Bronislaus drifted back to get an angle on the bandstand. In the corner, third violinist to the left, Jake, the narrow-faced Jewish musician who had joined Whitey and Sally for lunch at Michal's, and who had gotten them in the joint, sat with his eyes glued on Bronislaus waiting for his cue. He played his violin, skipping the charts. Bronislaus looked back at Whitey who was again being jerked around by Walter like a signpost in a typhoon. Bronislaus tried to signal him without being too obvious. But Whitey had a hard time seeing straight.

Behind Bronislaus, the rest of the band paused when Jake rose to do his solo.

From somewhere in the middle of being violently yanked around, Whitey managed to let out an extensive scream, "Get your filthy hands off me, you creep! I'm a married woman!" And Whitey smacked Walter as hard as he could. Walter's face went halfway across the table and his false upper teeth flew the rest of the way, clinked off the empty milk glasses and clattered onto the dance floor.

Jake's solo ended two notes later and he sat back down. He calmly reached under his chair to his music case and traded the violin for a Thompson submachine gun without anyone taking notice, and held it behind his bony leg. He waited, hoping with all his saved up prayers, wishes and mumbo-jumbos that he wouldn't have to use the damn thing. True he owed the Niemiec family a few favors. Who didn't in the neighborhood? Plus some cash, and his mother's hospital bills, but did it have to come to this? Shooting up the DA's Fourth of July party. Bronislaus, you're my pal, but not this, please, he thought.

Sally looked down in horror at the poor woman being manhandled at the table as the rest of the room went silent. Men!

Lorenzo and Walter grabbed Whitey to shut him up and instead made it look like they were gang-assaulting her. Bronislaus raised his teenage voice barely above the clamor, trying to sound as tough as possible.

"All right, you mugs, throw another kiss at my friend and this girly gets it." He put his gun to Nicole's head. "Now get your mitts off my wife."

Every thug in the room reached inside their coats.

Chances were Bronislaus wouldn't get to blow eighteen candles anyway. He hadn't felt this much tension in one joint since his father discovered he'd quit school after the eighth grade and spent his afternoons fishing and playing ball. He kept his eyes focused on Walter and Lorenzo. He needed a glass of water, and calling timeout while he went to the bathroom wouldn't hurt. "What are you waitin' for? Get your mitts off her."

In the back of the room, Bartolommeo rose out of his chair. "Let him go, boys." They let go. Walter plucked the blond wig from Whitey's head and threw it into Whitey's face.

"Whitey!" Sally yelled.

"Ssshhuuudddup!"

Jake stepped up behind Sally and pulled her aside as the restaurant filled with laughter, then quickly fell silent again.

"Table-top the canisters," Bronislaus ordered.

Lorenzo and Walter put their guns on the table. Whitey picked them up, toppling the table to the floor, and stepped over it to the dance floor with his purse on his shoulder and a gun in each hand.

"The rest of yous," Bronislaus continued, "very slowly, let's see scrap metal. Real happy-like."

The thug who had bumped Bronislaus earlier now sat at a table up against a window on the third tier. He made a fast move for his coat and Whitey shot his water glass to pieces, wetting down the whole table. His date to his right slapped him for being so stupid. The thug resisted belting her back and slowly withdrew his handgun from his coat pocket. After it was in clear view he tossed the gun out onto the dance floor.

"Let's go, shower-down-time." Bronislaus said to the general public.

No one else moved. Jake revealed his Thompson and sprayed the ceiling above their heads, pinging off a few of the fans. Plaster rained down on the people filling the room full of screams, but still no one moved. So much for prayers, wishes, and mumbo-jumbo... see you at the Synagogue, yeah Lord. Jake could see his musical career draining from the faces of his fellow players.

Sally held her hands over her mouth. This wasn't happening. Why in hell were they doing this... the girl? And Whitey in that girly getup, though those shoes were cute, it's still nuts. She looked from Bronislaus to Nicole. Could this be...? Oh my God, she thought, Bronislaus was bleeding! And bleeding badly. Suddenly she understood. Whitey was helping Bronislaus stay alive. So was Jake, and somewhere, probably Moe. All because of the girl in the car... how romantic! Dames.

"That's my last warning," Bronislaus told them.

Slowly, people across the room stood up and threw their guns down around Whitey's feet. All kinds of guns. Annie, the old flower lady, took out a sawed off shotgun from the false bottom of her flower basket and laid it on the floor and kicked it over.

"Annie!" Nicole said in shock.

Annie shrugged. "A lady's got the right to protect herself from brutes, ain't she?"

Bronislaus looked up at Bartolommeo. "Nice respectable establishment you've got here."

Bartolommeo took the hand-rolled out of his face. He exhaled a face full. "You won't get away with this, kid, none of ya will," he said through his clenched hippo teeth.

Bronislaus cocked his gun behind Nicole's ear. Nicole's eyes lit up. "All I want is for you and your buddy the DA to nix a certain bank note you've taken out on me. Am I making myself clear or do I need to add it all up for you in front of all these nice people?"

"Don't be..." Bartolommeo said.

"Try me."

Bartolommeo threw his hand-rolled back at his face and clenched down on it with his fat teeth until he clipped the end off and it dribbled down his belly to the carpet where he was forced to stomp on it before it burnt a hole.

"Now gentlemen," Bronislaus shouted, "drop your drawers."

No one moved. Jake sprayed the rafters again. Men started dropping their pants. Bartolommeo, Anthony, their two political friends and their sons were the last ones left to shimmy down. Bronislaus pointed his gun at Bartolommeo and sank a bullet into the cushion beside him. "Maybe you need my help?"

Bartolommeo and Anthony signaled for their sons to undress. Women laughed at Fourth of July print with flags on Robert's boxers. Anthony, Bartolommeo, and their two important guests remained dignified to the end.

"Now listen, son," Anthony said with his pants unbuckled, "this man to my left is running for governor. I think this has gone far enough. Don't you?"

"Let's see him run for governor with his pants down around his ankles. Now button down or the only thing to run will be his blood." Bronislaus took another shot that sank into the cushion beside Bill Fisher. Anthony, Bartolommeo and their two guests dropped their pants to the floor.

Jake got down off the stage under the glare of the band leader and made his way to the stage exit where the two forest green curtains hung down. Sally wanted to follow but Jake made it clear for her to stay out of it. He turned and held his violin case on the room. Then quickly switched to the Thompson.

Bronislaus backed Nicole toward the curtains, leaving a trail of blood. Whitey, with the two guns still drawn followed, walking backwards. At the exit Bronislaus stopped and yelled back to Bartolommeo. "Stay close to the horn, you'll hear from me."

Jake stepped through the curtains and stopped at the door. Bronislaus glanced back at him when he heard Jake fighting with the door knob.

"What are you waitin' for?"

"It's locked."

"What? I thought…."

"I did, twice. Someone must've' come along behind me and locked it again."

Whitey stood facing the room alone. "What the hell are you guys waitin' for? Scram out of here!"

"Look out," Bronislaus said, and Jake backed off. Bronislaus moved back from the door and sank three bullets into the lock. The door remained tight, minus some wood.

"What now?"

"If we get out of this, Bronislaus, I'm gonna murder ya for sure now."

"Shut up or I'll personally bury you in that dress, shoes, wig, and all."

"Real professional," Nicole whispered.

"You got any bright ideas?"

"They're gettin' real restless out here," Whitey said.

Bronislaus looked at Nicole. "Well?"

"Let me try the Thompson," Jake said.

"Try it."

Jake moved back and let loose on the door. The door rattled from under the force of the bullets but remained locked. Jake and Bronislaus looked hopefully back at Nicole.

Whitey stuck his head back through the curtains. "Any longer and I'll be tap dancin' out here."

Nicole walked to the door. She turned to face Bronislaus. "Did my father really have that done?" Indicating Bronislaus' shoulder.

Bronislaus nodded yes.

"And all you want is him to stop?"

"You got the picture."

Nicole kept her eyes on Bronislaus' and reached up and pushed a button at the top of the molding, and the door swung open. Jake went to give her a hug but Bronislaus held him back.

"What?" Jake asked.

"She could've gotten us killed."

"See if I help you again," Nicole said, as Bronislaus pushed her out the door.

"Let's move it, Whitey."

Outside the door, Moe screeched the Caddy to a stop.

"Hurry up. It's goin' to rain any second."

"Yeah, bullets," Jake said, as he covered the front of the building by spraying the lights above the door as armed men leaped back inside.

Bronislaus put the gun back to Nicole's head as he made his way to the Caddy. The two thugs and the Maitre d' re-emerged from the front door, by peaking around the door jam.

"In the building!" Bronislaus yelled at them.

They ducked their heads back into the building.

"Get in."

Whitey followed them out, walking slowly backwards still covering the room through the open curtains, giving the others enough time to make it into the Caddy.

"Couldn't we just have lunch?" Nicole asked sarcastically as Bronislaus steered her to the back of the Caddy where Moe waited with a twelve gauge, holding the door open.

Bronislaus pushed Nicole in first. "Watch your head."

Whitey came out backwards. "We okay?"

"So far. You drive."

"Me?"

"No, your boyfriend. Move it! I don't want you heaving up, either."

"Moe ride shotgun, aim at the front door but watch for anyone coming out the back."

"I'll drive," Jake said.

"Forget it." Whitey moved around the car. "A guy heaves up one time…"

"Just get in," Bronislaus said.

Jake ran around to the other side and got in back while Moe scrambled into the front rolling down the window to stick his shotgun out. Whitey got in behind the wheel and slammed it in gear with a crunch. He skipped the driveway, cutting across the grass, taking out a flower bed.

"Look out for that…!"

The Caddy also crunched through the Mangione parking sign.

"Never mind."

"You want to drive?"

Moe shook his head and clutched the dash with his free hand. "Not like this."

"Then shuddup."

The Caddy hit Whittier Avenue from over the curb and sped down the avenue heading toward Grosse Pointe Park's outer neighborhoods. Whitey took off the pumps and threw them out his window. "Ah, freedom," he said as the color came back to his feet.

"Hey, those were nice shoes…"

Robert came out the stage door pulling up his pants, followed by the Mangione brothers and Walter. Lorenzo hopped on one foot trying to get his foot through his pant leg, but the shoe was stuck in his suspenders and the weight of his gun hindered his progress.

Bartolommeo came out behind them. "Shoot the tires out."

The boys opened fire, and Lorenzo fell over into the shrubs, putting a forty-five caliber bullet hole in his father's pant leg, just above the knee. Bartolommeo kicked Lorenzo in the butt for nearly shooting him. Number three thousand five hundred and thirty-five, Lorenzo thought.

Angelo, who was too drunk to see straight, only managed to nearly kill the Maitre d' who had rushed back out from the lobby.

Caruso's three shots skipped off the pavement below the car, sending sparks off the differential.

But Robert took close and deliberate aim and pumped three shells at the fleeing Caddy. The back window exploded before Robert squeezed off the third shot as the Caddy moved out of gunshot range.

"You fool!" Bartolommeo took Robert's gun away. "Nichol is in there."

Robert looked at Bartolommeo with murder in his eyes.

"Now what?" asked Lorenzo, who was sitting in the bushes still trying to get his foot out of his suspenders.

"We move at midnight, like planned." Bartolommeo clamped down on a new cigar. It was broken. He grabbed it from his teeth and threw it down in disgust. He stopped at the stage door and looked back after the fading lights of the fleeing car.

"Only this time, we put them more than out of business." He held his hand out to test the wind. Big drops of warm rain plopped into his fat palm. Perfect, a storm, ideal cover for an ambush. Bartolommeo chuckled to himself.

Whitey made a mad left on two wheels through a stop sign and passed a black sedan. It was Carlo. He had heard the shooting and knew immediately who was coming his way. He waited for them to get a good start then followed. Albert was right, they struck back. Sometimes timing was everything in his business… and luck.

In the backseat of the Caddy, Bronislaus and Nicole were huddled face to face down on the floor. Jake was crouched in the corner behind Whitey, whose driving resembled an insane hunchback in drag with a sliver in his bottom. Moe lay motionless with his head against the door as raindrops began to pelt the roof of the Caddy.

"Boy that was close," Bronislaus said sitting back up.

He Looked at Moe. "Moe? Moe!" He grabbed Moe and shook him. Moe slumped forward onto the dash.

"They killed Moe! They killed Moe!" Whitey wailed.

"Shut up, Whitey! Moe, can you hear me, Moe?" Bronislaus leaned over the back of the seat to get a better look. He pulled Moe up straight. Moe's head dropped back over the top of the seat in front of Nicole. His eyes were open and rolled back up into his head looking at her.

"Is he… dead?" Nicole asked.

"I don't see any blood," Bronislaus answered, lifting Moe from the back of the seat to get a look at his back. "Nothing."

"Maybe he fainted," Jake suggested, not looking up.

"They scared him to death. His Mother will kill us!" Whitey was near hysterics as he hunched over the wheel and continued down the side street with his foot to the floor. Streetlights streamed by in a blur and the engine raced at top speed. Whitey zoomed through a stop sign at Vernor Highway.

A green late model sedan swerved out of his way on the newly wet cement and careened into a parked car, bouncing off it into a street light. It went out. Carlo slowed at the intersection as the two women got out of the car and into the rain, apparently shaken but unharmed.

"Slow down, will ya, Whitey. You'll have every blue coat in town after us. I still don't see any blood, Nicole." Bronislaus said as he let go of Moe and picked up the chauffeur's cap. He stuck his finger through the hole at the top. "Look at this."

"Better check his head again."

Moe flopped against the seat and began to roll his head back and forth as he came to. He lifted his head and looked around, alive but confused. "Where am I?"

"Thank god, Moe," Whitey said, letting go of the wheel and trying to hug Moe. The Caddy went over a curve across someone's corner-yard and blasted a row of shrubs on its way toward another street. Everyone screamed, including a young couple under an umbrella, diving out of the way.

Moe reached for the wheel as the Caddy struck a car on the far side of the street. "What's with you, Whitey?" Moe pushed Whitey off him.

Whitey grabbed the wheel back and after three drastic maneuvers, managed to straighten out the Caddy while pumping on the brakes.

Moe touched the back of his head, dug his finger through his thick carpet of hair and felt his scalp. He looked at the finger. There was a spot of blood. "Dang, that bullet creased my skull," he said adding a low whistle.

"Bounced off, more like it," Whitey said.

Moe playfully punched his little friend in the arm.

"Ahhhh…!" Whitey's arms were already black and blue.

"There's a hospital right up here," Nicole said.

"Forget it. Find a phone, Whitey," Bronislaus said.

"Make a left here," Nicole told Whitey.

The boys looked at her.

"Don't look at me like that. It's okay. Barbara is my best friend. We'd do anything for each other. She's home alone, sick with a cold."

Whitey turned to Bronislaus. Bronislaus shrugged. Moe looked back at Jake. Jake sat back up, pulling his violin case up to his chest, wishing he was back on stage with his b flats and f sharps, and an occasional c minor. Damn it. What had he done, he thought?

Outside, the storm began to build and spread its way across Detroit in more ways than rain.

16 - SZESNAŚCIE

Barbara, an only child, lived with her parents in an immaculate red brick two-story home with six upper shuttered windows from the three front bedrooms. At the end of the drive, to the right of the house, servant quarters were built above a three car garage that featured four dormer windows, two in each room.

The hot stagnant air had rapidly evolved into a wet summer night wind, plucking innocent leaves from the safety of their branches high up in the oak trees only to have them plastered to the lawn by the oncoming pelting rain. High above, thick pressing clouds rode in on the crest of the night wind, gobbling up the moon and stars as they advanced, threatening to answer everyone's prayers by finally terminating the dreadful hell-sent heat wave. A four-foot painted Negro coachman cooled its heels patiently at the opening of the driveway with a brass hoop in his outstretch hand. It held up a miniature white lantern in the other. Its cardinal coat had pigeon gray buttons, matching its jockey pants that were tucked down into its ebony boots.

A light burned in each window above the garage. The Caddy was inside the garage below, and the doors were closed behind it. Barbara, dressed in a solid mauve colored, flowing evening robe, came out of a door at the front of the garage which lead upstairs to the living quarters. A few steps behind her were Whitey still in drag minus the shoes, Jake in his tails and violin, and Moe in the chauffeur's get-up — sans the gloves and cap. She led them to the back of the house and into the kitchen.

Back upstairs, in the two room living quarters, Bronislaus hung up the phone. Nicole paced in front of a single bed. The room was lit by a table lamp in front of a side window. Just outside, the wind blew through a young maple and the moon vanished as the rain spewing clouds continued their trek across the sky heading right toward them.

Another single light bulb glared from a small kitchen area across from a gray and black print hide-a-bed. A single bare wood beam ran across the center of the ceiling and the roof vaulted skyward above it.

"On his way to the warehouse," Bronislaus said, hanging up.

"So?" Nicole asked as she paced back and forth.

"So we wait," Bronislaus said. He tried to remove his tux coat. It hurt him bad. "Help me with this, will ya?"

Nicole assisted in getting his arm out of the sleeve. "You've gotten us in a lot of trouble this time."

"Me? What about your trigger-crazed boyfriend?"

Nicole winced at the contrast of Bronislaus' blood on his white tux shirt. "Oh, god, you're still bleeding." She took the coat with her finger tips and hung it on a hook in back of the door. "You're the one who showed up uninvited again," she emphasized. She touched his shoulder.

"Ouch! Thanks. Your father started this whole mess in the first place. I'm the one with the slug in me, remember?"

"Well, if you hadn't been such a pigheaded fool."

"And if you hadn't been such a double-crossing selfish little brat…"

Nicole drew back to slap Bronislaus.

"Ah, ah, ah, you wouldn't hit a wounded man, would you?"

Nicole swung at him and meant it. Bronislaus blocked the blow and held her forearm. Nicole drew back but Bronislaus pulled her down to the bed on top of him and kissed her fully on the mouth. Her violent resistance slowed to mild opposition as her passion escalated and she became the aggressor. Coming up for air, Bronislaus painfully rolled her over onto her back and pushed away.

Nicole slapped him hard. "Bastard!" She sat up and crossed her arms in front of her. Her cheeks flushed and her violet eyes flared with anger.

"That hurt."

They stared at each other. He looked drawn and anemic. The twinkle in his eyes that always made her smile, no matter what mood she had been in, was almost gone. Bronislaus cracked a weak smile. Nicole fought back the urge to hold the poor boy in her arms. This isn't like her, these feelings. They were just friends… but her heart fluttered when their eyes met again. Oh, Bronislaus, what are we going to do about this, she thought? Nothing. We can do nothing. This is crazy to even think being together a possibility.

Bronislaus took her hand and closed his eyes.

"This isn't funny, you know," she told him.

Bronislaus felt a little light headed. "Don't worry, I think I'm bleeding to death anyways." He eased down on his back, nearly spent.

"Good. Here, let me take a look at that." She began to remove his shirt. It clung to the dried blood. She became aware of the blood on her new outfit. "Oh, shoot. I may kill you myself. Look."

"So, I'll buy you a new one. It was worth it."

"How flattering."

"I only bleed on my best of best friends."

Downstairs, in the kitchen of the main house, Whitey and Moe recalled the day's adventures to Jake. Between the three of them, they managed to munch and chew until Barbara couldn't take the uncouth noise any longer and left them sitting near the backdoor where the help usually ate. They didn't notice her departure. Half of a ten pound ham sat on a cutting board in the middle of the table beside three kinds of cheese, including a block of the good stuff, a handsomely aged Limburger that was smelly enough to make the neighbors wonder if Barbara was boarding farm animals in the kitchen. Jake had cut a clump, added it to a slab of ham, put them between two pieces of rye bread, and tried to hide the taste of the cheese and the guilt of the pork by plastering them both with horse radish and homemade hot — very hot — mustard.

Whitey tried his best to chew, but wasn't having much fun, especially after the mustard found its way to his cut lip.

Moe helped himself to a triple-decker sandwich of just provolone cheese, tomato, and onion, having already had two helpings of Mangione's lasagna that he had scraped off four returning plates in the bussing area. Nobody had offered to feed him, so he was forced to fend for himself. A little trick he'd learned early on hanging out at the backdoor of Michal's as a kid, because crazy white folk sure threw out a bunch of high-quality food when they were pickled beyond rational thinking. Come to think, that's how he came to hangout with Bronislaus who, most often, was in trouble and sentenced to peeling potatoes on the back stoop or scrubbing floors.

He stabbed a hunk of ham with a knife and ate it separately, thinking he knew somehow it'd all come to this — running for their lives, hiding out, eating probably their last meal together, with one of them mooning over a dangerous dame. Actually, Moe wasn't a bit hungry, but free chow was free chow, and the way things were going, this might actually end up being that last meal he saw coming. He bit into the slice of ham and slipped a few pieces of bread into his coat pocket just in case, thinking maybe he should call his momma.

"Hey, and then what?" Jake asked, taking a big bite.

Moe washed down the mouthful of ham with a glass of water. "Whitey heaved up all over the place and stunk the car up to high heaven so bad I lost my cool and beat his head in. Bronislaus', too."

Jake stopped chewing. He looked at the Limburger. His nose twitched. He put down his sandwich and washed down what he had in his mouth with water. "Never mind, I'll read the book." He looked at Whitey with disgust.

Whitey still couldn't chew. "I'm gonna starve to death if I keep it up."

In the hallway closet leading from the kitchen to the front stairs, Barbara held a phone to her ear. She spoke with a stuffy clogged nose. She sneezed, and blew her schnozzola. "My sinuses are killing me. I feel like hell. This must be a cold. The other three are in the kitchen," she said quietly into the phone. She glanced out the crack in the door at the kitchen door. "Yes, he's up there with her right now. He used the phone. The car is in the garage. The back window is blown out and it's dented. I'll stall them as long as I can. Sure. Don't you dare tell her I called. Bye." She hung up the phone and crept back to the kitchen door and listened.

Carlo Axler rounded Barbara's neighbor's house thankful for no fencing and somewhat thankful for the rain. He stopped beside the young maple and looked up to the garage quarters. A white Chihuahua yapped inside the kitchen door. Carlo peered in through the door window. The dog locked eyes with him for an instant, soiled the entry rug before stuffing its tail between its legs and quietly hiding in his room. Nothing messes with and nobody gets away from Carlo, he thought. The nerve of this Polack kid makin' him look bad in eyes of his payin' clientele. Things like this could snowball, and before a guy knew it, he was at the dirty end of a paid ticket to yesterday-land just to keep his mouth shut to protect former clients. He was fully aware of the game, and how it was played. He flicked his cig against the garage wall. Having to take garbage from the likes of Albert and Johnny — two tapeworms one step from being crapped to death — didn't sit well. The nerve of those guys wantin' a refund. He wasn't throwin' away a perfectly honorable rep over some young punk who thinks he's too smart to punch out when his time is up. Nobody, but nobody, outsmarts Carlo Axler… and lives to tell his friends about it! It's bad for business… and bad business ain't good business.

Up above, Carlo could see shadows on the ceiling from the window lamp. He carried a deer rifle with a scope. He had once downed a twelve point buck with it. Its stuffed head still hung in a whorehouse's billiard room in South Chicago where he once worked security and took black-mail pictures for the old broad who looked after him while he mended from four bullets to his back, taken in her dark alley while robbing twenty bucks from the wrong guy. Too bad he couldn't hang the other twenty-three young bucks he'd plugged over the past couple of years. What a shame he couldn't tag his name on them, strap them to the hood of his car and drive them through town. He'd stop at a couple backwoods pubs on the way and pound back a few with the local color and brag about the hunt, how he tracked them down one by one and murdered them in cold blood… maybe even have them printed up on a scorecard in the sports page instead of unsolved murders on the front page or short notes in the obits. Ah, the irony, he thought, time for number twenty-four plus three if he was provoked by the three lack wits he saw feeding their faces in the kitchen. He wasn't sure who the big-nosed girl was, and didn't care to meet her, but also didn't like seeing her on the phone like she was spying on the others. She was no good, he could tell.

Carlo looked at the maple. He took off his wet trench coat and dry tux jacket, strapped the rifle over his shoulder, and began to climb. Three years of surviving in a reform school campground came in handy. He had learned how to climb fragile tree branches to pick apples and pears and feed himself because the bigger kids took his food; until the biggest kid horrifically died as shards of stain glass from the prayer room shredded his stomach. From that day on nobody messed with Carlo Axler. Nobody.

A sudden burst of wind shook the tree and the rain started to fall even harder, hitting Carlo square in the face. "Shit!" Sometimes Mother Nature held the cards, and the hand she dealt just outright stunk.

Out front of Barbara's home, Lorenzo's car pulled to a stop across the street. Robert, Lorenzo, Angelo, Caruso, and Walter got out. They put their collars up to ward off the rain and headed across the street toward the house through the slowly increasing downpour.

Above the garage, Bronislaus still lay in the single bed in the back room. Nicole sat beside him. The rain pounded on the windowpane behind her.

Lightening lit up Carlo as he sat like a morbid ghoul of death swaying in the young maple tree. Thunder rumbled a few miles away. His face strained as he tried not to break his neck taking aim on what he saw through the window through his scope.

"I wish your father would hurry up and call."

"He'll call."

"When he finds out what you've done he'll probably..."

"He'll get over it."

"We missed all the fireworks."

"Don't bet on it." Bronislaus was drowsy.

Nicole turned toward the other room. "Did you hear that? Someone is coming up the stairs."

Bronislaus sat up. "It's probably just Whitey finally finding it in his Scottish stone-heart to bring up his poor hurting pal some grub before there's a death in my family."

Again lightning lit up the sky around the house as the temperature dropped like stones. The thunder cracked closer this time. The eye of the storm was approaching fast. Carlo tried to take aim at Bronislaus through the window, but the wind blowing the tree made the kid a moving target. One squeeze of his finger and the night's job was over. Just one flash of gun powder and he could get out of this rain. One count to ten, that's all you have to live, Polack. Enjoy, he thought. "One, two, three..." he counted to himself aloud.

Nicole got up, crossed in front of Carlo's scope and closed the door dividing the rooms. She took Bronislaus' tux jacket from the back of the door and moved to the bed. "Can't believe it, it's actually getting cold.

You should cover up." She helped him on with the jacket. "Let me take this leg brace off."

"Leave it. I don't want to lose it. It belongs to somebody." He let her put the jacket over his freshly bandaged shoulder.

Nicole turned toward the door again. "Someone is out there."

Bronislaus strained to stand up. "Yeah, I heard. Sshhh. Stand back." He carried his gun to the door. He looked over at Nicole, reached over and hit the light switch. Carlo pulled the trigger, the door flung open as the window shattered, throwing Bronislaus to the floor. His gun skidded along the tile and slapped against the baseboard under an end table.

A crack of a young maple branch followed by a muffled, distraught cry came through the shattered window as Carlo fell from his perch. A short human figure teetered back and forth, silhouetted in the door from the light in the outer room.

Lightening lit the sky again, shortly followed by a clapping thunder from directly overhead.

"Whitey?"

No one moved. No one answered.

"Who the hell is it?!"

A hand reached around the corner and turned on the light.

Walter, Bartolommeo's chauffeur, stood in the door with a distinct, well defined bullet hole between his eyes. The back of his head was in the outer room. Nicole let out a scream. Walter tilted forward through the door jam and slapped onto the bare floor with as much finesse as a dropped slab of cold prime rib. Nothing left to move but the blood oozing from his nose.

Bronislaus reached out for his gun.

"Don't do it, Polack." Robert stepped into the room with a gun drawn and pointed at Bronislaus.

"Robert." Nicole was genuinely surprised.

"Shut up," Robert told her. "Slide your gun over to the door, real easy."

Bronislaus slid it over and Robert kicked it back into the outer room. "Get up." Bronislaus fought to get up. Nicole helped him. Footsteps came tromping up the stairs. Whitey, Moe, and Jake were pushed into the outer room followed by Lorenzo, Angelo, and Caruso. They all looked at Walter's body and his blood seeping onto the floor.

"Christ all mighty," Angelo whispered.

The three brothers crossed themselves.

"Is he…?"

"Can it."

"The old man's gonna…"

"Shut up, goddamn it."

"For Christ's sake, he was our friend."

"He was what he was, but he ain't no more. Now shut up about it."

"Yeah…" Lorenzo started.

"Who was it?"

"Don't know, Caruso answered. "He's gone whoever it was.

"You've got all kinds of friends," Robert said to Bronislaus.

"Everyone loves a winner." Bronislaus looked past Robert to his pals.

"Tie these three jokers up. We'll deal with them later," Robert said.

"It's gettin' late," Lorenzo said, "We better get to the warehouse."

Robert checked his watch. "We got plenty of time to make this one look real pretty,"

Robert threw Nicole out of the inner room. Nicole sprawled onto the floor. She picked herself up and brushed herself off. Her eyes bore into Robert.

"Find something to tie up their hands," Robert said.

Lorenzo nodded to his brothers as he went to the door and down the stairs. Caruso and Angelo bound the boys' legs and hands with silk ties Caruso found in the closet. They pushed them down onto the couch as Lorenzo came back in with some good strong ropes he had found in the garage. They threw the ropes over the beam and began hosting first Jake, then Whitey and finally, with great difficulty, Moe by their feet until the three of them did the butcher window dangle, their noggins swaying inches above the floorboards next to the foldout.

Robert watched with quiet satisfaction until he was sure the boys were no longer a problem. He smiled to himself as he stepped back into the inner room where Bronislaus remained heaped against the wall.

"Robert, you pig!" Nicole screamed at him when she realized what Robert had in mind.

Robert slammed the door in her face and locked it. Nicole began to beat on it again and again, screaming at the top of her lungs until her brothers were forced to pull her away and hold her down, only to get a few choice words, scratches, and bites for their effort.

Inside the inner room, Robert came at Bronislaus, grabbing him up by the front of his shirt, and began to beat him about the face, with an occasional blow to the body for good measure. Bronislaus sailed about the room, not being able to put up a fight, his legs wobbling as he could merely resist by remaining upright, not giving Robert the satisfaction of putting him down. This only made Robert hit him harder and harder until his own knuckles bled.

Finally the lamp went to the floor and broke plunging the room into darkness. Robert came at Bronislaus as the young Pole lashed out with the metal brace and caught Robert off guard amongst his prospective children. All of Robert's future generations let out a groan as his fingers found their way around Bronislaus' neck and began to squeeze out the pain that racked his body until Bronislaus stopped breathing.

Robert rolled off Bronislaus, got to his knees and fought back anguished tears and the need to vomit. Moments crept by like drying tombstones. He wiped tears from his violent eyes and with the same motion lashed out to hammer Bronislaus' bloody face once more.

Bronislaus fell from the hands of death. Choking on his own blood, spitting up a few teeth, he began to breathe again.

In the outer room Whitey and the boys continued to yell even though the Mangione brothers had gagged them. Whitey's dress hung over his face so that when he was gagged it ended up being wrapped around his head and shoved into his mouth as well.

Nicole opened the door when she heard Robert release the lock and pushed into the room. Robert threw her out again. He threw Bronislaus out behind her. She shrieked when she saw what Robert had done to Bronislaus' handsome face. The boys screamed obscenities under their gags. Lorenzo kicked their backsides until they shut up.

Robert came back in the outer room. He had Bronislaus' blood splattered on his tuxedo shirt. He wiped blood from his bleeding fist. Nicole slapped Robert's face. Robert wiped it off and slapped her back, smearing his blood on her. The brothers turned on Robert.

"She had it comin'." Robert picked up his hat and put it on. "Take Walter down and put him in the car with this one." He kicked Bronislaus in the ribs. Bronislaus didn't make a sound. Robert walked manly trying to hide the pain that rocked his core. Lorenzo started to say something smart but saw the crazed look in Robert's eyes and thought better about it.

The brothers carted Walter with a repeated thump of his dead weight down the stairs. Robert picked up Bronislaus' gun and put it in his coat pocket. He waited for the brothers to reach the bottom of the stairs then picked Bronislaus up, held him at the top of the stairs, let him go and pulled Nicole back out of the way so she couldn't hold him up. Barely conscious Bronislaus teetered at the top of the stairs. He battled his failing knee joints just to stand, unable to take the first step down.

"Still won't take a fall, huh, tough guy."

Bronislaus mumbled something through his broken yapper.

Robert nudged Bronislaus in the back and he pitched forward, not having the strength to stop, and tumbled down the stairs, ending up a shipwreck on the concrete, face-up into the driving summer rain. Lightning lit his contorted grin, a horrid harlequin mask at best, with thunder following moments later, echoing drums of pending doom.

Nicole broke away from Robert's grip, and went after Bronislaus. By the time she got down to him the rain had washed the loose blood from his face down into the cracks of the driveway, already on its way to the gutter. He had a wide gash above his left eye and another below the right. Blood streamed from them both. His mouth bled profusely from where his lower teeth had sunk through his lip. More blood soaked his coat from the top of his shoulder down to about three inches below his arm pit. To make matters worse, if possible, he began to choke on his blood again. Nicole sat him up and thumped on his back until he spat it up. He opened his eyes and blinked to clear the rain and again to clear his head. It didn't work. He shook his head to chase the webs, but it was no use. He focused somewhat on Nicole's shocked, pitying face and tried to smile but managed only another cocky bloodletting grin.

Nicole couldn't bear to look. Tears streamed down her face but who could tell with all the rain. She wiped her face clean as she cradled his head in her lap. She stroked his matted hair where she found another two inch gash just above his temple.

Robert came down after a quick phone call, taking in the painfully touching scene and picked Bronislaus up out of her arms and set him on his feet. "Let's go, Polack, walk it like a man."

"You bloodthirsty pig!"

Robert turned his back on her. "Next time you won't kiss him."

"I didn't...."

"Don't lie. Look at you. Look at your face. Look what you've done to all of us playin' with this dumb kid, playin' with my heart. This is what he gets for makin' a move on my girl. And you for lettin' him inside yours."

Bronislaus wavered, resembling a bloody bed sheet in the wind, but with the help of Nicole's unsteady guidance, he somehow managed to luck his way to Lorenzo's car. He thought of running but knew they'd shoot him in the back. So he took the steps as he could find them powered by the one chance in hell he'd figure a way back home again.

By then the brothers had Walter's body on the floor of the back seat. So Robert threw Bronislaus face down on top of him.

Nicole stopped before getting in and looked back at the house. Barbara stood at the front door on the porch protected from the rain by a green and white striped metal awning. She sneezed. Nicole knew that Barbara had betrayed her, and Barbara knew that Nicole knew she was no longer her friend. She sneezed again and went back into the house, closing the door behind her to protect herself from Nicole's purple penetrating stare and seal in the pain of being left behind.

Robert pushed Nicole in the backseat where she was forced with Caruso and Angelo to travel with her feet on Bronislaus and Walter. Lorenzo started the car while Robert claimed shotgun and they sped away.

"He'll suffocate down there," Nicole said.

"Where he's goin', he'll need gills."

Bronislaus lay mug to mug with Walter. Walter didn't look any better dead than alive. His taxidermy, alligator eyes investigated Bronislaus with intensity of an over-vacationed tourist. His gruesome cranial bullet hole was inches from Bronislaus' nose. Bronislaus' own blood trickled down upon Walter's tobacco stained teeth. Careful not to draw attention, Bronislaus managed to work his good arm free and closed Walter's eyes before the pain made him blacked out.

At the third stop sign from Barbara's, Carlo pulled onto the street from a darkened driveway and followed far behind Lorenzo's car. The rain came down in bar tubs by then, accompanied by more lightning and thunder across the tumulus sky. Dead branches snapped and indiscriminately fell from maples and oaks onto the streets and yards. The heart of the awaited summer storm had finally hit Detroit with vengeance.

Back above Barbara's garage, Moe, Whitey, and Jake still hung upside down from the rafters. The phone rocked in its cradle a second time begging for attention. Barbara crossed in front of them this time, sniffling as she tensely reached for the receiver. The boys tried to yell for help through their gags.

"Hello," Barbara said, trying to sound like the hired help. It was obvious she had pulled the routine before. "Who, sir?" She looked into the swollen faces of Moe and Jake.

The boy's protested as load as they could through their gags. Jake's face had turned beet red and Moe's had turned a deep mocha brown. Veins bulged on their foreheads and eyes. Saliva dripped from under the dress as Whitey tried his best to scream for help.

Barbara turned her back on them and cupped the receiver, enjoying the moment enough, knowing how loyal she was behaving, that her faint mustache twitched with nasty delight. "I'm most sorry, sir, you must have dialed a wrong number. The Mister and Misses are at the Yacht Club gala. Yes, sir. Fireworks if the storm passes and everything clears up, I suppose. Happy Fourth of July, then." She hung up the phone, turning to face the three young hoods hanging upside down. She wasn't sure what was about to happen to these young men, but she knew she had to escape their brouhaha, and didn't want to stay with them with all this thunder overhead until someone came for them as Robert had told her to do. So she took the stairs down, closing the door quietly behind her and slipped back to the house through the rain. She had done her part. She had shown Robert that she was the one he could trust, shown Robert and her brothers just who Nichol really was inside, someone who didn't belong with them, nor wanted to belong. Oh, how she had longed to reveal to Robert and the brothers what had been taking place behind their backs at the lake all these years. The little scamps, Nicole not knowing Barbara had hidden silently as a rat, spying on them from up in the barn, that Barbara had discovered them giggling endlessly since childhood in the tall grass where the deer slept, their little hideaway together all these years. Barbara didn't find anything funny in the betrayal Nicole was thrusting onto the families. What could she see in that skinny little kid at the lake when she had Robert at home to dream about? It was obvious that Nicole didn't deserve or understand the complexity of someone like Robert. Not like she did. Not like how she wanted to fulfill his every need every day. Still it was Nicole he had angrily taken away with him. And not her, and that tore at her heart as much as watching them be happy together always had.

Moe was furious again, he needed to find new friends. He started to swing back and forth out of frustration. Jake began as well. They rocked back and forth for about three minutes before Whitey caught onto the game going on outside his dress. He, too, began to swing. Before long the beam started to creak in protest. Then louder until finally it gave out a gasping croak, cracked and ripped apart, causing the boys to topple down in a platoon of ceiling planks, roofing tiles, rusty nails and dirty water.

Moe landed on the couch accompanied by a six inch spike sticking into the meat of his shoulder with a plank fragment still attached to it.

Whitey plopped with his upper body on the couch. His knees struck impolitely on the floorboards.

Jake banged down on his noggin on the throw rug, putting out his porch light. His bound feet slid down the wall as his dead weight pushed over an end table, knocking a standing lamp, causing its shade to end up over Moe's head and the room to go dark. Half the cracked beam finally swung down from still being tied to Jake and slammed against the wall smashing a glass covered picture of Barbara's grandparents, impolitely ending up on top of Jake. A moment of silence before a rush of water dumped in on all of them from the upturned gutters through the freshly designed jagged six foot hole in the roof.

Whitey, face down in the wet cushions, managed to remove his gag and dress trapping his tongue, by rubbing his face on the upholstery. But otherwise he was stuck with his bottom sticking vulnerably in the air and the dress still over his head on the couch. "Ahhh, I broke my neck."

Jake was brought back around by the water continuing to pour down on his spinning head until he was close to drowning. He pushed the beam away and hooked a finger in his gag and pulled it down over his chin.

By then Moe had uprooted himself from the couch and rid the unwanted lamp shade. He gingerly plucked the spike from his flesh and nearly had himself completely free when he looked over and spotted Whitey's protruding bottom inside the dress. He rubbed it gently. "Ohhh, boy, I'm in the mood for something young and fresh, to take my mind off how poorly you white folks been treatin' me."

"Very funny, Moe"

Moe finished unhitching himself.

"Moe? Moe!" Whitey said in a panic.

Moe got up.

"Moe, don't get cute. Moe?"

Moe held back a laugh.

"You numskulls, quit screwing around up there. I'm suffocating down here," Jake gurgled.

Minutes later, Jake waited outside for them with his trusty violin slash Thompson. Moe had to use the phone to find out what Mr. Niemiec wanted them to do, and Whitey had to get out of the dress and back into his clothes. The makeup wouldn't completely wash off. He looked crudely clownish with his toe head hair askew. They came down the stairs together. Jake gave Whitey a look.

"Shuddup."

"It's locked," Jake said.

Whitey examined it. "We'll have to pry it open."

"We ain't got time." Moe grabbed the lock and gave it a massive yank, ripping the screws right out of the wet wood plank.

Jake flung the door open.

Whitey got in the driver's seat with Moe riding shotgun and Jake in back. Whitey paused in the driveway when he saw Barbara rush out onto the porch.

"What are ya waitin' for?" Jake yelled.

"Timing," Whitey answered. He put the Caddy back in gear and turned four doughnuts in the front Lawn, weaving around the pine trees.

Barbara came out screaming obscenities at them with her squeaky sore throat. The car's tires spun on the wet grass and threw sod up behind it. A clump of which caught Barbara on her chest, face and wide opened trap — in the middle of her vex.

Barbara's parents arrived just in time to swerve out of the way as the boys made their exit. The stunned parents careened smack-dab into the little jockey statue at the bottom of the drive, severing its head and sending it rolling up the driveway like a ten pound bowling ball and into the open garage.

"Waa hoooo…!" Moe yelled out the window as the boys sped through the rain.

Barbara still picked sod from her gums. She spit as she looked after the fleeing Caddy. "I deserved that," she said, and went inside to gargle.

17 - SIEDEMNAŚCIE

By then the 1929 Fourth of July celebration had passed and muted over the Detroit River leaving the sound of insistent rain and a distant unloading coal barge to fill its void. The crowds that had turned to revel in the praise of such a great country had returned to the safety of their homes and night spots, leaving a trio of midnight bells counting down in the distance at the remote side of an old, seemingly abandoned warehouse yard. Blanketing rain came down with the wind at a two o'clock tick. Gigantic lightning bolts flashed in the distance over the churning Detroit River revealing quick, eerie, skeletal glimpses of the yet to open Ambassador Bridge, instantaneously followed by even mightier thunder claps. A dead tree had long ago fallen in the middle of the vacant trucking yard, trampled to rotted-bits where rows and rows of metal, wood and painted glass warehouses — some partially burned, sat stinking of emptiness. Down along the second row of warehouses, off to one end, next to one of the burned-out buildings, was hidden Lorenzo's car, Bartolommeo's Caddy, and Johnny and Albert's trucks. No one was in sight. After a few minutes Edju and Lip arrived in a Tasties Bread truck. They pulled up to the first warehouse as usual, and swung around not avoiding the dead tree, pulling to a stop before backing up. When the transmission stopped droning, Robert and Lorenzo leaped on the running boards of the cab. Robert smashed the glass with the butt of his gun and put the barrel to Edju's head.

"Don't even breathe."

Edju pulled the truck out of gear and braked to a halt instead.

Lorenzo opened the other cab door. "Don't even breathe," he said.

Edju and Lip looked at each other. Someone needed a tough guy dialogue coach.

Even though Lipinski towered over him, Lorenzo managed to drag him out of the cab and pull him face down into the muddy gravel. Caruso and Angelo each held a gun to Lip's head "Don't even breathe," they hissed down at him in unison.

Lip couldn't help himself. He gurgled a laugh into the mud puddle.

Caruso kicked him for it.

Johnny got in the cab of the truck and backed it down the ramp. Albert rang a delivery bell. Stashu came out and was nabbed by Angelo who put a knife to his throat and a hand over his mouth.

Inside the same rundown warehouse, under a small hanging green lamp, Michal went over a book ledger while sipping a glass of red wine. He raised his eyes at the sound of footsteps. "How did it…?" his voice trailed off, his blue eyes taking in the full scene.

Bartolommeo stood there with his boys. Fifteen in all.

Edju, Stashu, and Lip where thrown to the ground, still alive, in front of Michal's feet.

"You seem surprised, Michal." Bartolommeo thumbed his cigar.

"Should I be?" Michal thumbed his own cigar.

"Not at all." Bartolommeo tried to relight his damp Cuban.

"Then I'm not." Michal relit his dry Canadian.

"Take his gun. I didn't expect to see you here," Bartolommeo said.

Lorenzo took Michal's gun off the table. He picked the wine bottle up also, took a swig and threw it past Michal's head, shattering it on one of the stacked wooden crates that lined the walls of the warehouse. The crash was joined by a hollow echo from within the crate.

Michal didn't flinch. Bartolommeo didn't notice the significance.

Bartolommeo shot his eldest son a level eye. "It saves me a trip."

Michal glanced down at his two boys with Lip on the ground. They didn't let on. He stood up from his chair as he reached for his glass and brought it to his lips to carefully savor the last drop of red wine. He brought the glass down and waited.

Lorenzo turned his head from his father to Michal as the glass came hurling past his head, making him duck and cringe. The glass crashed onto a wooden beam that supported rafters filled with more wooden crates.

"My mistake." Michal looked down at the man with the unlit damp Cuban clenched in his hippo like teeth. "Gettin' your hands personally dirty is out of style."

"One man's style is another man's grave." Seeing Michal enjoying his cigar so much Bartolommeo' tried to light his own cigar again, but it wouldn't stay lit.

Caruso tried, Angelo tried, then Lorenzo went to try but Bartolommeo slapped his hand astray. "Try to remember that while you and your family are fit for cement kimonos."

"And using big words," Michal said. "This has gotten out of hand. And I was told by the police that you barely spoke English."

Lorenzo went to clobber Michal but Bartolommeo stopped him. "Your son and his friends have infringed upon my family's dignity, and pushed me to my limits'"

"Dignity? You and your friend the DA have spent a lot for the rights to use that word."

Bartolommeo clamped down on his cigar. His thick jaw muscles bulged. How dare Michal bring his friend's name into this.

Michal glanced down to his watch. "It's early, what do you say we just get comatose right here, shake hands and forget all this mobbish anger, Bartolommeo? After all it's America's holiday. And isn't it why we came here, to live freely away from those who would pose us harm in the countries we come from?"

"That was yesterday. Today your family owes me. So I'm takin' the booze and puttin' you and your family out of our lives forever."

"If I'm not mistaken, one of my sons has a bullet in him already. Where is he now?"

"He's taking a bath," Robert said.

"You stinkin'…." Edju began. Robert cut him off with a kick to the ribs.

"That's enough, Robert."

"Robert Bunniti. Surely our fine Wayne County DA doesn't know his son's hanging around with hoods like your boys.

Bartolommeo let that comment roll off his thick back. "We've got work to do. Put them over there and tie them up." Bartolommeo turned to leave.

"Not so fast," Michal said.

Bartolommeo turned around. His boys stopped.

"I'll offer you one more glass of my finest vintage before we both possibly end up in cold mud."

"I spit in your wine."

"We both have all our sons here. Think it over."

"I have, and only my sons will be leaving this place."

Michal cracked a smile. He kept an eye on Bartolommeo's face.

Bartolommeo's eyes slowly began to show recognition of the true situation. What an ass, he thought. He had unwittingly chased the mouse into an angry dog's cage. He looked about him, knowing he was about to be mauled. His boys did the same.

"Drop your guns."

"You wouldn't."

"The Polish Gang...," one of Bartolommeo's men whispered.

Bartolommeo gulped, not knowing how many men Michal actually had working for him.

Lorenzo passed a little air.

"Say hello, boys."

Michal's hired men, led by the two ghosts who played gin rummy in Michal's office, sprang from the rear of the bread truck and simultaneously appeared across the rafters. Guns began to pop as Bartolommeo and his boys shot back while running for cover behind vacant crates.

Albert got it first, once in the back from a shotgun blast from the rafters and again in the chest as he floundered amongst the empty crates. He lurched up once, then twice as his chest ripped opened like a detonating tuna can, only to slide his way down another crate, leaving a blood streak befitting the slimy rat-bastard that everyone, including his mother, knew he was.

Lip caught a slug in the back of his knee and crumbled to the floor as Edju and Stashu dove behind crates. Stashu, seeing that his pal hadn't made it, scampered out and slid Lip's tall, lean body across the twelve feet of open concrete. Edju covered them both with forty-fives in each hand. He blasted away at the empty crates where Lorenzo and Caruso hid. Wood splintered and sailed back around the Mangione brothers. Robert's bullets whizzed past Edju's face until Ducky pulled him down.

Johnny plugged the guy in the rafters who got Albert, his partner in slime, then took eight shells from a Thompson submachine gun that nearly severed his left arm and pierced his heart and lung. His limp body banged against the crate behind him as he buckled to his knees. Blood trickled through his rotten teeth as he coughed up one last time. His eyes rolled back into his skull as he began the final swan dive toward Hell. He was dead before his face embraced the cold concrete.

Behind the crates where Lip was dragged, Stashu pulled his belt off and made a tourniquet for Lip's leg whose knee cap was shattered so badly that parts of it were still scattered about the floor where he fell.

Stashu worked in a frenzy to stop the bleeding. His heart raced. "Your leg's all tore up!" Stashu said as he wrapped the tourniquet tight. Immediately the bleeding slowed.

"Aaaahhhhggg… You think maybe I can't tell?" Lip lay on his back with his arm across his eyes.

Stashu snuck a peak beyond their hiding place, a crate deliberately loaded with scrap iron. The cross fire raged on from across and above the warehouse. It only slowed down as randomly the men reloaded their weapons or aimed. Three bodies lay out in the open. Stashu couldn't make out who they were through the gun smoke that quickly filled The Polish Gang's warehouse.

Outside the rain poured down on the hidden cars and trucks. Inside Johnny's covered flatbed truck, Bronislaus lay twitching as pain rippled through his semi-conscious body. Next to him Walter's cold, lifeless corpse oozed body fluids. As if fighting to emerge from a bad dream, Bronislaus slowly boxed his way out of his near coma. He opened his eyes and listened to the pounding rain and the distant gun fire. He filled his lungs with air, over and over again as he looked at Walter's uninspiring face. His joints felt as stiff from the dampness as his muscles did from the beating and the loss of blood. He rolled onto his good arm and put his ear to the side of the truck. It was definitely gun shots. In front of them, or through them, Bronislaus could hear sloshing footsteps coming closer, then stop, tap, tap, tap, then they'd come a step closer through the water running under the truck with a shuffle and a splash, then another slosh and a tap, tap, just outside the truck. Strangely enough, if he wasn't nearly dead already, he would have put his life on it that someone, just outside the tailgate, was tap dancing.

Because just outside the truck, in the pouring rain, Carlo continued to kill night crawlers that had gathered by the back tire of Johnny's truck. The rain pounded down over his Fedora and black slicker. He lowered his silencer to the rusted lock and pulled the trigger. The lock popped off and rolled down into the streaming gutter below. He reached a black gloved hand over and opened the back of the truck. A whiff of death hit him square under the hat like the scent of squandered money.

Inside the truck he found Walter lying on top of Bronislaus with a trail of blood flowing from their bodies down between the truck's scarred and abused hardwood bed. It now pooled at the tailgate, then trickled down into the gutter with the worms, as Carlos lowered the gate, and diluted by the streaming rain water. Carlo admired the red beauty of it and nudged Walter's leg. No reaction. He nudged Bronislaus' non-braced leg, again no reaction. He sensed he may have lost his ten thousand potatoes if someone else had killed the Polack, and wasn't too happy about it. How dare someone else kill his pray, interfere with his livelihood, and tamper with his undaunted reputation. He reached way in and took Walter by the suspenders and rolled him off Bronislaus. Carlo looked down to make sure he didn't get blood on himself as he leaned in and reached to pull Bronislaus out of the truck to see if the Polack Kid still had a pulse. Alive was alive, and dead was still dead.

Bronislaus took that opportunity to kick at Carlo with all his remaining steam and caught him flat on the jaw with the metal leg brace. The totally unexpected blow to the teeth sent Carlo reeling to the left side of the tail gate. His Fedora whirled out into the rain, skidding to a stop nearly twenty feet away.

Bronislaus mustered up enough do or die adrenalin to pull himself up to the stunned hit man, eyes locked on each other, and jammed Carlo's head down against a protruding bolt on the tailgate latch. A large gash opened above Carlo's ear near the temple. He went down to the gutter fast with a firm grip on Bronislaus' tux, dragging him out of the truck, while with his other hand he still managing to hold the gun cleanly between them. Bronislaus had a choice of grabbing the side of the truck and flee or going for the gun and fighting for his life. He chose the gun and ended up in the gutter on top of Carlo.

Blood gushed from Carlo's gash as the torrent stream washed over his submerged cerebrum. A sight he would've cherished, in particularly it being his own life streaming away.

Now on top of him, Bronislaus struggled feverishly to keep the gun from pointing in his intimate direction. Without warning it went off. Carlo's eyes opened wider, more surprise than pain, still under the water, and bubbles of air gurgled to the surface from his mouth and the new blow hole in his chest. Blood colored the bubbles as it gushed from him. Finally finding the freedom he was destined to feel all along. Crazy Carlo's last thoughts were of who would find his will, and fulfill his wishes by dropping his roasted ashes into a spewing volcano. Who would figure out in which banks his safety deposit boxes were left under his many aliases, the names of the people he has killed, and earn the right to keep every last dime by fulfilling his gravely wishes? Even if they had to dig him back up to do it right.

Outside the water, the force from the gun was enough to buck Bronislaus off Carlo and he splashed face up into the gutter between the back tire and the dying hit man. The water was forced away from them momentarily by the impact of Bronislaus' body, but quickly enveloped both of them again, turning an even thicker red as blood from both flowed together. Bronislaus struggled to lift his head from the water. He tried with all his might to reach across his body and grab the tire with his good hand, but he was spent. His fingers could barely trace the fading tread. He fell back and tried a second time, but couldn't even touch the tire. He fell back again, his eyes still open. Carlo lay next to him with a new blow hole in his chest. Ironically a smile grew on Bronislaus face as he realized he'd won the battle but was about to lose the war despite himself. "Ma…"

The storm raged on and lightening flashed above the surface of the water, while the dull thud of thunder rippled down from the sky. He felt it more than heard it, the rat-tat-tat of gun fire bouncing off the water. His mind slipped peacefully through a spectrum of washed out colors to a distant white that seemed to teasingly keep him at arm's length. Unexpectedly, a large foreboding creature reached through the serene painting of his death and reached down-down-down-down at him. Bronislaus' mind swelled with the horrendous fear of angry demons coming for him and dragging him off to hellfire for being such a pain in the ass to his family and the so many others who have suffered from his hooligan behavior. He opened his lungs one last time to repent as his body was pulled out from the depths of the watery womb, back to the life between Heaven and Hell. Drastic pain tore through his body like an inner violent eruption of a seven point magnitude. He sat up and vomited water, dirt and blood. His eyes glassed over and stung shortly before they cleared. Solid colors dive bombed back into his brain as though they were dropped from a single prop plane and exploded at the back of his eyes.

He blinked over and over again until he began to recognize Moe as the person gently wiping the wet earth from what was left of his face. He sat motionless, held up by Moe, as Whitey reached over and pulled Carlo from the flowing water by his blood soaked slicker.

"Who is it?" Jake asked standing over them with a Tommy.

"Crazy Carlo." Whitey let Carlo flop back down into the water.

"Let's get Bronislaus to the car."

They stood him up."

"Can you walk?"

Between coughs, "Another five seconds and I could've flown."

"You're welcome."

Bronislaus continued to choke up water as they headed toward the Caddy. Bronislaus pulled up and lifted his face towards the gun fire. "We've got to stop them."

"You're bleedin' to death, Bronislaus," Moe said.

"Help me, please, we got to hurry. Get Nicole. She's in that sedan over there."

"Leave her," Whitey yelled. He put Jake's hat on Bronislaus' head.

"We need her."

"Yeah, like another hole in the head." Moe put his coat over Bronislaus' shoulders.

Jake ran to Lorenzo's car. It was locked. He smashed out the window with the butt of the Thompson. Nicole lay in the back seat. She had been bound and gagged by her brothers so she wouldn't get in the way.

Inside the warehouse the shooting had come to a near stop. Angelo had taken a slug in the forearm and three others from the Mangione's crowd had minor wounds to arms, hands and legs. Other than that, Mangione had lost four men, including Albert and Johnny, who were practically no loss at all when considering the money Mangione still owed them.

On the other side, three of Michal's men had taken the short way home. The two from the rafters were now dead on the concrete. But the ghost from Christmas past, who had led the charge out of the bread truck, had managed to crawl back into it, only to slowly bleed to death from a twelve gauge shotgun blast to his stomach. He lay slumped against the side of the truck, gun still in one hand, a wad of blood stained bills in the other. He had tried to plug his wounds with a hand full of Franklins. His hat was tilted back, his eyes were closed, and the scar under his chin was grinning again from ear to ear. The soul from his ghostly body seemed to dissipate with the reek of gunpowder as it rushed past the truck and out of the open warehouse dock doors, only to become lost in the wet night air.

The atmosphere in the room slowly began to clear, but not the lethal tension now that the shooting had come to a standoff, Italians on one side, the Poles on the other, and hired dead bodies from both sides stuck in the middle and bleeding out on the warehouse floor. The sound of the rain rose out of the oncoming silence until it and wind was all that was heard pounding on the roof and whitewashed windows. The light was out because the single green lamp that hung over the table had taken one of the first direct hits. The only other light seeping into the warehouse came from the single yard light sneaking in around the bread truck.

"Daddy? Daddy it's me," came the frightened female voice from the front of the bread truck.

"Nicole?" Bartolommeo yelled out.

"Yes," she answered.

"What are you doing, Nicole?" Bartolommeo was furious. "Go back to the car!"

"Hey, Pop."

"Bronislaus? That you, boy?"

"Most of me."

"Thank God."

"I'm here with Nicole. We're comin' in to talk. Okay?"

"I'm coming in, too, Daddy.

"Don't do it, Nicole."

"We're comin in, Pop. Together."

Robert, Lorenzo and Caruso aimed their guns at where Bronislaus' voice came from. Bartolommeo shook his head.

Michal looked at his watch again. He caught Stashu eying him.

"Like gum on your shoe, huh, Pop?" Stashu asked.

Michal shrugged. "He'll be here."

From The Polish Gang's side of the truck, Nicole and Bronislaus walked out to the middle of the warehouse stepping side to side, back to back. They were forced to step over Albert's body. Nicole fought not to look down and accidentally tramped on his hand. Her breath caught in her throat.

Anxiety rippled across the blood-stained concrete floor from family to family, gangster to gangster, bootlegger to bootlegger, killer to killer, as the two young friends from their shared lake reached the center of the room. A Thompson burst the silence and trimmed the top off the hat Whitey had put on Bronislaus' head. Then silence. The anxiety mounted. Then a gunshot blast exploded Nicole's little pear shaped purse. Again the room went silent.

"You done playin' games?" Bronislaus struggled to steady his voice.

"Hey, Bronislaus," Whitey O'Neal yelled from the front of the truck.

"Not now, Whitey."

"We got company."

"Yeah?"

"Yeah!" O'Garrity's voice boomed out from where Whitey was.

"It's O'Garrity!" Bronislaus whispered to Nicole.

"We just happen to have the place surrounded. Mind explainin' what's goin' on?" O'Garrity kept out of sight. Bosko and the other two dicks had Whitey, Moe and Jake face down on the wet dock.

"O'Garrity!" Michal called out.

"That you, Michal?"

"I got someone here I want you to meet."

"I ain't interested. You're all under arrest."

"Patrick, I'd like a word with you," came a low soulful voice from where Michal hid.

"Alusia!? What are you doin' here?" O'Garrity asked.

"For your sake," Bartolommeo said, "she better be someone's date."

Caruso started to laugh out loud. Bartolommeo slapped him. Caruso stifled himself. There was nothing funny about this to Bartolommeo.

O'Garrity looked about him. There was no place to hide.

"No good will ever come of this, Alusia."

Alusia stood up and came out from beyond the crates. She wore a dark purple gown with a black cape over her shoulders. Her long dark hair was pinned up in a bun under her black veiled hat. The light was dim but not so dim that it couldn't reflect off the wide teardrops that fell down and streaked the make-up on her cheeks. She had a deep, rich Polish accent and she spoke haltingly as she failed to fight back her broken-hearted emotions.

"At least I'll finally have a good night's sleep, Patrick. We did a shameful thing. I wanted that child so much." Her hands came to her face, as she sobbed.

Both Bronislaus and Nicole where completely confused. They watched as O'Garrity came to Alusia.

"Oh, for Christ's sakes, Alusia, don't start ballin' in front of the whole world." He handed her a clean hanky. "Here, wipe your face."

"Gentlemen," Michal said, regaining O'Garrity's and Bartolommeo's attention. "The noodles are just about stuck to the wall. Shall we talk in private? Bartolommeo?"

Bartolommeo looked at his three boys and Robert, they had no idea what was going on. He looked at Nicole, O'Garrity, Alusia then Michal. "We had better."

O'Garrity didn't say anything. He looked around him at the bodies and the mess. There was still nowhere to hide, no way out. He looked at his men who seemed even less intelligent than normal.

"We've all been introduced, O'Garrity," Michal said.

"You just couldn't let it go, could you, Alusia? You and Stephania, all these years. You just couldn't let the past be what it was, the past. The girl was happy. She had a future. Now look what you've done. You and your damn telegrams. And you, Michal. Why do you think Stephania and Alusia liked to go to the lake so often? Were you so blind? And your damn boy... didn't you know what was goin' on under your nose? That's why I hate this little bastard so much. I saw it comin' a long time ago. And here we are, dead men at our feet and all our asses in a sling. All because of your kid and you winnin' your side of that damn lake."

The sound of the pouring rain and thunder filled the room once more. The wind picked up again, whistling through the refurbished holes in the warehouse. A lightning bolt struck a tin roof nearby and thunder clapped directly over head.

Nicole stood motionless beside Bronislaus, shaking like a lost, bewildered little girl. Bronislaus reached over with his good arm and gently took her hand in his and squeezed it. He didn't understand any more than she did, but he wanted her to know that he was there, wherever this was headed. He looked out at the bodies that lay around them... the price, plus human tax of their clandestine friendship.

But the truth of what had taken place so many years ago had to be paid for, and would not come cheap. So the negotiations began right there, right then, in the eyes of the beholders. Even if no one could outright win, and no one would end up outright happy, regardless of which side of Detroit or the law.

18 - OSIEMNAŚCIE

Bronislaus healed fast. Two weeks after the storm he was out of the hospital, minus two molars with minimal stitching to his face, but still wore a sling on his left arm.

Out at the lake, Stashu's cabin had four carpenters sawing and hammering it back together. Two more bedrooms were being added and the kitchen was being extended out another five feet. All was to be paid for by Bartolommeo Mangione.

For Bartolommeo and his family now owned the cabin, the Niemiec side of the lake, Michal's restaurant, and a slew of other property investments along Telegraph Road.

As for the Niemiec's half of the negotiations, they chose from the two Italian families, what was referred to as "prime real-estate" in the heart of downtown Miami, though at that time it was still technically a swamp. This also included a double vacant beach front lot where Michal hoped to build a hotel and restaurant, plus a four bedroom home further south overlooking a gorgeous palm and overflowing coconut tree studded beach, where his family would reside.

It almost killed Bartolommeo and Anthony to let the properties go. But this was the prize Michal had chosen as his part of the deal. So Michal and his family and Bartolommeo and Anthony and their families had agreed to swap even up. Everything was legally signed and sealed within a day of the shootout. As part of the deal, The Polish Gang would leave Detroit; in return the Mangione family would leave The Polish Gang alone. All charges and allegations therefore would be dropped by both families, and any questions regarding the incident would be ignored; and according to Anthony Bunniti, the court would do likewise. Bottom line: Bronislaus and Nicole would remain apart from each other, their friendship permanently severed, leaving Nicole to marry Robert as arranged and planned from birth.

O'Garrity retired from the Detroit Police department and rumor had it that he had moved to New York City where he planned to set up a private detective agency funded by a private entity of investors but everyone knew it was a pool of money set aside by both sides to get him out of the way. No word of him ever having been on the take was mentioned or otherwise implied during his early retirement formalities.

As for Alusia, she sold her property, paid off her girls, posted adequate tuition for her driver, all secretly paid for by Anthony and would move with the Niemiec family to Miami where she had purchased a sprawling estate just north of the city. She could send Christmas and birthday cards but no personal contact with Nicole would be encouraged. It was a bit harsh on Alusia, but Bartolommeo and Anthony both thought it could cause future problems to have a Polish ex-Madame paying visits of any kind. So her price was met. And it was a high one. If, after the wedding, Nicole chose to contact Alusia on her own, that was entirely up to her. Though, all in her family hoped she wouldn't and from all indications from her there were no lingering maternal desires to do so.

Whitey, Moe, Ducky, and Lipinski were also bought off handsomely in the negotiations and Michal made an extended deal to take them along with his family and find them work in his new hotel once it was built. The boys wanted to go anyway and would have for free, except Michal insisted they be compensated for losing their jobs, though Whitey officially never had one, and a pension fund was created for Lipinski who would never walk without a limp again. They could return back to Detroit if they chose to after one full year, but were not allowed on any property owned by either Italian family, including close siblings and distant relatives.

Bartolommeo was more than willing to extend the offer if the results were to rid himself and Detroit of such low-life troublesome trash. For this comment, Whitey had personally traveled to the eastside to hear Sally sing in her last Detroit gig and punctured all of Bartolommeo's Caddy's tires.

However, on Jake's part, he suddenly found himself being pursued by so many booking agents that he couldn't afford to take Bartolommeo's offer until after Michal had completed his hotel. No one really bothered with the facts. Rumors had him actually killing people, shooting it out with Crazy Carlo, saving women, robbing banks, and affiliated with various mobs and gangs from Chicago to Philadelphia. But none of it was even close to the truth of him having actually soiled himself the moment he first pulled the Thompson's trigger, to the point where he threw his clothing away when he got home and locked the door behind him, then cried until he fell asleep fearing someone would soon come there to kill him. It didn't matter how he felt about his life, because he instantly became known as Machine Gun Jake amongst the high rolling party-going crowd, so his management started billing him as Machine Gun Jake and his Ammo Renown. Hoods tipped their hats to him on the streets, delis named sandwiches after him, The Jake, two dead meats and a shot of Tabasco because the sauce was invented in 1868 by Edmund McIlhenny, a Maryland-born former banker, and women sent wedding proposals, naked pictures and undergarments in the mail to his home. His band was starting to make future bookings out of town in places like Chicago, Cleveland, the Catskills, and Buffalo. Who would've figure this could happen to him over helping a friend stay alive?

Also, on a personal note, Bartolommeo and his family had made oaths to castrate him if any of the truth ever hit the papers, or became known through him so he did nothing to perpetrate the truth. He had his father and mother to consider too, so he was keeping his mouth shut tight, his bags packed with clean shorts, and his legs crossed.

No mention of that rainy night or of those who met their end in the warehouse, at least not the truth of it hit the papers. The deaths were attributed to Carlo Axler, and Crazy Carlo was said to have taken his own life after a long drawn out siege of being surrounded by a heroic O'Garrity and his three brave men.

In the end, Carlo Axler was buried in a cemetery off Eight Mile Road with a simple marker sporting only his initials: C.A., because his birth name was unknown, or forgotten, even rumored not to have had a legal one given to him, and there was nothing in any past public records of his youth due to unsolved arsons at out of state reform schools. Though these sad places were only mentioned once in an obscure article written by a murdered newsman claiming Carlo may have spent his youth there. No one came forward to substantiate these hollow claims or of knowing Carlo after that.

On the day, no one attended his funeral other than Bronislaus, Whitey and Moe and the two men throwing the dirt, apart from a petite elderly lady who might have, at one time, been attractive. Her chauffeur-driven limousine, which had with Illinois plates, had slowed and she had watch them from a far. As the boys were driving away, Whitey couldn't help himself and secretly wrote down the plate number and stuffed it in the inside band of Carlo's Fedora.

Since no one else cared, there was no mention if Carlo had a proper will, of his current residence, or what might have become of his contract money. No one thought to ask about his aliases used in out of way pubs and whorehouses, or his dying wishes to be cremated and his ashes dropped into a bubbling volcano. Instead, he was buried as a pauper in the all-day suit he died in, except for his Fedora now on Whitey's head.

Whitey, who had lost his cheaper hat to gunfire that night, had taken Carlo's more expensive black Fedora that smartly sported a shinny grosgrain ribbon band as bounty and he wore it with pride despite the evil glares he got from his girl about it making him look like a punk hood.

As for Bosko and the other two dicks, Anthony made sure they were promoted and awarded a medal for the capture and the death of one of Top-Ten wanted killers in America, the notorious Crazy Carlo Axler and neither of them were likely to pay for a drink again.

Three days before The Polish Gang's departure the sun was out and the heat was back on. The humidity had eased and what remained was a few days of some of the most God sent weather any state in the Union had ever experienced.

Out in the middle of the deep lake a new rowboat drifted quietly, bobbing on the gentle waves as Bronislaus and his two best pals, Whitey and Moe, on the sly dangled their lines one last time. The birds floated overhead and the frogs croaked along the shore grasses. Bronislaus would miss this place, it was written on his brooding face, thinking of all the hours he spent waiting for her to find him fishing, watching for a car, listening for the pounding of hooves, and for what, this hollow feeling inside, knowing how inside out he turned her life, his too. Whitey kept his eyes towards the sky. He couldn't wait to get his butt out of Detroit and away from these crazy Dagos and the stinkin' birds up above this stupid lake. Moe, of course, was concerned about his momma and poppa, but since they ran their own candy store they really didn't need him around much; and besides his sister got married last year and it was time her no-good husband went to work. He might as well hang around the store and sell candy as any other corner and eat candy.

But Bronislaus wanted to go fishing one more time. They had to pick up Stashu's rowboat anyway, which had been replaced by Nicole personally, and delivered across the lake. So, reluctantly the boys went along with it, because Stephania had asked and they hadn't a thing better to do. Even more reluctantly they later agreed to row to the other side of the lake so that Bronislaus could say good-bye to Nicole. Mr. Niemiec would've blown his stack if he knew what they were up to, but the two of them waited offshore exactly where Moe had fished once before when the barn went up in flames and these dang white fools started shooting up the place. Moe had his line in the water quietly trying to rehook the big one that got away, and Whitey read the soggy Detroit Free Press, gnawing his spent nails to the cuticles, and chain smoking like they stopped making them, wishing he was on the road South already, and hoping he wasn't the second unlucky punk to die in the hat he hid his face under.

Inside the freshly painted white equestrian stables Nicole groomed her Thoroughbred with a brush and comb. She wore light blue shorts and sandals, had her pink checkered blouse tied at her waist and wore a Tiger cap on her head. Other than eight or nine other Thoroughbreds and Warmbloods jumpers she was alone to her thoughts. The 16 hand horse shivered under the stroke of the brush, its massive toned muscles rocking back and forth as Nicole stepped back to find Bronislaus standing shirtless in the light of the stable door.

"Thanks for the flowers."

"Not you again."

"'Fraid so. Too bad you couldn't stop by. It's not all true what they say about nurses." Bronislaus came in out of the glaring sunlight to where Nicole could see him clearly inside the shade of the barn.

Nicole looked him over. Beneath his shorts, his legs looked thinner. He'd lost weight on his upper body as well. She turned away.

"How do I look?"

"Not half bad for someone who's obviously polka-drunk. How do you feel?" She set the brush and comb down and wiped her hands on a damp towel hanging on nail in the stall door.

"Like a pin cushion." He took his bare arm out of the sling and ran his hand over the back of Nicole's Thoroughbred. He looked at her. "Pretty."

Nicole looked into his eyes for a moment. He didn't mean the horse and she knew it. She turned away to spread straw over the stall.

"Thank you."

She had hoped he'd stop by so she could say good-bye. It was her reason for having the boat delivered to the lake. But now that Bronislaus was there in front her again she couldn't wait for him to leave. Her breath came hard and she felt heaviness in the pit of her stomach. She wasn't sure what it meant or why she was feeling this way but she wanted it to stop right away. Oh why had she done such a foolish thing?

Bronislaus waited.

Nicole finished with the straw and came out and led her bay into the stall and turned the water on over the water trough. "You shouldn't have come. I'm sorry, it was my fault, I know. I just wanted to…" she stopped herself. "But you should go."

Bronislaus fought off the urge to hold her knowing this could be his last chance. Nicole fought off the urge of wanting him to.

"I shouldn't have done a lot of things."

Nicole turned off the water. She went past Bronislaus to the grain bin and took out a scoop of blackstrap molasses soaked oats and dumped them into a wooden grain trough.

Nicole loved the smell of it and took a moment to take it in, "Please, Bronislaus."

He had never seen her like this… so vulnerable.

"I just, well, Alusia called. You're bein' awfully hard on her, you know. The least you could do is talk to her, let her explain herself."

Nicole turned on him. "Please, Bronislaus, I don't find the idea of a crooked cop like O'Garrity and this common whore being my true parents an engaging thought. I am a Mangione, that's all that matters now. I want nothing to do with either of them. I've been bought and paid for. End of discussion."

"Nicole, I don't blame ya none, honest. But, Alusia, she ain't a bad old gal. Ma and she grew up together like sisters in Kraków, Poland. Besides, she just owned the place, you know, it was given to her by people, it wasn't something she did on her own, or ever meant to be. She was never really one of those girls. It's just that O'Garrity wouldn't have her as his wife on account of his mother and father, and she was just a young cleaning girl back then anyway; barely even spoke English while visiting us. She had you out of love for him, not money. What can I say, O'Garrity was a strapping guy in his time, had a good job, you know the rest, and it ain't uncommon. Alusia was scared and didn't fully understand what her rights were here in the States. She just wanted what was best for you at the time. It was years before she even told my ma about you. Mangione needed a baby so Alusia let O'Garrity talk her into givin' you to them."

"You mean, sell me."

"That was O'Garrity's doin'. He wanted to make sure Alusia was looked after. I guess that's why he got on Mangione's payroll, so he could keep an eye on you, make sure you were being looked after. The money was just to keep her out of trouble."

Nicole pulled her English saddle off the gate and headed into the stables toward the tack room. Bronislaus followed. "One of these days I'll run across your busybody mother somewhere and I'll push her off a curb."

"You know, you're actin' like a spoiled little girl!"

"I was a spoiled little girl! And I liked it just fine!" She slammed the tack door. "No thanks to them."

"Don't blame them for all this."

"They sent the telegram, didn't they?"

"Well, ya. Alusia and, well look, it was a misunderstanding. Once, Alusia and Ma came out here to pick mushrooms in the woods, and saw us together by accident."

Nicole went to the stable door to leave. "Spied on me my whole life, you mean."

Bronislaus followed her out. "So, she cared. It's not a crime to care about your daughter."

Nicole gave him her well used, lethal forty-five caliber look. She glanced away and climbed up on a stable fence and picked up a book on horse grooming from a post to her right.

"You're gonna read that, now?"

"It's educational. You should learn how sometime."

Bronislaus couldn't help but admire the smooth tan skin on the back of her shapely legs, and the engaging way her bottom contoured her shorts. Even if she was being insulting to his lack of public education. He could read the newspapers pretty good he thought, in both Polish and

English and actually had money in the bank and everything. Looking at her he again fought the painful urge to pull her into his arms.

Behind Nicole the ashes of the old hey barn that had exploded still lay in a pile, but little sign of the tractor remained, leaving not only their lifetime friendship in ruins. A faint smell of charred wood wafted in the horse stables on the breeze. The grass within twenty yards of the charred barn was still black and brown from the heat, though new grass had already begun to sprout. The fence that had led up to the old barn ended abruptly with three blackened planks stretching out to the stubble remains of a fence post. Chickens picked among the ash. Behind the mess, three truck loads of green lumber lay in wait for a new barn.

"Anyway," Bronislaus said aware that he was now being ignored, "I guess it put some silly romantic ideas in their heads."

Nicole didn't look at him. "It must have." She thumbed through the book, not really looking for anything. Bronislaus watched her for another moment. It was useless. He didn't understand how he felt about her at that instant, but it really didn't matter. In three days he'd be exiled to swampy, bug infested Florida and she would be officially engaged to Robert. It had been a mistake to come. Moe and Whitey were right. He really hadn't expected to feel this way. Under it all they were just broken friends, and had no control of the things that were happening around them. He had to get out of there, get her out of his sight, his mind, his heart. But he had no control over his emotions either, so he did what he could to save face. He turned away, walking back through the stable and out of her life… forever.

Nicole looked back up as the stable door squeaked shut. Tears streamed down her face. Her chin quivered. "Good-bye, Bronislaus," she said aloud to herself. A fifteen hand chestnut mare Warmblood jumper trotted up behind her and nudged her behind. "What are you doing out?" She stroked it behind the ear as the tears kept coming. "I am a Mangione. Bought and paid for, just like you. That's all that matters now, right?" The chestnut just looked at her with her big brown eyes and nibbled on the knot in her blouse. "Right." She wiped away the tears.

Back at the rowboat, Whitey held the binoculars up to his eyes as Moe fished in earnest. The smell of chard barn wolfed in on waves of summer breezes through the marsh grass, as did the buzz of mosquitoes. Moe was determined to hook that fish again before Bronislaus returned.

"What's keepin' him?" Whitey asked. He couldn't see much from where they were hiding behind the marsh grass. He tossed his cig at the shore. "I'm on my last cig, already."

"Quit rockin' the boat, will ya?" Moe looked down in the water and searched the rocks below through the clear cool water. "That fish is down there somewhere. I swear he was nearly as big as my arm."

"Give it up, Moe." Whitey put down the binoculars. "Next you'll tell me it jumped out of the water, spat between your eyes, and insulted your manhood." Whitey laughed and lit his last cig.

Moe didn't look up from the water. "Yeah, well he sure put up a bigger fight than you ever did."

"How would you like to spend the rest of your life with that pole chronically peekin' out the back of your pants?"

Moe splashed Whitey. "Yeah?" he challenged him.

"Yeah!" Whitey splashed back.

Moe splashed him back and Whitey splashed back again trying to keep his last cig out of it. They kept it up, back and forth, back and forth.

By the time Bronislaus showed up they were drenched. Bronislaus slid his arm out of the sling and slipped silently out of the marsh grass into the clear water and dove down to the bottom of the sloping lake where large boulders lined the bottom. He passed under the boat where he could see Whitey and Moe's hands dipping in and out of the water.

Not far from the boat, at the lake's bottom, was Stashu's old boat that Lorenzo had nearly cut in two. Next to it were Bronislaus' tackle box and his best three rods and reels that went down with Moe's gun. One of the rods had its cut line wrapped around a jagged rock. So, Moe had himself a whopper after all, he thought.

The boys still splashed up above.

Bronislaus smiled when he saw Moe's bait lying at the bottom of the lake. He reached over and seized a hold of Moe's line and gave a huge yank and the pole came flipping out of the row boat and drifted down into the water with Bronislaus.

Back in the boat, Moe's eyes opened wide in astonishment, the whites of them beaming back at him from the water. "Did you see that!?"

Whitey pulled his hand out of the water and counted his sore knuckles. "Yeah," he looked cautiously over the edge. "As long as I live, I'll never stick a pinkie in this lake again."

"Me neither."

Whitey joined Moe as they leaned over the edge of the boat. The boat dipped that way under both their weight.

Bronislaus waited for the boat to finish its dip, another half inch, ready, now. He had about ten seconds of air left in his lungs when he finally pushed off the highest bolder at the bottom of the lake, striking the boat from the other side with his one good hand, sending Moe and Whitey screaming and flailing overboard. They both thrashed about like sparrows bathing trying to get back into the boat, nearly sinking it.

Bronislaus came up to refill his lungs, still hidden by the boat. He dove back under and began to grab and pinch his two buddies' legs.

After they had finally climbed back in, Bronislaus came to the surface with a big mischievous grin on his face, nearly choking himself from laughing underwater. He put two fishing poles in the boat.

"What's the matter, guys, afraid of a little pond shark?"

Whitey wiped tobacco off his cheek and gasped for air.

"You little creep, I could'a drowned or somethin'."

"Get in," Moe said, his heart still racing. He searched around the shore, expecting two Dagos to show up with his signed obituary at any given moment. "Let's get out of here. Someone's bound to 've heard Whitey screamin'."

"Me?! You was bellowin' louder than me."

"Was not."

"Was to, big ox."

"Was not, little shrimp."

Bronislaus handed Moe the oars from the water. "Relax, no one's here. You guys kill me."

"We ought 'a," the boys said eyeing each other, breaking out into smiles. Bronislaus got them good, and it'd been the first time they saw him smile in weeks.

Bronislaus dove back down.

"Should've seen the look on your face."

"Me? How about you holdin' your pug nose?"

"Ah, you and your damn fish, anyway."

Bronislaus dove down three more times and retrieved everything from the bottom. The last time up, he tossed an old turtle into the boat and climbed in.

"What's that for?" Moe asked, pulling the oars in and began to row.

"Lunch."

Whitey picked tobacco from his ear while he studied Bronislaus. "So?"

"So what?" Bronislaus turned his back on Whitey and put on a wet shirt and the sling.

"Sew buttons, how did it go?"

"She wants nothin' to do with any of us. Includin' you."

"See there, Whitey?" Moe said. "That proves she's your cousin."

Whitey threw a wet, lump of tobacco at Moe. "Poor Alusia." He thought for a minute. "Did you tell her about Alusia shuttin' down and comin' to Miami with us?"

"No."

Whitey and Moe looked at each other. "Did you tell Nicole that she was invited?" Moe asked.

"No, I didn't tell her."

"Then what did you talk about? Horses?" Whitey asked.

"She says that she's a Mangione and that's all that matters now."

Moe stopped rowing. "Didn't you tell her about the big fancy-schmancy hotel your pa's gonna build in Miami?"

"With pink flamingos and palm trees and all that," Whitey added.

"Didn't you tell her she'd love it down there with us?" Moe asked.

"And that you're crazy about her?" Whitey couldn't believe his best friend could be so lame.

Bronislaus had heard enough. "Will you guys shuddup?" Bronislaus looked back toward the stables. "I told her nothin'. Except about Alusia bein' sorry."

"You mutton-head," Whitey yelled. "She loves you! And that's worth some lumps. I should know. I'm the lumps king for my girl."

Bronislaus gave him another look. "How would you like a poke in the eye, Lumpy?"

Moe looked at Whitey and shook his head. Whitey looked back at him and shrugged.

Bronislaus was getting tired so he stretched back in the boat to catch a few rays and to contemplate things.

Moe began to row harder toward the sounds of hammering and sawing, wishing Nicole had bought them a damn power boat.

Whitey was having some thoughts of his own. For starters, he yearned for a cig. His best pal was in more than physical pain. It wasn't natural to see him mooning like this. Sure, Bronislaus was only seventeen but he had lots of young dames chasing him around. The kid had looks, money, good friends, family, a car, and hooch, more than he probably even rightly deserved. Whitey scratched his wet, beach-white head, and looked back at the barns across the lake as he continued to mull things over. Even if Mr. Niemiec wasn't picking up Whitey's tab he would've hung around with Bronislaus. They'd been pals for over ten years. After all, Bronislaus introduced him to Sally Korner, and life had been one beating after another from day one. He'd have to ponder the virtues of that favor some other time. If Whitey's new found cousin was just another dame, Bronislaus would've taken the bullet and spit it out. But he wasn't even chewing. He was holding it in his gullet and it was obviously eating at him. The thing that bothered Whitey most was that Nicole and Bronislaus had played around together for almost as long as he knew him, and Whitey never even had a clue. He could see the reasoning, with the pending wedding and all, but he didn't have to like it. Sometimes it was hard to figure a guy, even a best pal.

Whitey suspiciously eyed the birds drifting up above. He hated Mother Nature. Give him the sound of leather on dry wormless cement any day. It was no wonder Bronislaus had so much time out here alone, Moe working at Tasties, Bronislaus getting up at the crack of dawn to fish, and Whitey hating everything about this place, sun, bugs, water and the heat.

Whitey put the wet front page over his head, his hat half soaked again in his lap. The sun was cooking his noodle, yet Bronislaus could lay there like a scaled perch in a cast-iron fry pan. This new suntan craze was mindless. He glanced down at Bronislaus' closed eyes. The sound of Moe's steady rowing blocked out all other thoughts. Whitey looked up from under the news to find Moe's eyes on him. Moe knew it, too. Some new headlines needed to be written about this sad event.

Maybe if Whitey had a fresh pack of cigs he could let all these thoughts go, but he hadn't. So he couldn't lose the hollow feeling of riding a bike when his best pal was stuck at the curb. Imagine, Bronislaus, Nicole, and Whitey all being relatives together, one big family, with sweet Uncle O'Garrity as the father-in-law. Wouldn't that be a ride in a crap house? No wonder O'Garrity had it out for Bronislaus all this time. Life was getting complicated, like trying to read street signs at night with a face full of bathtub hooch and find the right way home. But one thing was for certain, Sally agreed to head south to the land of big bugs with him… and his gal was definitely not a bicycle built for two.

19 - DZIEWIĘTNAŚCIE

At high noon the following day, Michal's was virtually empty to the naked eye, aside from those who were considered family, best of friends; or who weren't able to make it through without their quota of belly slop.

Lunch really wasn't being served, but Stephania couldn't resist spending her last hours there bent over the hot stove. She prepared one last meal for anyone who stopped by to remember all the excitement, joy and even at times sorrow, as in Manny's resent passing, that the Niemiec family had shared with the neighborhood. On the surface she couldn't wait to get her husband and kids on the road away from Detroit during such a violent time as Prohibition. But deep down inside, her heart ached from thoughts of leaving her church and friends behind, even though her best friend from childhood, Alusia, would be in Florida waiting for her. She couldn't stop the tears welling up in her eyes and dropping down into and salting the fry pan, knowing it was as much the onion as her heart that made her weep. She did her best to keep from fretting and worrying the others by humming and singing an old Polish lullaby her father used to sing to her on the farm. Alusia and she would sing along and dance barefoot in the planted fields when she was just the young farm girl, Stephania Jwastek, while their simple Polish families picked beets and potatoes to take to market. Now look at her, a big city girl in big trouble.

Ah-Ah-Ah, Two Little Kittens:

Ah-ah-ah, ah-ah-ah,
There were once two little kittens.
Ah-ah-ah, two little kittens,

They were both grayish-brown.
Oh, sleep, my darling,
If you'd like a star from the sky I'll give you one.
All children, even the bad ones,
Are already asleep,
Only you are not.

Oh those were the days, Stephania thought. But the thought of how close they'd come to secretly bringing Bronislaus and Nicole together and how disastrously close they had come to killing them, and perhaps others in her family. It made her stomach ache and keep interrupting the song. This was all their doing, two meddling old country fools. She hummed louder hoping it would make the grim thoughts go away.

"Ah-ah-ah, ah-ah-ah,
There were once two little kittens.
Ah-ah-ah, two little kittens,
They were both grayish-brown.

Oh, sleep, because
The moon is yawning and he will soon fall asleep.
And when the morning comes
He will be really ashamed,
That he fell asleep and you did not."

But the dour thoughts were still there in front of her, and she'd have to live with what she and her childhood friend had done to everyone she loved. They had rocked the cradle and had almost broken the bough. Legally the kitchen now belonged to Bartolommeo Mangione. But to hell with that, toil she, on the stove at Michal's one last time for extended family and friends,.

Outside, the men from the moving company carried the Niemiec's belongings down the front stairs and onto a large flatbed. Whitey and the other non-family members, belongings went on a separate truck, already packed and parked around the corner. First thing tomorrow morning everyone was to meet at Michal's, if they hadn't already passed out on the floor, and together, following one after the other, they would drive down to Miami.

Whitey exited his house across the street where he rented a room on the second floor. He looked in a bitter mood. His body felt cramped from sleeping on the bare floor. Out front, he met up with Sally, who had spent the night at her mother's. She glowed with inner contentment. Whitey scowled at her pleasant smile. She gave him a peck on the cheek anyway, and together they wandered across the street. After eying the van they entered Michal's for lunch. Giving Stashu behind the bar a salute, they took their usual booth. Whitey propped his elbows on the table and held his chin with his knuckles. Actually, he hadn't taken any punches as of late, and his face looked better than usual. Sally checked her lipstick in the tin napkin dispenser after she noticed that Whitey was wearing some of it on his cheek. He saw her look and attempted to wipe it off with the back of his hand. When that didn't work, Sally took a napkin, spit in it and wiped her man's cheek.

Emily entered the bar from the lady's room, smiling at the site of Sally grooming White like a child. She wasn't dressed for work. Neither was Stashu behind the bar, but there he was as usual talking baseball and women with the neighborhood grandpas. They all sipped sparingly, like they had for years, from coffee cups trying to shed the blue johnnies, the woolies, the ork-orks, the uglies, the black dog and more than likely a wife or two with a house full of grandkids. Stashu refilled their coffee cups with the house's best whiskey.

"Listen to this one," the old-fart said, squinting through a magnifying glass to read. "Patrolman Arthur L. Pascolini wounded himself fatally at seven forty-five P.M., Tuesday, when his revolver was discharged accidentally as he was about to shoot a cat. Happened over on Theodore Street."

"Shootin' good kitty like that ought to be a crime anyway," said the pug-ugly bachelor near the end of the bar.

"How would you know?" said the man behind dark glasses at the center of the bar with the savage acid scars covering his hands and most of his face.

"This kitty was suffering," said the old-fart.

"Shit, a lot of that goin' around," answered the man who had kept his mouth shut until he got up to wave his pistol at Sir Harry.

"This was a cat, you dumb clucks. The likes to scratch your eyes out," said the old-fart.

"Women," the man with the dark glasses said.

"Ah, blow it out your… hey, Stashu, another round of that stagger-soup, and none of that cheap shit you make down stairs."

The men at the bar all laughed and emptied their cups.

"To Manny," Stashu said, filling their glasses and joining them.

"To Manny," they all answered and sipped.

"It's a good thing he ain't around to see you folks closin' up and sellin' us out to them wop-dogs across town."

"Would've kilt' him for sure."

"To Manny."

"To Manny," they all sipped.

"With you stealin' all his old jokes, it's like he never left."

"'cept Manny didn't laugh at his own dimwits."

"To Manny."

"To Manny."

"How's the market look today?"

"My boy's makin' a killin'."

"Shit, six months ago your boy was a punk rum runner and now all of a sudden he's a big time stock expertise sportin' three hundred dollar suits. What's the secret?"

"He's got smarts."

"If he was that smart, he'd get out before he hasn't a pot to spit in."

"That's pee in."

"This is modern times, Sam, we got in-door plumbin' now." Another roar of laughter came up from the crowd.

"Hey, you wanna know the truth about why they call them brokers?"

"I'll bite?"

"Why not, your wife does."

"You should know she's your sister."

"Shuddup. Because they leave ya broker than when ya walked into the place."

"I miss, Manny."

"To Manny."

"Who ya got your money on tonight?"

"Philadelphia. Tigers ain't got enough pitchin' to win on the road."

"Beat the Yanks last night nine to eight."

"That's because the Yank's defense couldn't catch a cold."

"Detroit sure needs some fresh bona-fide pitchin'."

"No catchin' the Athletics this year anyhow. Bet stock on it."

"Who's got who on tonight's fight? Hey, Stashu put me down for ten on Braddock."

"You're a bigger loser then your son. Tommy Loughran will murder the bum in two."

"Says who?"

"Says me and twenty bucks."

"Ain't you heard? Loughran's got glass hands and no jaw?"

"Ahh phooey."

"You're on and I'll double it if you give me the Tigers and a run."

"Write it down, Stashu."

"Anyone else?" Stashu refilled the two betters' cups.

Emily wandered across the room in her new red summer-dress and shoes that she bought yesterday on sale for $16.75 downtown at Russeks, after seeing the same outfit in a fashion magazine. Her copper hair was brushed out over her shoulders, and despite the fact that she was moving away from all her friends, she seemed extremely happy.

In fact, so was Edju who was on his way down to Miami at that very moment to straighten out some details, arrange rooms, and see his wife and kid.

Dames, Whitey thought when he got a load of Emily from across the room. She came directly to the table and slid in beside Sally who was still puckering her kiss-me-nots into her hand mirror.

"Hey, Sal, nice blouse. You and the animal here want fed?"

Sally held out her hand to show off her big diamond engagement ring. She rubbed her fleshy lips together and pressed an imprint of them onto a table napkin.

"No foolin'?" Emily said, taking Sally's hand and bringing the ring inches from her eyes. "And it's real?"

Whitey gave her a smug look.

"With all the fancy trimmings," Sally answered.

"Well aren't we nonchalant. When?"

Whitey eyed the bar. "As soon as we hit Miami sand."

Emily went to yell to Stashu but Whitey reached over and held a hand over her mouth.

"Don't go blabbin' it all over the place. I don't want these lugs makin' a big deal over nothin'."

"No one's makin' a big deal, Whitey."

"And what's wrong with a big deal, anyway?" the blond bombshell asked. "Hey everybody, you missed out on this, I'm gettin' married," she yelled to the bar.

"To anyone we know?" the old-fart yelled back.

"Not to you," Whitey yelled at him.

"Congratulations, Sal, Whitey," Stashu said. "Buy them lunch and drinks, Emily."

"Thanks… see nobody cares, so shuddup."

"Oh, you big spoilsport. He's just sore because Ma made him sleep on his own floor instead of spendin' the night with me on her couch."

"Wouldn't be the first or last floor I'll end up on, no thanks to you."

"Congratulations, anyway, you two. I can't believe it," Emily said as she got up. She went to the bar and came back with a couple of rums.

Whitey sniffed his and set it down.

"Here you go. Congratulations for real."

Sally tipped back her head, "For real," and pounded down the rum.

"Ah hell," Whitey said, "it beats takin' a punch." He slid his cup over to Sally. I'll take a glass of milk." He leaned in to Molly. "And you slow down on that stuff, ya hear me."

"I hear ya, grandma. Better take that, Emily."

Emily looked at them, not figuring what was up yet. "Bronislaus is out back if you're lookin' for him, Whitey."

"I ain't, but thanks. Give us the usual."

Emily wrote it down and walked away. Over her shoulder she said, "Yours is on the house, Sal."

Sal eyed Whitey coolly. Her face flushed from the rush of the rum.

"What's got you all up in a snit?"

"Bronislaus. He's been moping around like an eggless seagull ever since he got out of the hospital."

"So let him mope. Who's it going to hurt?"

"Me. I hate birds."

Out back of Michal's on the two step stoop in the afternoon sun, Bronislaus sat with his feet spread wide apart peeling a large pot of potatoes. Ma was still in the kitchen behind him, packing up odds and ends from her spice rack while cooking food for that night's going away bash. Michal was sponsoring a bender for the whole neighborhood. Everything would be on the house. Everything must go or be dumped down the drain before leaving Detroit. That meant all the booze from down in the cellar was either to be drunk or given away to their friends because no one pretended to want anything dumped. There wasn't anyone in the neighborhood that didn't plan on being there. So Bronislaus was giving Ma a hand and continued to peel potatoes, all after scrubbing the bar floors for her around four in the morning. He was just about done with the potatoes but didn't seem in any hurry to move on to anything else. Perspiration poured down his shirtless back. His tanned arms rested on his thighs. The peels piled up between his legs as they thudded onto page thirty-five, the social section of The Detroit Free Press, dated July 9th, 1929.

Whitey came through the kitchen, gave Ma a kiss for the free lunch, and traipsed out onto the back stoop. He stood behind Bronislaus and watched him for a second. What a sad sap. Whitey looked back to find Ma encouraging him on with her kind hopeful eyes wanting him to say something reassuring to her youngest boy that would somehow bring him out of his humdrums. Whitey gave her a little knowing smile and turned back to study his best friend. What a poor dolt, he thought, peelin' potatoes on a day like this. "How come you ain't fishin', numb nuts?"

Bronislaus didn't turn. Emily had told him that Whitey was inside so he was expecting his bullshit. "Because I don't feel like it."

Whitey sat down beside Bronislaus. He studied the peels on the paper like they would tell him something smart to do, then looked closer as he picked it up and dumped the skins into a tin garbage pail beside the steps. He examined a profile photo of Nicole and the caption that read: Miss Nicole Mangione's engagement to Robert Bunniti, son of District Attorney Anthony Bunniti, will be announced tonight by her father, Mr. Bartolommeo Mangione, of Grosse Pointe Farms. The wedding will take place in the fall.

"You feel like a Tiger game today?"

"Who're they playin'?

"Philly."

"Nah, not really."

"Too bad, wouldn't mind a little road trip." Whitey laid the paper back down and Bronislaus began to hit Robert's picture with potato scraps again.

"Sally and I are gettin' hitched. Guess gettin' pickled is on the menu."

"Don't feel like drinkin' right now, either. Come by tonight and we'll throw down a couple with the boys. But congratulations. It's about time."

"You haven't felt much like doin' anythin' lately, pal. You're startin' to give me the big yawn."

"Nothin' personal."

"By the by, me and the boys won't be comin' to your pa's so-long party to the neighborhood until late."

"How come?"

"We're crashin' a swank bash where Jake's playin' tonight. Kind of my bachelor party. You want invites?"

"Who's throwin' it?"

"Just a couple Dago families up on the crustier eastside."

Bronislaus looked at Whitey for the first time, checking to see if his ma was listening. "What makes you think I'd want to show up there?"

Whitey picked up the paper and dumped the skins again. He held it up and studied the picture. "I'm your best pal, ain't I?"

Bronislaus took the paper and wadded it up. Slowly a smile grew on his face. Whitey did likewise. Bronislaus slapped him on the back and they shook hands. "Yeah, I guess you are, ain't ya."

"Everything's all set. I got the boys on the horn and we worked it all out this mornin'. You in?"

"Yeah, you bet I'm in."

Behind them, Ma listened at the door. She was worried, but deep down inside she was as gleeful as a song bird. She began to whistle louder while she worked, happier like a canary in love. It was a beautiful day to move after all, and suddenly, she couldn't wait to get on the road and out of town.

"Ah-ah-ah, ah-ah-ah,
There were once two little kittens.
Ah-ah-ah, two little kittens,
They were both grayish-brown.
Oh, sleep, my darling,
If you'd like a star from the sky I'll give you one.
All children, even the bad ones,
Only you are not."

20 - DWADZIEŚCIA

In Grosse Pointe Shores, facing Lake Shore Drive, Anthony Bunniti inherited a sprawling, three-story cream brick home. It sat majestically behind thirty-foot, immaculately trimmed dark evergreen conifers planted together as a vertical screen hedge row, said to be the cuttings from the original Italian Cypress trees brought to Italy by the Romans from conquered provinces in the Eastern Mediterranean two thousand years ago. At last count, there was thirty-three hundred of the Italian Cypress lined flawlessly to either side and between two sets of intricately, yet manly designed wrought iron gates. The gates were strategically placed at each side of the one and a half acre, perfectly manicured, smooth as a putting green, front lawn. Anthony and his family loved their front grounds. So much so, that a rumor kept inside the gates, claimed that the first gardener was shot by Anthony's father for having the audacity to make love to one of the maids on it. Though it was more of a joke then a serious belief, no one really knew what had happened to the gardener, and the young maid wasn't talking. In fact she couldn't, seeing she had passed on mysteriously years ago.

A cobblestone, horseshoe driveway, ran from each gate and met at the front door, where four white pillars stood at the corners of a porch like Roman guards protecting a set of enormous green doors, with polished brass knockers, molded into the shapes of gleaming lion busts.

Low, flat top blue spruce shrubs sprawled purposely along the white brick, backed by explosions of raspberry ice bougainvillea, nothing less than a brilliant display of fuchsia-red flowers with green and white jazzy variegated foliage that sprang up beneath every window like a coordinated ancient Roman Holiday with the God Cupid — the son of Venus, the

Roman goddess of love & beauty — perched prominently below the balcony as though he was suspended in midair by his own wings. Cascading masses of other colorful flower bracts borne on arching stems added even more brilliant summer color to the landscape, flowing effortlessly around the perimeter of the house until they abruptly ended at the service drive near the backdoor, just in time to catch one's breathe, before having to take in the immaculately manicured wooded paths.

Valets, in red jackets punctuated with gold buttons, white shirts and black pants, drove the arriving guests' cars back out the front gate, around the corner to the service gate, where they parked them in an open extended parking lot between the house and woods. The head Valet, Stewart McKinsy, a willow of a man with lightly graying hair, greeted each guest with a sincere, groveling bow and a white gloved hand to help them from their class-ridden cars. Limousine drivers, of course, parked their own cars, and were to stay with them at all times.

Directly across the driveway, smack-dab in front of the main entrance, an oxidized bronze pride of amber-lit abstract lions splashed gleefully in an immense cement fountain. The four century old fountain had once adorned the front of Anthony's great uncle's home in Florence, Italy. Anthony's father had it shipped over when he first landscaped the grounds fifty-five years ago, much to the disdain of Anthony's great uncle who awoke in the morning light to find that someone had dismantled his precious fountain, coins and all and had stolen it in the night.

Anthony loved to show his more squeamish friends the bullet holes left behind when his grandfather and great grandfather had both been murdered by his mother's brothers, during a feud over his parent's marriage. Anthony was the soul fruit of their love. He told this story with great pride, much like the lions themselves, with love for his father, who had come to America and amassed a grand fortune developing Detroit. Needless to say it wasn't until on his deathbed did Anthony's great uncle receive a picture from America depicting what had become of his beloved fountain, purely to fulfill the last wish of a dying relative, if not a shimmer of guilt from his great nephew. It was said the oldest living member of the Florence Bunniti clan died with a proud smile on his face knowing that the fountain pride was still in his family possession and had made it to America, something he had only dreamed of doing himself.

The water that spurted from the lions' mouths ran down a cement stone channel lined with an assortment of small purple and yellow pansies. The water ran under the left drive and nearly half the width of the front grounds. It settled into a goldfish pond below a balcony at the foot of a stand of old oak trees. Yellow gas lights on cement posts were spread out amongst the oaks to light a series of paths that meandered through the giants down into a hidden ornate perennial flower garden, and around to the side of the estate where, since the advent of the automobile, it was partially cleared and turned into the quest parking.

The balcony, overlooking the lights reflecting in the pond, was romantically lit by three beveled glass double doors. Two of which opened out from the second floor ballroom, creating elongated shadows stretching across and over two foot thick marble railings, that rested upon the backs of another pride of carved marble lions. The railings enclosed the perimeter of the balcony just high enough for lovers to rest their elbows on, or perhaps a glass of champagne. A young couple hid there from those inside, entwined, their hearts on fire, stoked by the light and music, as it drifted serenely out from the rapidly filling ballroom.

Inside the beveled glass doors, the ballroom was overflowing with summer flowers. Some were spread about the room in vases propped on tall, thin, white stands. But most were used as part of displays on two identically designed buffet tables on either side of the dance floor.

Each buffet table had lilac-colored skirting boxed over three eight foot tables. Spacing was left to walk in between to get to the dance floor which was nearly sixty feet square.

Three double bars lined each wall. Male food attendants trimmed excess roasted fat from remarkable barons of beefs which stood on cutting boards at the end of each buffet table. On either side of the tables, white platters with six different kinds of pasta salads, antipastos, and sliced tomatoes with goat cheese and a sprig of mint waited for the guests. Silver chafers with their lids still on were filled with steamed vegetables and baby rose potatoes soaked in garlic butter. Baskets were overflowing with Italian bread, and white ramekins were filled with butter. A food server stood behind each dish and waited for dinner to be announced.

A third double sided buffet table held coffee, three different kinds of homemade cookies in white baskets, assorted nut pies with whipped cream toppings placed on silver trays, and a heavily spiked fruit punch in a priceless Mangione family crystal bowl heirloom belonging to his great-great grandmother who had claimed to the very end it was a gift from within the Vatican itself, though unsubstantiated rumors claimed a young Bartolommeo Mangione had stolen it at gunpoint during shipment.

Other male waiters passed hors d'oeuvres from silver trays while the buffets remained closed until after the anticipated formal announcement of Nicole and Robert's engagement.

Enough round tables were spread about the room to accommodate four hundred people, ten at each table. On each guest table were an identical center floral arrangement with an array of exotic flowers and ferns spread just large enough to not hide the person across the table. A different table number on each arrangement protruded from the top. The tables were fully set with flatware, water, white and red wine, champagne glasses, votive candles, and crystal ashtrays. Everything that was crystal, gold or silver reflected the light from the massive overhead chandeliers.

The orchestra, dressed in black, softly played from a platform built into the wall. A young redhead in a pink sequined gown sang with a low, husky voice into the microphone, and smiled a big toothy grin out at the rapidly filling room.

The Mangione and Bunniti families and their elegantly dressed, all Caucasian neighbors and friends, were too busy getting smashed and having a darling time to notice that someday the singer would be a star, or perhaps since she was there they expected it. After all, everybody who was anybody in Detroit in 1929 was there. That's why Jake was the band leader despite what he'd done, and surely wouldn't have the audacity to do again.

Even Henry Ford and three other rival auto makers were there. An actress by the name of Tallulah Bankhead, star of "The Little Foxes," had just ordered champagne while smiling that Broadway-bound smile for all to see. In fact, everyone was always smiling. Women were smoking cigarettes with holders; their hair cut short, cropped with waves and curls, and had silk hats that wrapped around their skulls with floppy brims nearly hiding their faces.

The orchestra broke out into a jazzy Charleston and the young men and women began to kick up their heels, swing their long pearl necklaces, and flashing their bare knees. After all, Detroit was in the grips of the "Roaring Twenties." Never had people seemed so unconcerned about the future. The War to end all Wars seemed to set the World free. The stock market was rising at a pace that put money in everybody's hands, and the thrill of cheap booze or a forbidden opium den tingled every nerve. And the thought of heroic bootleggers and killer gangsters in their midst and swarming the city, new sports cars like the Auburn boat-tail speedster, the Stutz speedster, and Packard's 734, filled with ring molls, stars from the stage, the radio, and silent pictures; all attending professional and college sports, made everything seem so… well… swell!

Behind the orchestra, with doors on either side of the bandstand, was a cavernous, gray-tiled, service kitchen filled with workers in white uniforms preparing hors d'oeuvres and backup food for the buffets. Waiters in black cocktail coats hurried into and out of either door. The kitchen door on the stage left side also led to a small unobtrusive hallway with service stairs going up to rooms on the third floor and leading down to the first floor's kitchen directly below and out to the back of the house. At the center of the hall, another service door led to a wide staircase beginning directly at the front door which ended three flights up in front of a widow's peak window. The somewhat breathtaking view took in the fountain, lawn, Italian Cypress at Jefferson Avenue, and the lights out on Lake St. Clair and beyond. On the other side of the main staircase were eight guest rooms, all of which were occupied by visiting guest, dignitaries, and family.

On the second landing, the main staircase led to the double oak doors of the ballroom. Just inside, bartenders worked three of the bars. Plush lavender velvet curtains hung down directly behind them from the twenty foot ceilings. In between the curtains, hung Seventeenth and Eighteenth Century oil paintings of succulent naked women with beautiful children, cowering from victorious warriors in red uniforms and black boots on horseback. The fierce men in the paintings peered down upon the newly arriving guest with life shattering contempt.

The entire ballroom, despite its magnitude, barely took up three-quarters of the second floor. At the far side of the ballroom, Anthony's study and a small art gallery completed that side of the house. From the art gallery, glass doors led out to the marble balcony. The gallery was also accessible to the ballroom through large wooden doors. The lights were out in the gallery and its doors closed.

Another door hidden in the panels of the darkened back corner of the ballroom led directly into Anthony's study, where a small thick carpeted, spiral stairway spun down to the first floor's plush living room. Except for the two windows and a fireplace, the study was completely encased in dark stained book shelves of first edition nautical and law books. Anthony had read them all. The room was heavily draped with dark olive velvet curtains. A single brass lamp with a green glass shade sat on a mahogany desk. Not a sound from the ballroom entered Anthony's refuge.

In front of the desk, just beyond the reach of the light, Anthony and Bartolommeo sat in two overstuffed chocolate-colored leather chairs. Large brass upholstery tacks lined the perimeter of the chairs' backs. A cloud of cigar smoke hovered near the ceiling and around the lamp. Bartolommeo and Anthony sat in quiet reflection as they sipped from their near empty brandy snifters. A half-filled ornate brandy bottle sat on a small serving stand between them.

Anthony seemed deeper in thought than Bartolommeo, which didn't seem that significant when considering the shallowness of Bartolommeo's mentality. Bartolommeo twitched his olive hippo face while he studied his long time friend's sullen expression for a clue as to what he might be thinking. After a while Bartolommeo broke the silence.

"What is the matter, my friend? We should be happy, you and I."

Anthony remained silent for a moment longer, not wanting to voice what he knew in his heart he must, for himself as well as for his family and future family. Finally, as though it took great effort to come back from where his mind had wandered off too, he gradually looked up from his hands to Bartolommeo's face. His expression varied little. "My mind is full of memories," he said, "and troubled thoughts. I have no problem with the past. It's gone and we cannot touch it. But the present grips me by the throat and I fear may choke the very life out of me."

"Anthony, please." Bartolommeo's eyes held great sorrow to see his friend like this. "You're driving us both out of our minds. I swear, once The Polish Gang reaches Miami and O'Garrity is settled in New York, we'll never hear from them again. I promise you. It's all been arranged. And cost me plenty, I tell you."

Anthony studied Bartolommeo's eyes. He didn't want to know what Bartolommeo had planned for O'Garrity in New York and he cared even less to hear what Bartolommeo had in mind for The Polish Gang in Miami. "O'Garrity, that fool, I told you he couldn't be trusted, Bartolommeo. But selling Michal Niemiec that piece of swamp in Miami was not such a bad idea."

"Swamp? That land will be worth a fortune someday. And giving up your house nearly killed me, but now the lake is ours.

"The lake. I wish you would've told me the truth about Nicole from the start. We could've spared everyone a lot of heartache, and me having to give my wife's family home away to some Polish cleaning woman."

"I just wanted to keep everything like we planned, one family, one blood. I did it for the good of the family, for you, Anthony, and Nicole."

"And you, of course. When will you stop being that poor little boy with the painful inferiority complex? You're a grown man, Bartolommeo. Let go of those torrid memories."

"I can't forget, not the pain, the jokes or the rejection. I'm an ugly man, my friend. I must be better and richer than others to even have decent families talk to me. But you, you didn't care. You became my friend that summer, such a skinny kid on vacation from America. Remember the beatings we took?"

"Yes. But the pain has gone."

"Not for me. They beat you only once because of me, but I was beaten repeatedly many times because of hatred, because of who I was, who my parents were and what they weren't, and because of what I looked like. A boy doesn't forget that pain, and a man can't help but remember the shame their family lived with."

"You are richer now than most of those men could ever dream of. Most of them are even dead, thanks to you with help I hope of Mother Nature. Your restaurant is the place to be here in Grosse Pointe and you are renowned in two countries for your find foods, entertainment and generosity. Rejoice in that. It is not by faux pas on my part that you are still my best friend after all this time. You have heart, Bartolommeo, whether you choose to acknowledge that virtue or not. You make things needed to get done happen."

"And I thank you with all of this heart for allowing me to be useful. Believe me, I do. My whole family does."

"Then watch your step."

"I swear, when that child was stillborn and Nicolette lay dying in my arms, she had no idea her child was with God, but she knew she herself would soon be gone. She wanted to see her child. I couldn't tell her she had failed to birth a live one. 'Bring me my beautiful baby,' she pleaded. 'I want to see my baby, just once, Barto.' I couldn't refuse my love, my life, that one thing she wanted more than anything in the world, to hold her newborn baby girl just once before she was gone. How could I say no to those eyes after giving her three boys of the likes of my genes produced? Or even let her see the truth in my eyes. I had to lie — I had to do something to give her peace. Surely you understand that. But I was at a loss. Me, who always took care of everything, turned all the wrongs into rights for anyone who asked. There I was, dying from the inside out — humanly powerless to help the one person I loved with all my heart and soul. She was the one. My one and only true love. She was the only woman who really loved me back, who saw what lay inside of this, who may ever love me the way she did. She was dying for Christ's sake, there in my arms, and all my money, all my power, could do nothing. Nothing.

"So I went looking for a solution, searching my soul as well as those halls, for an answer to my prayers. I needed a place I could pray to God. I was nearly out of my mind. The child was another boy, you know, and she so wanted a little girl, trying once more, putting her life at risk at her age. I had to do something. Then it hit me. I could borrow a baby girl for a bit of time, I thought. I swear that's all I meant to do. I approached a young doctor with my desperate plea and a fist full of dollars, and it was he who introduced me to O'Garrity pacing outside the delivery room.

"It was he who suggested we strike the deal. The doctor switched the birth certificates. O'Garrity didn't want the child, and the young Polish girl had no way of raising her on her own. He swore to me she didn't want the baby.

"I knew then, and I believe it now, that God placed that child, that beautiful baby girl in my hands. How else could I explain how a stunning little girl of Nichol's magnitude, a diamond amongst millions, would be born unwanted that very night, that exact time, in the same hospital?

"I did what I had to do. The doctor brought Nicolette the child himself and she named her Nicole. O'Garrity named his price and I doubled it and made him promise to take care of the Polish girl, and they put my poor stillborn child to rest for me. I swear I thought you'd never have to find out, and I prayed to God I'd never have to tell Nicole. Surely you must understand. It was for Nicolette, for us, for our families, and for our plans, not just for me."

Anthony sat in silence contemplating Bartolommeo's words. He'd heard it all that night, of course, after being called to the warehouse. Hearing it said aloud again with such passion, after hearing it in his mind a hundred times, made it somehow seem like an old fable and it somehow didn't bother him so much. But his mind went back to earlier thoughts. Thoughts that really bothered him. "All right, Bartolommeo, I forgive you. But I'm out of our little business deal. I don't need the money bad enough to jeopardize my family standing in this city."

Bartolommeo nodded his head. He knew this was coming.

"And as a law abiding District Attorney, I don't want my son affiliated with it in any way. Marriage or otherwise."

"I understand. My hands are washed. To hell with Prohibition. It won't last forever."

Anthony drank from his glass, draining it. He reached to the small table between them and tipped the bottle to the glass in Bartolommeo's out stretched hand and refilled his own as well. "One more thing, my old friend. Believe me when I say this."

Bartolommeo nodded. Knowing what was to come.

"If Nicole doesn't snap out of whatever is going on inside her foolish young head, we postpone everything. And call it off if we have to."

"But."

"No buts. I won't stand to have my son make a fool of himself over her again. Is that clear? I don't care whose daughter she is."

Bartolommeo thought for a moment then chuckled. "Of course, I fully understand the reasoning behind your being angry."

"Being angry?" Anthony raised his voice. "You son-of-a-bitch, you almost ruined my family. I should've let you rot in jail. You're all just damn lucky you had my backside bent over a picket fence with my only child being involved." Anthony eyed Bartolommeo as he fought to cool down. His nostrils flared like his best running horse on a Saturday hunt.

Bartolommeo just waited for it to pass. He had seen it many times over the years. Anthony pretended to be above it all, but like all politicians of their time, their hands were not as nearly soot free as their feet.

"One small hitch and it's over."

Bartolommeo lit his cigar, then Anthony's. "I agree. We'll let it go."

"I mean it."

"So do I."

Anthony's cigar glowed bright. A satisfying smile grew on his face. "Now my mind can rest. I believe in what this country stands for. Freedom of happiness means a lot to me. It meant a lot to Father. I don't want to be a part of what is wrong with her. I need to live in peace, mind and soul. So will my son and his." He closed his eyes behind his cigar.

Bartolommeo watched Anthony carefully, knowing things were out of his hands, and didn't like it one bit, as his cigar went out again.

21 – DWADZIEŚCIA JEDEN

As the two men smoked, an ice delivery truck pulled into the Bunniti service gate, pulling past all the color, and set its brakes just short of the back door that led directly into the downstairs kitchen. The driver got out and a tall well-hulked thug, meant to be security, sauntered out of the kitchen door shadow and opened his coat to show he was carrying. The driver gave him a big grin.

"Yeah?" the thug asked.

"Ice."

The thug looked to the end of the drive to see if his pals were watching. He saw a cigarette burning in those shadows. "Who called for ice?"

"Beats me, friend. I just deliver the stuff.

"Yeah. No one tells me nothin'," the thug said.

"Yeah, me neither. My boss is in there swingin' some dame. And all I got is five hundred pounds of chipped ice to dance around. You got the authority to sign or do you want to go up and get someone who can okay this?"

The thug looked up at the house knowing how chaotic the kitchen was and what a prick the head chef could be after catching him plucking finger food off the trays. "I guess I can. Where?"

"Right here."

Just then a figure slid out of the dark and thumped the thug over the back of his head. His knees gave away and his hat dropped into the hands of the driver. The thug fought to regain his balance and this time Ducky had to step into the light to finish the job. The thug fell back into Ducky's arms. Ducky recognized him as one of the guys from the warehouse, so he was disappointed when he checked and found the man was still breathing as he pulled a thirty-eight out of the thug's waistband. He looked to see if the coast stayed clear while he dragged the body to the side house and stuffed him into a basement window drainage hole. Ducky looked back across the drive to find Bronislaus and the boys helping the driver unload his five hundred pounds of chipped ice. They hustled it over and piled it against the house over the window drop to hide the thug from anyone looking for him. Ducky emptied the shells from the gun and threw it into the shrubs across the service drive. A young valet ran by but didn't notice a thing. Bronislaus handed the driver a roll of bills. The driver tipped his hat and backed out the drive without a word.

"Is he still breathing?" Bronislaus asked. He pulled on a white tux coat and Lip straightened his bow tie for him. The boys brushed off their black waiters' coats, and used the ice water on their hands to slick down their hair.

"He'll have a whopper of a drop-over when he comes back to life."

"Watch yourself on the way out. There are two biggies asleep up in the bushes. Lip recognized them from the warehouse the other night."

"That one, too," Ducky said.

"Good, then they had what they got comin'. The others are along the back drive near the limo." Bronislaus looked at Moe, Whitey, Lip, and Ducky in their waiters' outfits. "Keep in mind what Jake told us about the layout. Everyone should know what to do, so if you have any questions, now would be a good time." The others kept quiet having planned all this themselves. "Good. Work fast before they start to recognize us. Let's not bust up the party unless it's self-defense. I mean it."

They all agreed and entered the kitchen and went up the service stairs one at a time, to the upper event service kitchen where the boys picked up trays right where Jake told them they'd be. One by one they blended in with the other waiters, while Ducky and Bronislaus walked to the door leading to the main staircase and listened for footsteps. Bronislaus eased out into the hall and followed three couples into the ballroom. At the door was another thug trying his best to look as though he wasn't working. He wasn't good at it. Bronislaus approached him from the front, deliberately obtaining the heavyset man's attention.

"Everything okay?"

"Everything's fine." The thug looked Bronislaus over.

"Good, good, then no suspicious characters?"

"No."

"You want a drink?"

"Who are you?"

"You don't recognize me?"

Ducky eased himself out of the door behind the thug.

He passed by Bronislaus. "Would you care for a drink, sir?"

"Two champagnes, please."

"No, I don't recognize you. Should I?"

"I'm sorry. I thought by the way you looked at me..."

"Yeah, well, I kind of did. Oh yeah, I remember you. You were in that, ah..."

Ducky showed up with two glasses of champagne.

"Yes, I was. Say, I know a director looking for a guy just like you."

"Yeah? Me, an actor?"

"Why not? Just look them in the eye and tell them the truth or at least what they tell you to say."

"I could do that if it pays good."

"Hell, if a numb-nut like I can, you're a shoe-in. Say, my friend is here tonight, somewhere. I'll introduce you to him before I leave."

"That'd be swell, buddy.

"You still want that drink? Relax you a bit just in case. You got nice teeth, too."

"Sure, sure, good idea, but in here. These are all real." He smiled big showing his nice teeth as he led Bronislaus back toward the service door. Ducky followed. Moments later Bronislaus reappeared with two empty champagne glasses. Ducky followed behind him and passed without saying a word, smoothing out the nice teeth marks on his knuckles.

Out in the middle of the ballroom, Caruso and Angelo stood with their dates pretending not to be guarding the Crystal punch bowl to the left of the stage. Nicole and Robert danced near them. Lorenzo danced not far away with Barbara. Barbara's eyes followed Robert with longing needs and only looked away when Nicole looked up.

Whitey, Moe, and Lip had entered from the left of the stage behind Caruso and Angelo.

Bronislaus went over in his mind the diagram Jake had laid out as he reached for fresh champagne and kept his eyes on the room. He located Whitey and Moe on the far side passing hors d'oeuvres, while not far away, on his side of the dance floor, he could see that Ducky had joined Lipinski with an empty tray. They began to sweep the room of dirty glasses and napkins from the crowded tables. He glanced up to the band and toasted his glass toward Jake when he finally caught his attention. Jake nodded pleasantly, nodding his head slightly towards Nicole.

While still dancing, Nicole looked up to find Moe a few tables over. She tried not to react, but her back stiffened anyway. This wasn't happening again, she thought.

"What's the matter?" Robert asked.

"What? Nothing. I… these heels, a twinge shot up from my ankle."

Nicole's eyes followed Moe's eyes to where Whitey was.

Whitey glanced toward Bronislaus and Nicole followed his eyes to him. Bronislaus motioned her to join him in the service hall. She looked away, rolling her eyes up into her head in disbelief as she continued to dance, feeling a bit faint. She glanced back only once to make sure she wasn't hallucinating.

A heavy set woman, in a black shiny overstuffed gown, with three rows of frills, tapped Whitey on the shoulder and spun him around with her big meaty paw. She wore the same material on her head. She rubbed her fat stubby, diamond studded fingers as she examined the tray of hors d'oeuvres.

"Hors d' whatever, ma'am?"

She wiggled her thin mustache in anticipation. "Oh, and what do we have here?" She already held a handful of wadded up stained napkins.

Whitey wasn't sure what he had. "Mozzarella cheese balls or something woppish is my guess."

"Really, I must try one." The fat woman picked three of them up by their toothpicks. Whitey handed her another napkin. She flashed him a handful of diamonds.

"Knock yourself out. Here, take a bunch more, they got plenty."

"I shouldn't."

"Go ahead, they look good on you."

"Oh, I guess I'll just take a couple more. Don't want to spoil my dinner, you know," she said with her mouth already full. She wavered on her feet and Whitey caught a hold of her flabby underarm. "Oh, such a gent. And what is this?" She pointed to the tomato based sauce on Whitey's tray and stuffed another cheese ball in her already full mouth.

Whitey tried to remember what Moe had told him it was. "It's, ah… some merry-memory sauce." He looked away as he said it, hoping she wouldn't hear him.

"Is it really?"

"Go ahead, try some. I did."

She dipped and stuffed them into her mouth. "How wonderful."

"Thanks, you ain't so bad yourself."

She just laughed with her mouthful. Whitey couldn't stand to watch. He gave her a nod and walked away. What a delightful little man, she thought, and continued to stuff the deep fried cheese balls between her triple chins and bleached out mustache. She looked away and belched. "Excuse me."

The song came to an end and Nicole excused herself to go to the powder room to check her nose. Robert protested slightly, but Barbara came over and insisted that he dance with her. Nicole was still refusing to speak with Barbara. So she didn't acknowledge her presence and used the intrusion to head toward the main entrance. She looked up at the band as she crossed the dance floor and Jake nodded to her. She smiled menacingly, and mouthed the words "I'll kill you." She covered up her anger as she greeted a young couple at the door.

Once in the hallway she made a sharp left and went into the service door that led into the long service hall.

Bronislaus sat on the steps. His glass was empty. He pretended to tie his shoe in case it was someone else. He got to his feet when he saw it was Nicole.

"You've come to take me away again, haven't you?"

"I'm not takin' you anywhere this time. However, if you want to come to Miami with us, the car leaves in five minutes." Bronislaus looked her square in the eyes.

"Bronislaus, I can't." She looked away.

"You can't tell me you're happy here."

"I'm just a little confused. Who wouldn't be?"

"What about Robert?"

"What about Robert?" For some reason this irritated her.

"Does he know you're in love with me?" He kept his eyes on her face searching for the right answers.

Nicole was surprised by the brazenness and angered even more. "I never said I was in love with you."

"You never said you were in love with him, either."

"I don't have to say anything."

"My sentiments exactly."

Nicole's first reaction was to leave. She turned toward the door, but stopped. Bronislaus watched her. She looked back at him with an uncertain look of what to do. She studied his face. Bronislaus was right and it frightened her to think it was true. She was in love with him. But he wasn't what she wanted in life. He was uneducated, hung around with hoods, and was dangerous. Kind of like... her brothers. What she thought she wanted was right here, all around her. But something was missing, something she had longed for all her life... true love and a sense of rightful belonging. Bronislaus was right, she never belonged here, and that was the hole in her heart that being part of all this could never fill.

She studied his face. "I can't believe I'm even considering it. I can't go with you. It's insane."

"Look Nicole, I hate to have to go and get sappy here, but if it means feelin' the way I've been feelin' inside lately, thinkin' I'll never see you again, I..." he stopped when he saw a tear in her eye. "Well anyway, I've never felt this way about anyone before. Maybe I have for awhile about you, since maybe that night we watched the stars together, and you showed me the constellations and what they all meant to the world around us. I don't know, but I can't see a star without thinkin' of you these days. So, maybe I fell for you that night and just wasn't aware of it until all this happened. I'm not sure what's insane or what's not insane. All I know is that I want you to come with me. And ah, so do the boys. They set this all up themselves and sprang it on me this mornin'."

A waiter went by with a tray of food and went out the door to the ballroom.

"Why are you doing this to me?"

"Because you want me to, goddamn it."

"I do not."

"Then tell me to leave. And I'll go. End it now. Cut me lose, because I can't stand thinkin' I'm leavin' the best thing that ever happened to me behind without a fair fight."

Nicole opened her mouth to say the words but they did not come forth.

"You're wastin' time."

"I can't just disappear like this. They'll go crazy looking for me."

"Let them go anywhere they want. They can't do anything to us if you go willingly. Meanwhile you've got one minute to make up your mind."

Nicole turned the knob on the door. "I won't walk out the back door. I'll leave out the front like I came in."

"We can go down these stairs and out right now. You don't owe them anything. The boys will meet us outback in thirty seconds."

"This one is for Alusia Pochinski." She came to Bronislaus and gave him a kiss on the lips. He held her, not wanting her to go, wanting to hold on to that first kiss forever, but let her ease out the door to the main hall. He waited a few minutes then followed her out. This would get a lot uglier before anything started looking good again.

Robert still danced with Barbara as the brothers watched over the punch bowl.

Nicole crossed the room.

Whitey was near the bar. He watched Nicole cross the dance floor, cut in on Barbara then lead Robert out to the balcony. Whitey grabbed a glass of champagne from the bar and downed it. Bronislaus stepped up beside him.

"Whitey."

Whitey nearly dropped his tray. "What?!"

Bronislaus took an hors d'oeuvre from Whitey's tray.

"Relax, will ya. Take Lip down and bring the cars around front."

"The front door? She's comin'?"

"She wants to leave in style. We'll be outta here in five minutes."

"Yeah, feet first as usual."

Whitey headed off toward Lip, while Bronislaus headed toward the balcony.

22 – DWADZIEŚCIA DWA

Out on the balcony, lights from the ballroom continued to cast long romantic shadows. Jake's violin drifted softly on the breeze and laughter came and went from the ballroom.

Nicole stood at the marble railing and rested her elbows as she looked out over the grounds. Robert came up behind her after he made sure they were alone. He ran his hand along her shoulder. She shuddered.

"What's the matter, Nicole?" He wanted so much to love her it hurt. "You don't seem to be having a good time."

"I'm having a pleasant evening so far. Look, there's the little Dipper."

Robert looked up to the sky. "There isn't a star in the sky."

"See," she pointed down to the pond. "There in the pond. I never noticed it before."

Robert looked. "I don't see it."

"The reflection."

"Those are the lights from the grounds."

Nicole didn't say anything. She just sighed. Robert tried to see her face but Nicole wouldn't let him. "What is it, Nicole?"

"I'm uncomfortable."

"Why should you feel uncomfortable? You're among loving friends and family."

"Tell that to Lorenzo and Caruso."

"A lot has happened in the last couple of weeks. They'll get over it. After we're married and get a place of our own, I promise things will smooth out."

Nicole turned to Robert. The dams broke behind her eyes and tears streamed down her poetic face. He handed her his hanky. She tried to wipe her tears but they kept coming.

"I'm sorry. I promised myself I wouldn't do this." She dabbed away the tears trying not to mess her makeup. She looked at Robert when she finished. How could she tell him she didn't love him and was leaving right now? She took in a deep breath. She let it out as she turned toward the pond.

"It's okay, Nicole, I…."

"Robert," she said turning to him, "It's no use. Too much has happened. I can't go on pretending I'm a part of all this, any of this."

"Please Nicole, don't," he tried not to plead. "I don't know what I'd do. Don't you understand? All of this around you," he opened his arms to signify everything in sight, "will be ours someday."

Nicole cleared her eyes. "And the lights in the pond?"

"Yes, of course the pond." Robert could feel an uncontrollable rage building up in him. The same rage Nicole had always been able to bring out of him. He fought it back. He fought it back just like he always had except for recently when that Polack started getting in his way.

Nicole sensed Robert's rising anger. She knew she had to move cautiously. "I'm sorry, Robert. This wasn't meant to be. I wasn't meant to be. I'm a lie. My whole life has been nothing but a lie."

"It's that Polack again, isn't it?"

Nicole didn't have to say anything, Robert knew. He knew it from the start. He felt himself going crazy inside. Nothing meant anything. Life had to be the way they had planned it all these years. It was that damn Polack. I'll kill him, he thought! "But, this whole party is for our engagement," he said, losing control of his voice so that the words squeaked out. "Your father will announce it any minute now." If he had been a steam kettle his head would have whistled.

"We'll have to tell them right now, I guess. I want to say good-bye."

"You guess?! Good-bye? You'll marry me or I'll, I'll…"

"Or you'll what?" Nicole didn't like the implications of physical danger. How dare him?

Robert slapped her face hard. "I'll kill you!"

Nicole didn't flinch. By then her tears had dried, as had all fond feelings for Robert, into crystals of salt.

She stared him down. "You'll regret that," she said and stepped past him to leave.

Robert grabbed her by the arm and swung her around and took a hold of her and shook her until Nicole thought her teeth would fall out.

"That's no way to treat a lady."

Robert let Nicole go and she stumbled, almost falling. She reached and caught hold of one of the lions for support. "Bronislaus," Nicole said. More scared for him than she was for herself.

"You!" Robert couldn't believe his eyes.

"Now let's not get all hairy-chested out here," Bronislaus said in a low calm voice. He didn't want to get Robert any crazier then he already looked. He had been listening from the darkened art gallery and he had heard enough. He just wanted Nicole and then out of there. No trouble, no getting even, no nothing. He didn't even have a gun with him and he assumed Robert didn't either. But many dead men had assumed wrong in love tangles before and there was no reason to believe that they were any different. He began to regret on insisting that the boys leave their rods in the car. "I believe the lady's leavin' with me."

"That's it," Robert said. He started for Bronislaus. "I'll break you in half."

Bronislaus slipped under Robert's first lunge, ducking a left jab. He backed away as Robert swung twice more at his nose with wild abandonment and missed by a city block. All Bronislaus wanted was to gather up Nicole and get, but Robert managed to keep himself between them, and keep Nichol away from the ballroom door.

"Look, pal," Bronislaus said in that same soothing tone he once heard O'Garrity use on a crazy armed man, "Let's try to be sociable about all this."

"I should've drowned you out at that lake a long time ago."

Using the soothing tone worked out better for O'Garrity.

Robert moved within reach of Bronislaus' right millhouse and took the young Pole's best punch to the side of his head, followed closely by a quick left jab to the right of his nose. The millhouse sent a spiking pain through Bronislaus' knuckles. That ought to hold him off for a while, Bronislaus hoped.

But it didn't. Robert shook it off like a pea-shooter on an armored truck and kept coming. Blood trickled out of his right nostril. He wiped it with the back of his clenched fist. The sight of his own blood only made him stronger.

Bronislaus tried to shake the pain from his right hand, thinking maybe it was broken.

Robert faked to his left and Bronislaus drifted to his own left to avoid the sloppy punch and wandered blindly into Robert's trained right uppercut to the jaw. Bronislaus felt his teeth clamp shut and stars volleyed through his temples as his brain bounced around inside his skull like dice on a craps table. He felt his knees cave in as he battled to regain some kind of dignity, but Robert already had him by the necktie and the crotch of his pants. He picked Bronislaus up effortlessly over his head and shook him like a sack of potatoes until change fell from Bronislaus' pockets and rolled off the balcony to the shrubs below.

"Say your prayers, Polack." Robert stepped over to the marble railing.

Bronislaus looked down over the edge. The view was a little too spectacular in his predicament. "Hey, what are ya, daft? Put me down."

"I'll put you down." Robert hung Bronislaus farther into the open air.

"Ah… let me rephrase that."

Robert shook Bronislaus over his head a few more times, playing with his captured pray.

"Come on, Robert, this is a fresh suit I'm supportin'."

Robert stopped to look into Nicole's eyes. "Say good-bye to your little fisher boy, Nicole."

Meanwhile, out front, Whitey and Lip had pulled up in Moe and Bronislaus' cars. Stewart, the head valet was by himself. The others were eating pizza out back. All the expected guests had arrived. And no one was expected to leave until after the announcement. So Stewart eyed the two unexpected cars apprehensively. Whitey and Lip got out. Whitey was still in a waiter's uniform. Stewart noticed Lip's stiff leg right off.

"You're supposed to enter through the servant's gate out around the side," Stewart said gentlemanly.

"We came to pick someone up," Whitey said, pulling out his pack of cigs. He scanned the grounds to see if any of the thugs had risen from their involuntary naps.

"I'm sorry, but you still can't leave your cars here."

"Hold on to your dentures, Mac, we ain't stayin' long," Lip told him.

"Riff-raff, are we?" Stewart said disdainfully.

"Yeah," Whitey assured him. "This is Riff and I'm Raff."

"Very well, sir, I shall have to call security."

"Don't get huffy on us. We just stopped in to pick up an important guest," Lip told him.

"Got a match?"

Stewart reluctantly lit Whitey's cig.

"What's takin' him," Whitey said, blowing out a cloud of smoke into Stewart's face.

Stewart merely closed his eyes and let it pass. "Thank you, Sir. Now please leave."

The music ceased, and over the applause, Bronislaus' voice drifted down from up above. Whitey and Lipinski looked up.

"There he is now," Lip said.

From the balcony, Robert gave Bronislaus the final heave-ho while he fought off Nicole from behind with an elbow to her chin. Bronislaus gave out a yell on the way down, "WwwHHAAoooo." He crashed into the low line of manicured blue spruce, just missing Cupid, and stayed there.

Whitey got to him first. He tried to pull Bronislaus up but couldn't, so he waited for Lip to limp over. Together they sat him up straight in the shrubs. Bronislaus was a rabbit in wonder-wonderland. "Bronislaus." Whitey slapped his face. Nothing. "Bronislaus." Whitey slapped him again.

Bronislaus slowly began to come around. He opened his mouth but only drooled.

"Hey, Bronislaus. You in there?" Whitey shook him a little more.

Bronislaus' eyes rolled counter clockwise in his head.

"Look, you dumb lug, snap out of it."

Bronislaus shook his head. A good sign. "Okay, Ma, I'm up, I'm up. I ain't got school today."

Whitey backhanded Bronislaus again. "Bronislaus."

Lipinski picked Bronislaus up and held him by the arm. Bronislaus wobbled, unable to stand by himself. His feet still among the broken spruce. "Try to clear your head, Bronislaus, this ain't no time for a nap," Lip insisted, shaking Bronislaus.

"Where are we?"

Whitey held three fingers in front of Bronislaus' face. "How many?"

"Six."

Whitey clobbered him again and held up the same three fingers. "How many now?"

Bronislaus fought to focus his eyes. "Three. And if you slug me again, I'll maim ya."

By this time Robert had reduced Nicole to tears again with his verbal abuse. He leaned over the railing and yelled down. "All right, Polack, you've had your jollies. Now get out of my bushes and get the hell off my property."

Bronislaus looked up at him. "Oh, are these bushes yours?" He deliberately stomped on them, breaking branches as he did.

"Stewart," Robert yelled, "See to it these punks are put off the grounds."

"Yes, sir.

"And where the hell are the men we hired?!"

"I don't know, sir."

This was too much for Robert, the incompetence of it all. He would have to take care of this himself. He turned back to Nicole. She wasn't there. He looked to the glass door to find Moe, Ducky, and Jake with Nicole standing behind them.

"All right, tough guy, she's comin' with us," Ducky said.

"Over my spilt blood."

"Funny, we was thinkin' the same thing?" Moe said, pounding his big fist into his open palm.

Robert charged them like a bull and the boys grabbed hold of him and pinned him back against the marble railing, impolitely bending him over it while adding three quick jabs to the side of his head.

"Let's give 'em a taste of his own," Jake said.

"Wait." Nicole moved to Robert and looked into his eyes. He sneered back at her with nothing good left between them, their childhood dreams together shattered beyond forever. She suddenly slapped his face as hard as she could. "There, now throw the Dago-crud over."

"I like this dame already," Ducky said.

Robert struggled but the boys managed to flip him over the railing into the bushes below. He hit his head on the floating Cupid on the way down. Making it swing out and back at him as he tried to sit up, elbowing Robert right in the chops, and mercifully knocking him out cold.

Stewart, who had been unsuccessful at keeping Bronislaus and Whitey from reentering the house, ran to Robert's aid. Robert got up unsteady as Stewart reached him. He fell forward onto Stewart, taking them both down.

"How was that?" Moe yelled down to Lipinski.

"Could've used a little more top spin," Lip called up from the cars.

"Ahhh." Moe turned to find Lorenzo and his two brothers had entered the balcony with two of Bartolommeo's men who apparently were not just guests.

"I thought you guys looked familiar," Lorenzo said.

He looked at Nicole. "Where's Robert?"

Nicole jerked her thumb toward the ledge. "Trimming the bushes."

"What?" Lorenzo went and looked over the edge. He turned back. "You guys packin'?" he asked the two guests.

"We ain't officially workin' tonight, so Mr. Bunniti had us check them at the door."

Lorenzo reached under his coat and Ducky snatched a hold of his arm and jerked it out. The gun clattered onto the marble flooring. Angelo went for it and got a knee from Jake. He sat abruptly on his backside.

Nicole picked up the gun and tossed it over toward the pond below.

"What'd you go and do that for?" Moe asked.

"Use your own guns."

Moe, Jake, and Ducky looked at each other.

"Oh, yeah, no irons, huh?" Lorenzo helped Angelo up, "Come on, boys, let's take 'em."

"Now we got us a hoedown!" Ducky said.

Inside, Bronislaus and Whitey made their way back into the ballroom as Ducky and Lorenzo crashed through one of the balcony's glass doors. Screams and shouts filled the room. Moe hurtled both Caruso and then Angelo through the shattered doors after them. Jake came in right behind them through the doors, stepping over the broken glass, with one of Bartolommeo's men on his back. Moe picked him off Jake and flung him into a floral display against the wall. He bounced off the wall in a colorful explosion of flowers and staggered to where Henry Ford sat with his wife. As Henry, unfazed, slid his chair back, the stunned man belly flopped onto the table and slid off with the table cloth, glasses, and center piece showering down onto his chest. Glass and flowers clung to him. Henry seized the moment to pluck a pink daisy off the man's body and handed it to his wife.

"For you, dear."

"Oh, Henry."

Other waiters seeing that some of their crew members were in a fight with the guests began to wade in to stop it and soon the fracas began to spread across the room. Women were screaming as food and drink sailed through the air. Tables and chairs were knocked to the floor, flowers and vases crashed. A champagne bottle struck one of the innate soldiers hanging on the wall and ripped a hole painfully suggestive in his groin.

"This is suicide," Whitey said.

Bronislaus looked for Nicole. "Gather up the boys. Don't forget Jake and meet us downstairs." Bronislaus stepped away from a knuckle sandwich, having already eaten, and it caught Whitey unexpectedly on the side of the head.

"Hold the Mayo," Whitey said as he dropped to the floor to make his way under the buffet tables. Twice he got kicked but he kept going. After the third time he bit into a black pant leg. It turned out to be Moe.

Meanwhile, as Jake had instructed, the band played on. By then, Nicole had the balcony to herself. She leaned over the lion's faces and looked down onto the lawn to where Stewart still tried to revive Robert. "Better get him some water, Stewart. Use the pond. It would be fitting for the scum."

"But... yes, ma'am."

Bronislaus crept quietly through the broken glass. He hesitated to take in the view as Nicole leaned over the railing. Her deep blue sequined dress shimmered in the light. He cracked his knuckles. Nicole turned to see him. He held out his hand. "You done sayin' your good-byes?"

Nicole came to him and they kissed long and hard until an apple came flying out of the ballroom and struck Bronislaus square between the shoulder blades. He turned to find Whitey making gestures that he would like to scramola.

"I'm ready."

Bronislaus kicked the apple away. "You see any snakes around here?" They entered the ballroom and sidestepped through the struggling bodies.

A tall man wandered around with a woman on his shoulders while she bopped people over the head with a bottle. Bodies lay about the floor. A waiter held a baron knife to Angelo's throat making his eyes bulge until Caruso clobbered the waiter from behind with a whole baron.

Barbara hid beside a pillar completely unscathed by it all. Bronislaus and Nicole walked past her. A waiter and a guest came up struggling over a platter of cold pasta, each trying to spill it on the other. Nicole walked up to them and scornfully demanded that they give it to her. Bronislaus couldn't watch, but they reluctantly handed it over. He peeked through his fingers as Nicole went back to where Barbara hid.

"Barbara," Nicole said coming up from behind her.

"Yes?" Barbara turned around. Nicole dumped the pasta over her head and the cream sauce and strands of noodles dripped and hung down from Barbara's head and shoulders. Nicole gave the platter back to the waiter who promptly clobbered the guest with it. Barbara looked at Nicole through her pasta blinds.

Nicole smiled. "Robert's all yours now," she said and walked away.

Finally Bartolommeo and Anthony finished drinking, and together, not sensing or hearing a thing, opened the heavy study door to make Nicole and Robert's engagement announcement. Instead, they found the room in a shambles and their guests and families in an all out brawl with their employees. Their jaws dropped simultaneously in disbelief and their cigars fell out of their mouths.

Just then Bronislaus and Nicole passed by. Nicole stopped in front of them. Bartolommeo went to say something but Anthony stifled him. Apparently, the visuals had said enough already.

Bronislaus pulled her away and they scrambled across the bandstand to the main stairs and went down.

Hell burned in Bartolommeo's eyes as he watched the plans for the rest of his life flee from the room.

In the center of the room, Whitey danced around with Caruso and Angelo close behind him. At full speed, Whitey dove onto a dessert table and slid the length of it through the mounds of pastries, crumbled cakes and smeared whipped cream. At the end of the eight foot table, Lorenzo waited with murder in his eyes. He pulled Whitey skyward by the hair and was about to punch his lamps out when the fat lady with the bleached mustache came down with a wine bottle on the back of Lorenzo's skull. Lorenzo let go of Whitey with a splat on the table and sank to the floor.

Whitey bounced up on his knees and gave the lady a big messy kiss, leaving whipped cream and cake all over her face and gown. She loved every calorie of it.

Two waiters jumped Angelo and Caruso from behind while Whitey leaped from the table and headed for the main door. The Mangione brothers and the two waiters stumbled to the bandstand, where Jake's extinct Band Renown had finally packed up and were headed down the back stairs. It's soon to be famous singer, was left unnoticed at the bar getting drunk.

Out front, Stewart helped Robert up the stairs past the Roman soldier like pillars. Ducky, Moe, and Jake came running out the front door with their hands full of goodies. Ducky had the almost empty Mangione family's crystal bowl heirloom, while Moe tried to juggle a whole baron of beef and a platter of pasta. Jake carried three bottles of champagne and his trusty violin.

"What do you think you're doing?" Stewart yelled at them and let go of Robert who toppled backwards off the porch and fell into the spruce.

Moe grabbed Stewart. "The Polka," he said and danced with him, getting pasta and baron grease down the back of Stewart's coat.

Bronislaus and Nicole rushed out of the house, hand in hand.

Robert stood back up. His feet still in the dirt at the side of the porch. He saw Bronislaus and Nicole together. "You've had it now, Polack."

Ducky gave Stewart the punch bowl and drew back to hit Robert.

Bronislaus stopped him. "I'll handle this one."

Robert swung and missed Bronislaus by half the porch, and Bronislaus, using the leverage of being on the porch to his advantage, flew up with an upper cut to Robert's jaw, flipping him one last time back into the shrubs.

Led by Jake, they all ran down to the cars where Lipinski waited with the doors open and the cars still running.

Stewart suddenly realized that they were running off with the guest of honor. "Hey, you can't do that." He ran after them, spilling the rest of the punch over his hands and down the front of his pants. "Oh, buggers!"

Jake got into the backseat of the convertible Buick while Bronislaus and Nicole climbed in front. Moe slid behind the wheel of his beat up 1915 Dodge 4 door convertible sedan with all his food and Lip and Ducky got in with him. The two cars pulled away, and then halted.

Bronislaus turned around and looked at Jake. "Where's Whitey!?"

Jake shrugged and looked back into the other car… no Whitey! Just then, a rapidly accumulating, hysterical clamor from a growing maniacal mob flooded down the double wide main stairs of the house. In front of it was a dessert stained Whitey, leaving sticky foot prints as he went, and keeping about three unhappy steps away from a severe beating.

Robert crawled up onto the porch and Whitey sank a shoe into his back and leaped right over the head of Stewart.

Stewart covered his alarmed eyes with his arms and the crystal punch bowl crashed to the ground with an immense shattering at his feet, as though the ghost of its history escaped into thin air, keeping the mob pinned inside the doors just long enough to give Whitey a fresh start to make it to the cars first.

Bronislaus and the others cheered Whitey on at the top of their lungs as he splashed through the fountain's stream and cut a path across Anthony's manicured lawn.

Gaining on the winded Whitey fast, three guests got tangled up with Angelo as he dove for a foothold of Whitey, causing all three of them to unwittingly attempt half gainers into the stream's rocks.

Jake couldn't resist the irony of the moment, and took out his violin to put the whole scene to razzmatazz while Bronislaus and Moe put the cars back in gear, making Whitey dash along after them. Just when they reached the middle of the drive, Whitey passed Moe's junker and dove at the back of Bronislaus' open Buick, latching a hold of the convertible's boot, flipping head over heels into the back seat. "Hey, you're stainin' my leather seats."

"Shuddup."

Behind them, Moe swerved his junker Dodge sedan onto the DA's perfectly manicured lawn, cutting horrendous grooves across it, while Lip and Ducky fought off Lorenzo and two of Bartolommeo's men, prying their grips from the car. One by one they were left sprawled across the lawn or rolling on the cobblestone driveway while The Polish Gang sped away.

Bronislaus made a right onto Jefferson Avenue when Moe's Dodge emerged from the other gate making a left. Distant police sirens approached from the north.

And the one-man-band lead by the infamous Machine Gun Jake himself, fiddled on into the Detroit summer night.

23 – DWADZIEŚCIA TRZY

Across the street from Michal's, a dark plump figure stood in the shadows beyond an overhanging lamp that splashed down onto the walk in front of the closed Tasties Bakery building. The figure stood motionless as Bronislaus drove his cream-colored convertible over the curb and parked it on the front lawn of Michal's.

Moe pulled his sedan up and double parked on the bakery side and everyone filed out waving champagne bottles, brandishing a partially eaten baron of beef and throwing cold pasta at each other.

The door was locked at Michal's, but loud noise and music escaped through the cracks and drifted out to the street. Bronislaus led Nicole and the boys to the front door and pounded on it. The Skyscraper looked through a peephole and let them in.

Michal was behind the bar handing out bottles of booze as gifts. The usual four musicians played a drunken version of "Roll Out The Barrels" to the backdrop of breaking furniture as the Skyscraper's blond bombshell, barely clothed, danced on the pushed aside pool table. The place was sardined with smoke and laughter and old drunken friends.

In the back booth, Stephania sat with Emily and Sally. Three tables were pulled together in front of them and they were stacked full of sandwiches, potato salad, coleslaw, stuffed cabbage, ham, and all kinds of Polish delicacies brought by Stephania's friends from around the neighborhood. Just about everyone there was comboozelated, gorey-eyed, moon-eyed, impixlocated, parboiled and stuccoed, including Michal. Stashu tried his best to get Molly Korner off the pool table, to the boos and jeers from the packed room.

Bronislaus stopped inside of the door to take it all in. The boys crowded in behind him forcing him forward. Nicole held back out of sight, waiting for an okay from Bronislaus, and ready to run. Whitey pushed past Bronislaus, still dressed in his dessert-stained waiter's get-up.

Alusia entered from the ladies room. She froze when she saw the condition of Bronislaus and the boys.

Michal waved his arms until the band caught on and the rounds of barrels faded to the corners of the room, until only the old-fart, minus his teeth, sang a cappella while lying under the booth nearest the kitchen. Someone dragged him out and attempted to shut him up.

"To Manny," the old-fart yelled.

"To Manny," they all toasted.

A new hush traveled across the room. Stashu took that moment to get Molly down off the pool table by letting her leap into his arms, giving the crowd one last show, and laid a wet juicy one on his nonplused lips. The Skyscraper rumbled over and Stashu reluctantly deposited Molly safely into his arms.

Bronislaus shuffled his feet and waited for his pa to speak. The drummer picked up the step with his brush sticks on his snare, and the room filled with snickers.

Michal waved the room quite. "Where've you been, boys?"

"We went across town for a while." Bronislaus uneasily shuffled some more, shooting the drummer a look to shuddup.

Michal took a good look at his boy's clothing. "What happened to your monkey suit?"

"I, ah, took a fall."

"You just fell?" Michal looked around the room until he found Stephania. "The boy just fell, Stephania." Stifled laughter spread quickly across the crowded room and just as quickly disappeared.

"In some bushes," Whitey defended his pal. "From a balcony."

"In some bushes," Michal repeated. "Did you hear that, Stephania, Romeo here fell from a balcony into some bushes?"

"I can hear, Michal."

"Just making sure. And what happened to you, Whitey? You have problems digesting your food?"

"He ordered a knuckle sandwich to go," Moe said, from behind them, still holding the gnawed beef. Its blood dripped on the floor and his shoes. Whitey elbowed Moe in his belly. Moe sucker punched Whitey lightly in the kidneys.

Michal poured whiskey into a tumbler of ice and splashed a tad of water on it. He eyed the boys quietly, sobering quickly anyway. "You want to tell me or do I get so many guesses?"

Bronislaus shuffled some more. The drummer picked up on it this time by raking a hi-hat with his brush sticks. Bronislaus quit shuffling. The crowd got a giggle out of it still.

Michal shot a glance at the drummer again. The drummer quieted his symbol smirking to his buddies.

"We went to see Nicole at her engagement party."

Michal slammed down his glass, splashing the whiskey all over everyone near him. "At Bunniti's home?! Holy Joseph! Tell me I'm dreaming this. Stephania, my own stupid kid is trying to get me deported back to Kraków."

Whitey pushed forward. "It was all my fault, Mr. Niemiec. I twisted his arm."

"I ought to twist your head. What happened, Moe?" If anybody, Michal always knew Moe would tell him the truth.

"We kind 'a busted up the place a little bit."

Michal downed what was left of his drink and poured another.

"But we didn't start nothin'... and no guns."

"We just finished it," Lipinski said.

"It was kind of what you might call a mutual disagreement," Bronislaus said.

"Yeah, they swung first so we pounded their heads in," Ducky added.

"Did you have anything to do with this, Jake?" Michal asked.

"Yes, sir, I told them how to get in, and I threw my share."

"I suggest you go home and pack."

The boys looked at Jake and smacked him on the back.

Jake held up his violin. "I'm packed, sir."

Alusia came to the center of the bar. "Did you see her? How did she look?"

"Kind of like this, but not as happy." Bronislaus pulled Nicole into the room. "Come on in. It's okay."

Nicole hesitantly moved into the room. Her cheeks flushed red. Every set of eyes were on her as she looked around the overstuffed bar. "Hello."

"Does Mister Mangione know you're here?"

"Yes. Sort of. He knows I left with these gentlemen.

"Looks like we'll be leaving Detroit earlier than planned, boys."

"I think I'm gonna cry," Alusia said.

"For sixteen years you've been saying, if only I could say hello. So say it already, before I do."

"Hello, Nicole"

"Hello, Mother."

"Did you hear that? Did you hear that, Stephania? Mother. She called me mother. Now I know I'm gonna cry."

Nicole went to Alusia as the elegantly dressed woman stood in the center of the room and allowed tears to stream freely down her cheeks. They hugged. Stephania came over and the three of them hugged. There wasn't a dry eye in the bar. As an instant bonding of mother and daughter took place, her mother holding her for the first time, Nicole knew she had never felt like this before. She wasn't sure what it was, but whatever it was, it felt good. It felt warm. It felt like finding a home.

"I'm sorry for crying like this," Alusia said, as she wiped her eyes.

"So go ahead. Who's it gonna to hurt? Look at me. I'm blubbering like an old fool," Stephania told her. Stephania turned to the crowd who still watched with damp eyes. Sniffles filled the room.

"What's the matter, you never seen a mother hug her daughter before?" Emily came to her and they hugged too. She reached out her hand to Nicole and Nicole took it and squeezed it tight. Every daughter and mother in the room reached for one another as hugs spread throughout the crowd.

"Hey, I may be on my way back to Poland now. So we got a party here or what?" Michal poured a setup for the boys and a glass of milk for Whitey. "Drink up this booze." The crowd broke out in a cheer and the band picked up where it left off. The crowd sang along as if there was no tomorrow because there might not be at this point, and if it was possible, became even wilder than before.

"Come on in, you guys. Let me buy you a drink." The boys went over and downed the drinks waiting for them at the bar. "Come on, Stephania, I need to dance," Michal yelled and a polka broke out across the room.

Nicole and Alusia went and sat at the back table. Sally gave both mother and daughter a hug, and Emily gave them even a bigger one before leaving them alone. Sally went over and joined Whitey at the bar and by the time the room was well into its tenth chorus, Whitey pulled Sally up on stage and interrupted the band.

Whitey raised his arms to quiet the crowd. “Look, I’m sorry for the interruption, here. I’m sorry, I’m truly sorry.”

“You always were, Whitey,” Moe yelled and was followed by laughter and applause.

Whitey raised his arms again as Sally pulled his dessert stained coat from him. “Keep it up, wise guy,” he said to Moe after the crowd calmed down.

“What I have to say is, that is, most of you heard that Sal and I are gettin’ hitched and all. Well the truth is, ah…” Whitey had problems finding the right words. He looked at Sally for help.

“The truth is that Mr. Romantic here, is gonna be a father. I’m pregnant!” Everyone cheered and a pickle flew from the crowd and struck Whitey on the forehead.

“Very funny,” Whitey said, and wiped the pickle juice from his face.

“Sing us a song, Sal,” the Skyscraper said from the door still holding his drunken wife.

“Yeah, Sal, sing us one of those pretty slow ones you used to do,” the old-fart said from on his back at the center of the floor.

Sally turned to the band and told them what to play. Whitey came off the stage and was slapped on the back so many times he was thinking twice about having a second kid.

“Let me pour you another milk, Whitey,” Michal said.

“Make it a double, and sprinkle something sweet in it, please.”

“Nicole, Bronislaus, everybody, grab someone to dance with. I want to sing something new for ya. Come on, Jake. Grab a horn up here for me. Jake wrote this.” Jake came on stage and one of the musicians gave him a horn and pushed over a chair for him. Jake took a moment to explain how the song went.

Nicole came out and met Bronislaus on the dance floor. He took her gently into his arms and held her close as Jake began to play a few bars until the rest of the band caught on to where he was going with it and Sally began to sing Jake’s new song called “Doin’ The Gangster.” The room filled with dancers, laughers, drinkers, smokers, sinners and criers of lovers and joyers. The Polish Gang rejoiced.

But outside, the dark plump figure still lurked in the shadows of the bread factory, standing motionless as the fun drifted across the street under the sound of Sally's sweet voice and the subtle rhythm of Machine Gun Jake and his temporary Band Renown.

Halfway through the ballad, Mangione's Caddy pulled around the corner and heaved a sigh behind Moe's Dodge. Another sedan pulled up behind it. The Mangione family got out, followed by four of Mangione's men who got thumped at the party. They were heavily armed. Lorenzo carried a Thompson, Caruso had a shotgun, and Angelo had two handguns. One of the other men pulled out five wrapped sticks of dynamite. Mr. Mangione nodded and the man lit it. They waited as the two foot fuse burned down.

"Nice night for a walk, huh, Bartolommeo?" the voice came from the shadows.

Bartolommeo turned around, so did his boys, to find O'Garrity behind their Caddy fingering a double barrel at Bartolommeo's fat gut.

"O'Garrity? What are you doin' in town?"

"Like I said. It's a nice night for a walk." O'Garrity motioned toward the thug with the lit dynamite.

"How's your night goin'?"

The thug with the lit sticks began to look anxious to rid himself of them.

"We came to put the finishing touch on this story."

"Sorry, Bartolommeo, that ain't the ending I had in mind."

"This ain't your story to tell, O'Garrity."

From beside O'Garrity, farther off into the shadows closer to the Niemiec garage, a man spoke up. "You got troubles, O'Garrity?"

O'Garrity looked almost startled. He didn't take his eyes off Bartolommeo. "Evening, Captain. No, no troubles."

The Captain took a step into the street light. His road map face under his hat stayed calm as he eyed the rapidly burning fuse. "Seems like we have a little excitement around here tonight."

"A little," O'Garrity said.

"Keep out of this. I told you if you didn't take care of that Polack kid, I would," Bartolommeo said.

"This is still my side of town. Now, Mangione, if you feel it necessary to blow your fat ass to hell, please do it in your own precinct. Sergeant?

Bosko moved quietly out of the dark and behind the thug with the dynamite, pulled the fuse and tossed it into the middle of the street. The thug holding it looked relieved. He dropped the sticks and kicked them away. They all stood in silence, listening to the music as the fuse burned down and mercifully finally fizzled out. The rest of Bosko's men came out from the shadows, all fifteen of them.

"Throw down your guns and get back into your cars. Do it now." The Captain said keeping his voice low and calm.

"Don't be telling me what to do. This is my property."

"Not until tomorrow at noon it ain't," the Captain said.

"They broke the agreement, not us. They took Nicole, so we're here to take her back!" Bartolommeo said.

O'Garrity cocked back the hammers on his twelve gauge shotgun. "I don't think so, Bartolommeo. I made a bad mistake that night to think Nicole would be better off with the likes of you. Nicole is where she should've been all along. And I'm here to see she stays there. Now drop the guns, like the Captain said.

Bartolommeo and the boys didn't move.

"You're not a policeman anymore, O'Garrity. If you shoot this fat little runt, you do it as a civilian."

"Yes, sir, I know."

"But Bosko here is. So are the rest of these men. And if they shoot at you and happen to hit the rest of these boys, well I guess that would just be tough luck.

"I guess it would, sir."

Bartolommeo looked around him. I'll get you for this, Captain."

"Mind if I don't sweat it?"

Bartolommeo ground his hippo teeth as he figured the odds.

"All right, boys, drop them."

"We can take them."

"You heard me, Lorenzo. Drop 'em and get into the cars. All of you."

They dropped their guns and Bosko picked up the dynamite. His men picked up the artillery. The Mangione men got back in their cars. Bartolommeo stopped and looked at Michal's, then at O'Garrity and the Captain. "You haven't heard the last of us, O'Garrity. None of you have." He got back into the Caddy, and Lorenzo, who was stuck driving now that Walter was gone, drove away. The other car followed. O'Garrity put his gun away.

"You stayin' out here?"

"Yeah."

"Why not just go on in? Hell of a lot more fun than standin' out here."

"I don't think so, Captain. Maybe some day."

"I want you out of town when their trucks pull out."

"Sure, Captain. Thanks."

"Bosko and the boys will see them out of town."

"I appreciate that. Good night, boys. Bosko."

"Never happened," Bosko answered.

"Well, boys, like the man in the shadows said, it's a nice night for a walk. Shall we?" The Captained led Bosko and his men back down Petersburg Street. They shook O'Garrity's hand as they passed him by.

O'Garrity watched as they went, then turned back to the shadows and stood as he had before. Someday, he thought.

Sally sang on:

"Doing the Gangster.
Nineteen-twenties' Gangster.
Crazy Carlo, working for the mob."

Late that night, just before dawn, the Niemiec family and friends, hung over to the gills, loaded themselves into their respective cars and trucks and drove off, leaving their old Detroit Westside neighborhood behind.

So it went in Detroit, as time passed by, except for one newsprint article and an occasional old-timer's porch-swing tale, memory of the small band of young men known as The Polish Gang… just slipped away.

In memory of Bronislaus (Benny) Niemiec
(Awarded Silver Star and Purple Heart WWII)
He is survived by his three sons and one daughter
1919 - 2005

About the Author

Karl J. Niemiec is Benny's youngest son of four children, three boys and one girl. Karl wrote the first draft of The Polish Gang on a 1929 Underwood at the corner of Santa Monica and Vine, three flights up. Today, Karl is Publishing Director of LapTopPublishing.com, creates enrichment programs at YoungStar Studios, is the proud father of three boys and one daughter, and lives with his wife, Erin, in Carmel, Indiana.

CPSIA information can be obtained at www.ICGtesting.com
Printed in the USA
BVOW06s1737140615

404575BV00006B/29/P

9 780983 366331